Also by Alyssa Maxwell and available from
Center Point Large Print:

Murder Most Malicious
Murder at Rough Point
Murder at Chateau sur Mer
A Pinch of Poison
A Devious Death
Murder at Ochre Court
A Murderous Marriage
Murder at Crossways
A Silent Stabbing
Murder at Kingscote

**This Large Print Book carries the
Seal of Approval of N.A.V.H.**

A
SINISTER
SERVICE

Center Po
Large Prin

A SINISTER SERVICE

A LADY AND LADY'S MAID MYSTERY

Alyssa Maxwell

CENTER POINT LARGE PRINT
THORNDIKE, MAINE

This Center Point Large Print edition
is published in the year 2021 by arrangement with
Kensington Publishing Corp.

The text of this Large Print edition is unabridged.
In other aspects, this book may vary
from the original edition.
Printed in the United States of America
on permanent paper.
Set in 16-point Times New Roman type.

ISBN: 978-1-64358-901-5

The Library of Congress has cataloged this record
under Library of Congress Control Number: 2021930432

CHAPTER 1

November 1920

The Rolls-Royce took the bend in the road sharply, sending Phoebe Renshaw and her three siblings hard to the right. Amelia, several years younger than Phoebe, took the brunt of their collective weight against her and let out a yelp. As the motorcar righted itself, the eldest, Julia, assumed a cross look and leaned forward to speak to the driver. "Really, Fenton, do you wish me to have my child two months early?"

That elicited a gasp from Amelia, a smirk from their youngest sibling—and only brother—Fox, and a shake of Phoebe's head. Julia was seven months along and not due until after the holidays, but that didn't stop her from threatening the imminent arrival of her child whenever it suited her purposes. From the front seat, poor Fenton, their new chauffeur, stuttered a mortified apology. Julia sighed and leaned back against the pomegranate-red leather seat.

Anyone peeking into the motorcar windows would surely guess they were siblings, with their varying shades of blond hair, ranging from Julia's bright flaxen curls to Amelia's darker honey tones, to Fox's dusky wheat color, and Phoebe's reddish gold. They resembled one another in their features as well, though in varying ways. Julia rivaled the most glamorous film star, Amelia might have stepped right out of a portrait by John Singer Sargent, and Fox showed promise of becoming handsome in a distinctly patrician manner. Phoebe had no choice but to acknowledge being the plain one of the family, the one who could blend into a crowd and move through a room without being noticed.

They resettled themselves. Why the four of them had had to squeeze into the motorcar was beyond Phoebe. Another perfectly roomy touring car followed them, its boot crammed with the luggage that hadn't fit in the Rolls-Royce, while their two lady's maids, Eva and Hetta, enjoyed the backseat all to themselves. Personally, Phoebe would have appreciated spending the hours with Eva for company, but Julia wouldn't have it. One does not travel in the servants' motorcar, she had admonished, much to their grandmother's agreement. There simply had been no arguing the point.

They'd been driving for hours now, having left Little Barlow before the sun had shone properly, stopping for lunch outside of Worcester, and then continuing relentlessly northward toward their destination: the small town of Langston in the county of Staffordshire.

Phoebe's attention drifted once more beyond

the motorcar window. Mid-November had stripped the waning colors from the fields and bordering forests and left the world a drab, lifeless gray. Other than a few halfhearted flurries earlier in the month, there had been no sign yet of snow, which always lifted Phoebe's spirits from their late-fall doldrums.

The Rolls-Royce soon left behind hilly countryside prone to steep, if not overly high, slopes and rugged promontories. They entered a wide valley, the center of which played host to a crowded jumble of homes and industry, the tall stacks belching smoke and turning the sky a rather sickly yellow-gray.

"Is that Langston? Not very appealing," Fox commented as he leaned past Phoebe to see out the window. "And to think I'm missing the most important rugby game of the season tomorrow. We're playing Harrow, you know." He said this last with all the wounded dignity a fifteen-year-old could muster, which was considerable.

Julia shrugged one shoulder in her habitual way and smoothed a hand over the belly that protruded like an overripe melon beneath her cashmere cape. "What's more important, some silly rugby game or our grandparents' anniversary?"

Fox let out a sound somewhere between a *pish* and an oath that would have had him simmering in his room for two whole days, had their grandfather heard him. "What do I know about teacups anyway?" he mumbled into his shirt collar. "Don't see why I had to come."

Phoebe hid a grin. She had nothing but sympathy for him, really, and had it been up to her, she'd have spared him the trouble of this outing. But Julia had insisted, and in her delicate condition there was simply no debating with her. She had become rather like Grams that way.

"It's not just teacups," Julia announced with a sniff. "It's an entire set of china by the very same company favored by Queen Mary. And Grams and Grampapa have not *had* a new set of china since long before the war."

"I doubt Grampapa very much cares either way," Fox retorted once more to his collar. Julia pretended not to hear him, and paid no mind when he added, "Who cares what Her Majesty favors? It's not like she's coming to take tea at Foxwood Hall anytime soon."

"Well, *I* think it's a perfectly lovely idea and will make a splendid anniversary gift," Amelia announced in a bright voice.

"You think everything is a perfectly lovely idea," their brother murmured with no small sarcasm and sank lower in the seat. His knees hit the back of the seat in front of them, revealing how much taller he had grown over the summer months.

Amelia shook her head in resignation. "Really, Fox, can't you make even the smallest effort to be cheerful and enter into the spirit of the occasion?" When Fox raised his chin to respond, Amelia didn't give him the chance. "This is the first time the four of us are on our own, our *very* own, you understand, and wouldn't it be jolly if we could simply get along and accomplish something worthwhile as a family? Don't Grams and Grampapa deserve that from us? I'm not speaking merely of the china, but of showing our gratitude to them for raising us by assuring them they've turned out four thoughtful, responsible, and *sensible* individuals rather than a pack of squabbling geese."

"I . . . er . . ." Fox swallowed whatever he was going to say, or perhaps he couldn't find the words at all. A surge of color engulfed his face. He stared back at Amelia, his eyes, so like Julia's dark blue ones, swimming with surprise and perhaps a smidgeon of shame.

And no wonder. This Amelia, the one able to gather her courage to say whatever she felt needed saying, and do it eloquently, had emerged only recently, to the surprise of them all. She was no longer a little girl, and the truth of that startled even Phoebe at times.

Fox finally pushed out, "Sorry."

Amelia turned her attention out the window. "There! Is that it? Is that the factory?"

The driver had rounded another bend—more gently this time. The view revealed a collection of redbrick buildings huddled in the snaking curve of a river. They formed a large quadrangle with several smaller enclosures within. Scattered among the buildings were rows of towering, bottle-shaped structures that sent out spirals of smoke. Beyond the factory precincts, row houses fanned out in all directions. Phoebe supposed many of Crown Lily's workers lived in those houses.

Fox leaned to see around Amelia's and Julia's shoulders. "Good grief, it looks like a prison. I hope we're not going *there*."

Ah. His contrition had proven all too brief. But in fairness, he wasn't far off. Even from a distance, Phoebe found the place grim to the extreme, and she couldn't imagine some of the country's finest, most delicate china being fashioned within its bleak walls.

"What *did* you expect?" Julia didn't bother glancing out the window, but sat examining the manicure she'd had the day before. "Did you think china was made in fields of wildflowers? It's an industry, and is manufactured much like anything else. Phoebe should know all about manufacturing from her many conversations with Owen." She injected subtle yet unmistakable innuendo when she spoke of Owen Seabright, who owned textile mills in Yorkshire, and whom they all considered Phoebe's beau.

They weren't entirely mistaken, at least generally speaking. She and Owen did have a special regard for each other, yet the traditional meaning of *beau* no longer applied when it came to them. Did they wish to marry? They had discussed it, yes. But as to when, Phoebe couldn't say. She didn't wish to rush into being a wife and mother—as Julia had done last spring when she'd married Gilbert Townsend, Viscount Annondale. Look where that had gotten her. Yes, Julia had become the Viscountess Annondale, but she was also widowed and soon to give birth to a fatherless child.

Phoebe simply wished to do a thing or two first, achieve merits of her own, which she could bring with her into marriage and motherhood, but would always remain hers. Hers alone.

The rim of the valley fell away as they entered the precincts of the town of Langston. Here, two-story edifices, many of brick, others wood-framed, lined the main thoroughfare on either side while side streets disappeared into the distance. Signs and shop windows rushed by in a blur. Their driver had to move far to the left, practically onto the pavement, as a trolley rolled past on its rails. Motorcars and lorries weaved in and out among horse-drawn carriages and pony carts, while overcoat-clad pedestrians hurried along on their errands.

The sight of uniformed children filing from a school prompted Phoebe to consult her wristwatch, an accessory Grams had termed *thoroughly modern,* which Phoebe knew

11

translated to *decidedly unladylike*. Wristwatches had become popular during the war—pilots had worn them to keep time without having to remove their hands from the controls. Phoebe liked the modern touch, and perhaps even the slightly unladylike touch it lent her.

"It's noon already," she said. "It feels like we've been traveling for days."

"Not you, too." Julia fussed impatiently with the strap of her handbag. "Honestly, is complaining all you and Fox can do?"

"I wasn't . . ." Phoebe didn't bother. She and Julia had been getting along fairly well in recent weeks, and she understood her sister's present tetchiness had more to do with the worries on her mind than any real displeasure in her siblings. Julia wanted this anniversary gift to be perfect and had thought of little else lately, except for impending motherhood. But that wasn't all. This trip would entail more than choosing china patterns for their grandparents. Julia planned to assert her rights among her deceased husband's family for what would be, really, the first time since her marriage. And that set her nerves very much on edge. Yes, Phoebe thought with a sigh, their day was only going to become more stressful.

Eva Huntford, lady's maid to Phoebe and Amelia, watched as the Rolls-Royce carrying her beloved ladies—and their often taxing younger brother—passed beneath an arching sign that proudly announced CROWN LILY POTTERIES, in a script Eva found entirely familiar from seeing it on the bottom of countless pieces of china at home.

The motorcar she and Hetta Brauer, Lady Annondale's maid, were riding in followed close behind, driven by Douglas, one of Foxwood Hall's footmen, who doubled as a secondary driver whenever needed. Both cars stopped at the gate. The watchman made his inquiry of the first motorcar and waved them both in. Sooty buildings closed around them, cutting off the outside world. Eva could see little else but endless walls of brick filling the motorcar windows.

An instant later she stepped out onto a paved enclosure, the cobbles rough and uneven beneath the soles of her low-heeled pumps. The Crown Lily factory had been in this precise location for nearly two hundred years, a fact that drew Eva's admiration. Simply surviving the war years without spiraling into bankruptcy could be considered quite a feat, never mind maintaining solvency generation after generation.

She hurried over to the Renshaws' Rolls-Royce to assist the passengers out. Hetta did likewise, her face a mask of bewilderment. Eva suspected Hetta had little or no experience with industrial towns in her home country of Switzerland, a hunch bolstered by Lady Annondale's having spoken of Hetta's nerve-ridden perplexity whenever they visited London.

Eva made a quick mental assessment of her surroundings as she smoothed the wrinkles from her ladies' overcoats. The sense of being closed in persisted, a sensation past experience had taught her to distrust.

A low building sprawled beside the two motorcars, every window radiating the yellow glow of the electric lights inside. Three other, taller buildings formed the rest of the enclosure, but for two wide openings—the one they had driven through and a second leading to another part of the factory complex.

A stillness pervaded the immediate area, but the air just beyond the enclosure pulsated with the dull rumble of the factory's workings. The breezes carried eddies of heat and brought ash floating around them like drab snowflakes. Eva brushed her hands across the shoulders of both Lady Phoebe's and Lady Amelia's coats and inwardly sighed. If they spent much more time outside, the soot would be embedded in their clothing. A fortunate thing, then, that among her luggage was her case of garment brushes.

"Well, Fox, I suppose you were right." Lady Annondale emerged from the rear seat of the Rolls-Royce with a critical frown. "Quite prisonlike. Ah, well. We have to be here only long enough to meet with the designers and choose a pattern. That shouldn't be too difficult."

Two men presently came bustling around a corner. They wore dark business suits, were hatless, and appeared somewhat out of breath, as if they had been very busy, but suddenly realized they had visitors—important ones. The taller of the two buttoned his suit coat and smoothed his peppered hair as he approached. The other, a pale man with hollow cheeks and wisps of hair pomaded across a balding pate, pulled a pair of spectacles from his breast pocket and carefully set them on his aquiline nose.

"Welcome, welcome. You must be the Renshaws." The first man extended his hand, then snatched it back and bobbed his head as if he were meeting royalty.

Eva judged him to be older than the second man, yet in better health generally, his shoulders straight, his hair still thick, his complexion robust.

"I'm Mr. Tremaine. Mr. Jeffrey Tremaine." A breathy laugh tumbled from his lips. "The owner of Crown Lily. You are most, most welcome to my establishment. I . . . er . . . trust you had a pleasant trip?"

Eva pressed her lips together. Poor man seemed to be battling a case of nerves. And while Phoebe and Amelia would strive to put him at his ease, Eva knew Lady Annondale would enjoy playing the part of imperious viscountess. What had begun years ago as a defense mechanism had quickly become second nature to Julia Renshaw, and later, Eva suspected, a source of amusement for her.

"Oh, dear me," Mr. Tremaine blurted as if startled by some development none of the rest of them perceived. Two spots of color stained his cheekbones. He gestured to the man waiting silently beside him. But patiently? No, Eva had caught several clipped sighs and the tapping of his shoe on the cobbles. "May I introduce Ronald Mercer. He's the head of our design department, responsible for the majority of our most successful patterns."

"Goodness, then you're the man we most wish to speak with." Lady Annondale extended a hand first to Mr. Tremaine, then turned her attention fully to Mr. Mercer. "You received my letter?"

"Indeed, Lady Annondale, and I've worked up some preliminary ideas for your perusal." While Mr. Mercer might have been Mr. Tremaine's inferior in terms of rank within the business, he displayed none of his employer's agitation. "They all incorporate the Wroxly coat of arms. I think you'll be delighted with what you see."

"And tell me," Lady Annondale said with an inquisitive lift of her eyebrow, "have you designed anything lately for Her Majesty?"

Eva understood the question was meant to

detect whether Crown Lily still enjoyed being the favored pottery of the Royal Household. She and the four Renshaws turned their faces toward the designer.

He smiled pleasantly. "Of course. I designed a luncheon set for the Princess Royal's birthday last spring. She was quite enamored of it, as was the queen."

"Splendid." Lady Annondale cast a significant glance at her brother. "You see, Fox, this shan't take long at all." She received, in response, a half-hearted shrug.

"Yes, well . . . While it's . . . er . . . true that Mr. Mercer here has been working on patterns for you, Lady Annondale, another of our artists has been doing so as well." Mr. Tremaine's cheekbones glowed with color. "He's quite talented as well, and eager to take up the project, and, well, you understand, I don't wish to play favorites. Especially when your ladyship"— he raised his gaze to take in the other Renshaw siblings—"and the rest of your charming family should have the very best of choices to consider."

The balding art director compressed his lips, then sighed again and nodded. "Indeed. Our Percy Bateman does fine work, if sometimes a bit overly bold in line and color. He's young, of course, and at times could use some reining in. Raw talent, you understand. We're very glad he joined our art department."

"Yes. Yes, *we* are." Mr. Tremaine stressed the word *we.*

Eva narrowed her eyes and studied this Mr. Mercer. He didn't seem at all glad the younger man had joined what he obviously considered *his* art department. She allowed herself a small smile, knowing each young Renshaw to be of strong opinions and unafraid to express them. They would soon see for themselves which artist embodied their vision for their grandparents' anniversary gift.

But would they be able to agree? She had her doubts that it would be as easy or quick an endeavor as Lady Annondale believed.

"All right, then." Lady Annondale glanced at the nearest building. "Shall we go and meet this Percy . . . ?"

"Bateman, ma'am," Mr. Tremaine was quick to offer.

Lady Annondale nodded distractedly. "Go and meet him and see what our choices are?"

"Of course, ma'am. Right away." The owner of Crown Lily half stumbled as he led them around a building and into another enclosure. Eva no longer felt an urge to grin at the man's jitters. Perhaps meeting nobility had unnerved him, but he won Eva's respect by seeming disinclined to allow his art director to take on the project without giving the younger artist an equal chance. "We've arranged a tour of the factory," he said as he held a door open for them. "This is our main administrative building, where we house our designers, accountants, clerks, and salesmen, and where we entertain prospective clients, like yourselves. Let's begin in the showroom."

"A tour won't be necessary." Lady Annondale breezed by him through the doorway.

The man looked crestfallen, until Lady Phoebe spoke up. "I would love to see the facilities. Amelia?"

"Oh, yes, I'm very curious to see how the china is made."

Fox added his consensus with a shrug. "Count me in."

"Phoebe," Lady Annondale murmured, but Mr. Tremaine came to the rescue. He stole a quick glance down at her rounded belly.

"If you'd care to wait in our conference room, Lady Annondale, I'll . . . er . . . have tea served and you can look over the various shapes of our teacups. They're already laid out on the table. It's those shapes, you realize, that will determine the look of the rest of the service. In fact, that was part of the plan. A tour, followed by tea and refreshments served in a variety of cup shapes and sizes."

"Oh, what a wonderful idea!" Amelia exclaimed. She pulled the pin from her hat and removed it, allowing her honey-golden hair to fall forward around her shoulders. "Thank you,

Mr. Tremaine. Julia, you can wait here with Hetta while the rest of us take the tour. It won't take very long, Mr. Tremaine, will it?"

"Not at all," he assured them.

"Very well." Lady Annondale pulled off her gloves. Hetta went to her side to help her off with her overcoat and smoothed the sleeves of her frock. "Perhaps Mr. Mercer will keep me company and tell me about his ideas for the design?"

"Nothing would give me greater pleasure, Lady Annondale," the designer said. "Truly, there is nothing like holding each shape in your hand, and actually sampling tea from it, for helping to find the exact right product."

Lady Annondale turned to her maid. "Hetta, would you care to join the others? I'll be fine here with Mr. Mercer, I'm quite sure."

Hetta shook her head vigorously. "I stay with Madame," she said with a possessiveness that ended the matter. She also issued Mr. Mercer a stern look from under her blond brows. Not that she had any reason to distrust the designer. Hetta merely assumed that manner with any individual new to her lady's acquaintance.

After a brief word to a young man Eva supposed was his secretary, Mr. Tremaine led them along the main hallway. Sounds of typing, of telephones ringing, and muted conversation reached her ears from behind closed doors. He opened a set of double, frosted glass-paned doors. Unmistakable pride brought a renewed flush to his cheeks. "This is our showroom."

Good heavens. Eva gasped as she peered over Phoebe and Amelia's shoulders. Bright electric lights and the sunlight pouring through a wall of floor-to-ceiling windows illuminated china of every shape, pattern, and color—florals, geometric designs, crests, and picturesque scenes. Porcelain gleamed and glimmered everywhere Eva looked. She had never seen so many cups, saucers, and dishes in one place, not even in the china department at Harrods. There were porcelain teapots that ranged from short and round to tall and tapering, creamers and sugar bowls, serving bowls and platters of many different sizes on stands to display their designs.

"And through here is our conference room, where we've set up an exclusive display based on your initial thoughts on what you might like." Mr. Tremaine opened another door into a well-appointed room, with a long mahogany table and at least a dozen leather chairs ranged around it.

Lady Annondale, the first to enter, approached the table. She reached out a fingertip to stroke the graceful line of the nearest vessel, a fluted teacup sporting a bright burst of flowers. She raised the cup by its delicate pink handle and held it to the light from the windows. Even from where Eva stood in the hallway, she could see the transparency of the porcelain, which rivaled an eggshell in its thinness. Hetta followed her mistress inside a good deal more timidly.

"*Ach du meine Güte,*" the Swiss woman murmured. Eva had spent enough time in Hetta's company to know this loosely translated to *good gracious.* Eva nodded her agreement.

Once Mr. Tremaine saw Lady Annondale and Mr. Mercer settled with a pot of tea and plate of biscuits, he gestured to Phoebe and the others. "This way, if you please."

He preceded them to another, heavier door. They stepped outside to an expansive enclosure between buildings that stood several stories tall. Directly behind a row of them, the tapering stacks of those odd structures Eva had seen on the way here poked against the sky. Lorries lumbered slowly across the open space, jostling over crisscrossing rail tracks that connected one building to another. Men were methodically loading and unloading barrels from railcars.

Eva helped Lady Amelia back on with her hat to prevent the bits of floating ash from settling in her hair. They crossed the quadrangle and entered a building. The industrial humming Eva had noticed earlier grew stronger now, seeming to vibrate up through the linoleum floor and radiate from the tiled walls. The first room they came to reminded Eva of the cellars back home at Foxwood Hall, with their stone walls and floor and utter lack of adornment. Ranged about the room were several wide, round vats made of steel. They were at least a dozen feet in diameter and nearly met Eva's shoulders; she was just able to peer into the interior of the nearest one. Curved blades fanned out from a center axle. There was no one working here, and these particular machines stood idle. Still, she heard the rumble and grind and felt the vibrations of what must be several others of these contraptions in nearby rooms like this one. She supposed these lay dormant for their tour, for safety's sake.

"This is one of our grinding rooms," Mr. Tremaine said. "This is where the ingredients for our porcelain—beef bone, stone, and clay—are ground and mixed."

"Looks like Mrs. Ellison's hand-cranked dough kneader," Fox exclaimed, "only giant-sized."

"It's not much different," their guide informed them.

Perhaps not. Eva had more than once wondered what might happen to a finger caught in the dough kneader's blades. Now she shuddered to think what would happen to someone unfortunate enough to fall into one of these vats while the blades were churning.

"And what exactly is the mixture?" Lady Amelia went to the vat, stood on tiptoes, and peered over the edge. Eva felt half tempted to pull her away. "How much of each do you use?"

"Our formula, my lady, is the strictest of secrets." Mr. Tremaine seemed to have shed his nerves and replied with enthusiasm. "You see, our special ratio of bone to stone to clay is what makes our china not only the thinnest of Staffordshire bone china, but the strongest. It appears delicate, but it's made to last, to be passed down through generations. If you'll all come this way . . ."

He led them into an adjoining room, another chilly, damp space, where Eva beheld several long metal tanks that stood even higher than the grinding pans. "These are rotary cylinders, which further mix the clay into a smooth and creamy slip. Once that's done, the slip flows through this trough—or *ark,* as we call it—and over a powerful magnet to remove any metallic particles remaining in the mixture. Once that's done, the clay is run through the pug mill to remove any air bubbles that might have formed."

"Are bubbles bad?" Amelia asked.

"Very bad," Mr. Tremaine confirmed. "They can cause an item, whether a cup or plate or what have you, to explode in the heat of the firing."

"I'd like to see that!" Fox exclaimed.

"Fox," Phoebe admonished in a whisper. "Behave." Then to the rest of them she said, "This is so much more scientific than I'd imagined. Quite an elaborate process." She turned to Eva for consensus.

Eva nodded, impressed and slightly intimidated by what she'd seen so far. "To think, all this for an object as simple as a teacup. It's rather like magic, isn't it?"

"This is only the beginning." Mr. Tremaine smiled proudly. "There are many stages to producing our china."

"What happens next?" Amelia gazed around her, her eyes alight in her eagerness to learn more.

The owner walked them out of the building and across the cobbled yard to yet another section of the factory. If Eva had to find her way back to Lady Annondale by herself, she didn't think she could do it, not without a map and a compass.

Now she found herself tilting her head back until it could go no farther. This area played host to several of those bottle-shaped structures. Up close they were huge, several stories high, round and wide at the base, tapering to narrow chimneys at the top. Each sent black smoke curling against the afternoon sky. If Eva had felt intimidated by the grinders and rotary cylinders, she was doubly so now. The notion of these looming brick structures posing a danger might be irrational, but she couldn't shake the sensation. They were simply too big, too foreign to anything she had ever encountered before.

"These are the bottle kilns," Mr. Tremaine was saying. "They're where the first firing takes place—fifty-five hours at twelve hundred fifty degrees centigrade, followed by a cooling period of seventy-two hours. We light several kilns at a time, on a rotating basis." He went on to describe the series of heat-dispersing flues that ran beneath each kiln, fed by coal furnaces, or what he called fire mouths, set at the base of each kiln.

"They're colossal!" Lady Amelia shaded her eyes as she gazed up at the tops of the kilns. "Has anyone ever been trapped inside?"

"No, indeed, my lady." Mr. Tremaine sounded almost scandalized. "Not in our nearly two-hundred-year history. There have been other kinds of accidents, to be sure, but not here. We take the utmost precautions to ensure the workers have cleared out before the kilns are sealed and the heating process begins. Nothing organic can survive inside at those temperatures."

"No, I would imagine not." Lady Phoebe moved closer to Eva as if by instinct. "I'm sorry to say I find them rather unsettling."

"I think you'll appreciate the next part of our tour, then." Mr. Tremaine ushered them away from the kilns. "Now you'll see more of the artistic side of the business."

Before they could enter the next building, however, a voice behind them called out, "Renshaw! Good heavens, is that you?"

They all turned, and Eva beheld a youth of about Fox's age, with close-cropped hair and a prominent nose. He reminded her of someone . . .

Fox strode to the other boy, kicking up dust on the cobblestones in his haste. "What the devil are you doing here? We all thought you died."

CHAPTER 2

Phoebe watched her brother hurry over to the other boy. He had a dog with him, a hulking creature with a muscular body, broad at the shoulders and narrow at the rump. His fur was sleek and short in a brown-and-white pattern. More significantly, the dog possessed a wide, flat snout that assured her that once he set his teeth into something, he wouldn't release it until he was blasted certain he wished to.

"Who on earth could that be?" she asked Eva, though she didn't expect a reply. "Fox didn't mention knowing anyone in Langston, much less at Crown Lily Potteries."

The two boys shook hands and fell into a conversation Phoebe couldn't make out, though she heard their short bursts of laughter. The dog jumped once toward Fox, but at a word from his master, he set his rump obediently on the ground. Then the pair appeared to become serious. She started toward them.

"Fox, who's your friend? Do introduce us." She stopped some yards away, hoping the animal wouldn't change his mind about behaving.

Amelia stopped beside her, perhaps with the same thought in mind, while Eva came up behind them. Then Mr. Tremaine spoke.

"Trent. Shouldn't you be filling saggars?" At the sound of his voice the dog gave a friendly bark and trotted over to the factory's owner. The man bent down to pet the top of his head and gave his shoulders a rub for good measure. He was rewarded with a few affectionate licks before the dog ran back to his master.

That young man made a face. "I have been, Mr. Tremaine. I'll go back in presently."

"Don't leave yet." Fox turned toward Mr. Tremaine. "Don't send him off. We're schoolmates at Eton. Or we were before Mercer here disappeared into thin air." Fox regarded his friend. "What happened to you? And what are you doing here?"

"Mercer," Phoebe repeated as a realization dawned on her. "Are you Ronald Mercer's son? The art director?" she added. Behind her, Eva said, "Oh," as if this answered a question she'd had.

"I am," the youth said, but with little apparent satisfaction. His eyes were hazel, a trait he must have gotten from his mother, for Mr. Mercer's eyes were dark. "Ronald Mercer is my father, and he's the reason I'm here." He relayed this latter information to Fox, who shook his head in puzzlement.

"I don't understand. Why did you leave Eton? You were near the top of our class. I only wish I had your marks."

The other boy shrugged, staring down at his

dog. He bent down to stroke the animal's stout head and nonexistent neck.

"Trent is here learning the business." This came from Mr. Tremaine. "He's to follow in his father's footsteps someday." Phoebe distinctly sensed the word *perhaps* in Mr. Tremaine's tone, as if he doubted the boy's abilities.

Another glance at Trent's sagging posture suggested it wasn't the boy's abilities in question, but his willingness.

"In light of your reunion, Trent, why don't you join us on the tour and leave the saggars for later." Mr. Tremaine smiled indulgently.

Trent Mercer brightened at the prospect, but Fox frowned. "What are *saggars?*"

"They're special containers we use for the firing," Mr. Tremaine explained. "They're made of clay, and have separate compartments into which each item of china is placed to protect them from discoloring in the intense heat. They prevent the glazes from fusing one piece of china to another during the second firing."

Fox looked incredulous. "You left Eton for that?"

"Father has me learning the china industry from the ground up." Trent shoved his hands in his trouser pockets. His lips flattened for an instant, further revealing his displeasure. "I've shoveled ash and stone, been a packer, worked the glost oven—"

"What's that?" Amelia wanted to know. "Is that different from the bottle kilns?"

"Why don't we continue our tour, and you'll have the answers to all your questions." Mr. Tremaine held out an arm to usher them into the next building. They saw the glost ovens, where glazes were melted by electricity into a clear glass finish—a different process than that for the colored glazes. Next came the throwers, who shaped cups and other round items on wheels, and then the molders, who poured liquefied clay into molds to produce more intricately shaped items, such as the fluted cup they'd seen inside.

They watched an engraver etch one of Ronald Mercer's designs onto a copperplate. The plates were then covered in pigment and applied to tissue paper, which would be used to transfer the pattern onto the china. From there each piece was given to a painter or enameler, who painstakingly applied colors according to the designer's explicit instructions. Along the way there were various inspection rooms to ensure the quality of every piece. The rooms in each department were vast, nearly as large as the ballroom at home.

Phoebe's head nearly swam with all she'd learned. "I might not remember all of this tomorrow," she joked with Eva as Mr. Tremaine led them back to the administrative building and the conference room, where Julia awaited them. "But I certainly have a new appreciation for how much effort goes into creating china. I'll never take a teacup for granted again."

Eva chuckled. "Now comes the difficult task, choosing a pattern and shape for your grandparents."

"Why difficult?" Amelia had caught up to them, once more removing her hat and swinging it by her side.

"Because, my lady, there are four of you and only one pattern to be chosen."

Phoebe stepped inside ahead of them as Mr. Tremaine held the door open. "I'm fairly certain we can rule out Fox having an opinion one way or the other." She glanced over her shoulder at him, lagging with his friend several yards behind their little group. The dog—Jester, Phoebe had heard him called—lumbered along beside them, his tongue lolling. None of the trio appeared particularly enthusiastic about the prospect of going inside. In fact, Phoebe guessed, if given the chance, they'd take off—the boys running, the dog bounding—somewhere no one could find them for a good long while. But she had no intention of giving her brother that chance and having to explain to Julia how she had lost him.

"Fox, come along. Julia is waiting. And you know how she gets when her patience runs out."

That did the trick. Fox hurried his steps, and moments later they all filed into the conference room. The mingled scents of various teas—

spicy, sweet, smooth, bold—filled the air. Julia and Ronald Mercer occupied two places at the far end of the table, Julia at the head and Mr. Mercer to her right. Hetta stood near a window, her hands folded at her waist, her eyes fixed on her mistress.

Julia and Mr. Mercer were leaning toward each other, appearing deep in concentration. Each held a teacup aloft, sipping occasionally, while around them was ranged an assortment of cup shapes and sizes. Julia had been busy in their absence, apparently. She glanced up and blinked. "There you all finally are. I was beginning to think you'd never return."

Jeffrey Tremaine once more colored with embarrassment. "I'm so sorry, Lady Annondale. I . . . I hadn't realized we kept you waiting such an uncomfortably long time. I do apologize."

"Oh, Julia, you should have come." Amelia walked the length of the table and plunked into the chair opposite Mr. Mercer. "We learned so much! All of it fascinating."

Julia issued one of her shrugs and tilted her head. "One doesn't need to know how a motorcar works to operate one." She drained her teacup.

"Try *this,* Lady Annondale." Mr. Mercer leaned forward to retrieve a teapot; he turned to Amelia. "Choose a cup and saucer and tell me what kind of tea you fancy." Then the man noticed his son standing behind Fox. Or hovering, looking

33

as though he hoped not to be seen. His father's pleasant expression dimmed. "Trent. What are you doing here? You have work to do." Phoebe saw his gaze land on the dog, but he gave the animal no sign of welcome. Neither did Jester trot over to the man in greeting.

"We're mates from Eton," Fox explained when his friend only stared back at his father in tight-lipped silence.

Ronald Mercer leaned back in his chair and viewed the boys down the length of his curving nose. "Is that right?"

Fox nodded. Trent continued to gaze mutely at his father. Phoebe couldn't help but notice how his eyes became larger and how his bottom lip protruded. His withdrawal from Eton had been a contentious topic between them, she concluded. Still was.

His father smiled. "Not anymore, I'm afraid. Trent has left academia behind. He's learning this business and will eventually train as a designer. Like me." He touched his fingertips to his coat front.

"That's splendid." Julia sampled the tea the man poured for her, then announced, "Mr. Mercer and I have made some preliminary decisions."

Phoebe took a seat beside Amelia. "I thought this was supposed to be a family decision."

Before Julia could reply, a bustling sounded in the doorway. A man practically skidded in from the hallway. Compact in size, with unkempt dark hair and uncommonly green eyes, he appeared out of breath and flushed. A bundle of papers, the corners sticking out this way and that, filled his arms.

"So sorry I'm late." He came to a sudden halt beside Mr. Tremaine, who rolled his eyes slightly and looked as though he'd like to melt into the floor tiles. "Got caught up with a project." He attempted to straighten his papers on the tabletop, to little effect. He laid them down instead. "You're the Renshaws, yes?"

Phoebe and her siblings regarded the young man in perplexed silence, until Phoebe overcame her surprise at the manner of his arrival. "Yes, we're the Renshaws. Let me hazard a guess. You're Percy Bateman, the other designer."

"I am," he replied in equal surprise, as if he credited Phoebe's knowledge of his name to mystical powers. "And I've brought some ideas for your china."

"That might not be necessary, Percy." Mr. Mercer looked downright triumphant. "Lady Annondale and I appear to see eye to eye on what the family requires."

"But . . ." Percy Bateman visibly wilted. "I've worked so hard. Surely . . ." His glance darted from Phoebe to each of her siblings, landing lastly on Julia. "Surely, you'll at least take a look."

"Of course we will." Phoebe ignored Julia's intake of breath, yet another sign of her impatience. "We haven't made any decisions yet."

"Have a seat, Percy." Mr. Tremaine gestured the younger man to the table. "Before our guests decide on a pattern, they must choose a cup shape, which will determine whether the design will be traditional, modern, romantic, Baroque, etc."

"Modern," Julia uttered without hesitation. She pointed to a cup with sleek, tapering lines, a small round foot, and a triangular-shaped handle.

"Romantic," Amelia said over her, reaching toward a fluted cup that mimicked the petals of a flower.

"Traditional," Phoebe said with emphasis. "Grams and Grampapa are traditionalists in every way. They won't want anything modern, Julia. Or too fussy, Amelia." Her gaze landed on a footed cup with a wide bowl and scrolling handle.

"Nonsense." Julia sniffed. "It's a new decade. A new era."

"While I couldn't agree with you more," Phoebe said evenly, "we can't impose our tastes on Grams and Grampapa. This gift is for them, not you or me."

"I agree with Phoebe about not wanting something modern." Amelia reached into the center of the table, looped her finger into the handle of the fluted teacup, and lifted it carefully. "But traditional is boring, Phoebe. This is for their anniversary. It should be a romantic shape, with a lovely floral pattern worked around the coat of arms." She turned to their brother, who sat with Trent farther down the table. "Fox?"

"I say we scrub the whole idea of teacups and bring Grams and Grampapa a pair of Staffordshire bull terriers, like Jester here." He pointed down at the dog, sitting placidly beside his master's chair and appearing thoroughly bored by the humans around him. "That's what Foxwood Hall needs nowadays. A good pair of dogs like we always had about the place before the war."

With Phoebe and Amelia's permission, Eva left the siblings to squabble over teacups. Mr. Tremaine had said it would be all right for her to return to the building where the artwork was done and quietly observe, but to stay clear of the industrial areas. No risk of that, as she had no desire to return to the subterranean-like chambers that housed the vats with their lethal-looking blades or the ovens, where nothing living could survive the temperatures.

What held her fascination in the room she returned to were the rows and rows of worktables, nearly all of them occupied by women, each with a good two dozen teacups on trays before them.

Each woman wore a simple cotton dress of light blue or gray, covered by a thick white apron. It surprised her that those aprons, in most cases, were virtually unblemished. That showed their great skill and care in handling paint. Brush in hand, prepared pigments arranged beside them, each artist painstakingly applied an array of color to each item of transferware, bringing the patterns to vivid life.

She walked slowly down one of the long aisles, of which there were nearly a dozen. Large windows let in a good amount of natural light, augmented by the electric lights overhead. Eva understood this last detail would have been added only within the past few years. Before that, artwork would have depended on the weather cooperating with abundant sunshine. Days without must have put production behind schedule.

Only a few of the artists glanced up as she passed them. Most seemed undisturbed in their concentration and unaware of their audience of one. Or perhaps they were accustomed to being observed. Eva would imagine Mr. Tremaine, as the company's owner, and Mr. Mercer, as head of the design department, would wish to ensure their workers produced only the finest quality.

She was about to make a turn onto the next row when a woman sitting in the corner at the far end of the room stood abruptly. She was a sturdy, large-boned woman, much like Hetta, with a round face, wide chin and brow, and small blue eyes above a short, upturned nose. She and Hetta were even about the same age. But here the resemblance to the congenial Swiss woman ended. Eva could imagine *this* woman as a head matron at a hospital, one who ruled her nurses with an iron fist, especially judging by her displeased expression, which was aimed wholly upon Eva.

"Can I help you?" Nothing about her tone implied a desire to be solicitous. On the contrary, she appeared about to order Eva from the premises. "You shouldn't be here. I can't imagine how you got in."

Eva decided to be acquiescent rather than defensive, even if she did have Mr. Tremaine's permission to be there. "I'm terribly sorry, I didn't mean to disturb anyone. I was here earlier, touring the facilities with Mr. Tremaine. Perhaps you remember?"

"And? That doesn't explain what you're doing back here now." The woman narrowed her gaze as she took in Eva from head to toe, surveying her charcoal traveling suit beneath her plain wool coat, and her sensible pumps. A little gleam of judgment entered the woman's small eyes. She had sized Eva up and made a deduction, though whether for good or ill, Eva couldn't yet say.

"You see, my employers are planning

to commission a table service for their grandparents." She smiled and tilted her head apologetically. "They're deciding on the particulars now and don't need me, so I slipped away. This part of the factory fascinated me, and Mr. Tremaine said it would be all right if I returned to watch. Honestly, I didn't mean to disturb your work."

She quickly gazed to her right and left to find several of the workers had turned their attention on her, but they just as speedily returned to their tasks. Perhaps it wasn't that they found the encounter dull, but that they feared being censured by their supervisor—for Eva decided this woman must be in charge of this department.

"Your employers, you say? Are they the family of the Earl and Countess of Wroxly?"

"Yes, the very same." Eva made sure to smile and speak cordially.

"*Hmph.* That's an important commission. All right, then, you may stay." The woman's gaze traveled over Eva once more. "What are you, a lady's maid?"

"I am, yes."

"*Hmph,*" the woman uttered again, giving Eva the impression she disapproved of the position. "I'm Moira Wickham, head of painting and enameling."

Yes, Eva had guessed correctly. "It's a pleasure to meet you. I'm Eva Huntford. Thank you for letting me stay." She glanced down at the woman's left hand and saw no ring. Not even that slight, telltale indentation of the finger that said she sometimes wore one, but removed it to work. In all likelihood none of these women had husbands, or they wouldn't be working here at all.

Miss Wickham began walking, signaling for Eva to join her. They slowly made their way down the row Eva had been heading for before Miss Wickham had waylaid her. As they passed by each desk, Eva silently admired the efforts of each painter. "Do you have artistic ambitions, Miss Huntford?"

"I wish I had the talent, but, no, I've only an appreciation for the work you're doing here. I must admit to being slightly envious."

"You don't like your position, then."

"Oh, I don't mean to imply that at all. I love working for my ladies. I tend to two, you see, the earl's two younger granddaughters. It used to be all three, but now that the eldest, Lady Annondale, is . . ." Eva trailed off, having little desire to explain the circumstances of Lady Annondale's widowhood. Besides, Miss Wickham could hardly be interested in such particulars. And yet, the woman nodded.

"Yes, the Viscountess Annondale, that was Lady Julia Renshaw. I read all about her in the papers last spring."

41

Eva's face heated. How she loathed the thought of any of her ladies being subjected to the scandal sheets. Yet, she could hardly blame the newspapers for running the story of the Viscount Annondale's murder on the very night of his wedding. How, then, could she blame the public for reading those same stories?

Best to change the subject altogether. "How long have you been working here, Miss Wickham?"

"Over ten years now. Before that, I worked for a competing pottery."

"If you don't mind my asking, how is it that most of the painters here are women?"

They stopped beside a blonde of about thirty who held one of the modern cups Lady Annondale had admired in the conference room. She appeared to be working with a palette of blues, with white, lavender, and subtle pinks bringing highlights to the elongated trees in the design. The woman smiled up at them and immediately refocused on her work.

"Women have smaller hands, better for such fine details."

Eva couldn't help stealing another glance down at Miss Wickham's hands. They were hardly small. In fact, they were wide and muscular, the fingers were short and stubby. But Eva could only surmise the woman possessed the necessary dexterity nonetheless, or she would not be head of painting and enameling.

"Our few men are only here temporarily, as soon enough they'll be promoted to assistant designers. As for the rest of us, there isn't much work out there for female artists, other than what we do here. It's not creative, you see, but carefully laid out for us. Creativity is left to the men. You met Mr. Mercer."

It wasn't a question, nor was the observation without its implications—being that women were relegated to a secondary role in the creation of Crown Lily china, and this did not please Moira Wickham.

"I also met Percy Bateman," Eva said. "He seemed most eager to present his design ideas to the Renshaws."

"Poor Percy, he's a bit of a nervous wreck sometimes, but a first-rate designer. I hope he wins the commission, but we'll see." Her brow creased. "There are others who'd like the commission as well, who have fine ideas for the pattern design, but they won't be considered."

Again, the implication seemed to be that Mr. Mercer held the reins of creativity tightly in both fists. Eva hoped Mr. Bateman would win out merely on principle. Then again, was Miss Wickham speaking of herself as having fine ideas for the Renshaws' pattern? How frustrating it must be, and infuriating, to have one's talents dismissed merely on the basis of being a woman.

"How did you receive your art training?" Eva

asked, at the same time surprised that after such a frosty beginning, they should find themselves speaking almost as confidantes.

"My parents saw my potential early on and found the means to send me to one of the local art schools. There are plenty in the region, you know, because of the many china manufacturers."

"Were they artists as well?"

Miss Wickham laughed quietly. "My parents, no. My mother was in service before she married. A lady's maid, like yourself." She nodded at Eva, and Eva suspected the coincidence was largely responsible for Miss Wickham not sending her packing earlier. "And my father was a vicar before he retired. They very wisely wanted me to have choices, and I often wonder, nowadays, where I would be if they hadn't."

"What do you mean?" The comment left Eva truly curious, and she looked up from studying a bold black-and-white pattern, strewn here and there with brightly colored balloons, on the plates a woman was painting.

"The war, of course," the woman said succinctly. "I'm a surplus woman, as are most of the others here. Women without husbands, and who'll likely never find husbands. Like yourself, if I'm not mistaken. You're about the right age, I'd say."

"*Surplus women* . . . such a callous term." Eva wasn't admonishing Miss Wickham. She had heard those words before and read them in the newspapers in recent months. Miss Wickham had defined the term perfectly: women who would likely never find husbands because the war had taken so many men of their generation. That much Eva knew to be true. What she couldn't understand was why such women were blamed for their circumstances, as if they should apologize for existing and slink off into oblivion, where society would no longer have to acknowledge them.

Yet, she didn't mention that, unlike so many women her age, she very likely *would* marry one day. It wasn't a lack of prospects that kept her single at present, but duty toward her ladies—and genuine love for them. Having been motherless from an early age, and fatherless since the war, the Renshaw girls needed Eva as so much more than a lady's maid. But when they no longer did . . .

Then perhaps she and Miles Brannock might build a life of their own. A constable made too little money to support a family, but someday he would be promoted . . . and her ladies would no longer need her as they do now . . . And then, they would see.

"I'll have you know it was us women who kept Crown Lily going during the war." They had reached the end of another row, and here Miss Wickham drew Eva aside. "Pulling double duty not only painting and enameling, but filling in for the men who went off to fight. We packed barrels and loaded lorries and train carriages. Backbreaking work, I don't mind telling you. But we did our bit. It was the patriotic thing to do, keeping an old English company like this one afloat. We were painting quite a lot of commemorative patterns, too, town and city crests, military insignia, tributes to our victories on the continent. Many was the day we toiled long into the night, but not a one of us complained."

"I'm sure Mr. Tremaine is very grateful."

"Is he? *Hmph.*" Moira Wickham set her hands on her fleshy hips. "The moment the men came back, we were patted on our heads and told to return to our proper places. And when I asked him if some of us might be allowed to submit original artwork for new patterns, he bowed down to Ronald Mercer, who insisted women hadn't the skill to compete in the china industry, that Crown Lily would be taking a frightful risk to allow it." She rubbed her hands together as if to brush away crumbs. "And that was that."

CHAPTER 3

Phoebe arrived at Lyndale Park feeling as though she'd been submerged in murky water and wrung out to dry. She wanted only to retreat to whatever guest room she'd been assigned to and sleep until dinnertime. They had achieved little at the Crown Lily Potteries, other than to establish that she and her siblings had a far different opinion as to what her grandparents would prefer. Fox had stood firm on his recommendation that they should forget the china altogether and bring home dogs instead. As outlandish as the notion seemed at first, she wondered now if perhaps he had landed upon an ingenious solution to their dilemma.

There had once been a full host of hounds at Foxwood Hall, before the war. Each autumn, Grampapa and Papa would host a hunt for some several dozen guests lasting four or five days, with teas, dinners, and other entertainments planned around the daily rides across the estate. They'd had pet dogs as well, and they had enjoyed the full run of the house. A pair of spaniels, a Great Dane named Horace . . .

Phoebe's throat tightened, remembering how most of the animals, including the horses, had been given over to the war effort. Dogs had been used to relay messages through the trenches. It had hurt Grampapa dearly to see them go, but he'd done his part to help the soldiers.

She blinked away the memories and turned her attention back to the property they'd just entered. The approach to the house appeared peaceful enough, with twin lines of laurel trees, all trimmed to a uniform size, casting their wintry, skeletal shadows over the drive. The lawn sprawled to either side, framed by thick forest and, in the distance, rolling hills. Closer, stone benches, an arched bridge over a stream, and flowerbeds, however dormant now, created a picturesque scene. The house itself was a three-story redbrick manor in the Carolean style that dated from the mid-seventeenth century, charming and understated, yet grand nonetheless.

Phoebe had been here before, but only once, and that nearly a year ago when Julia and Gilbert Townsend had first become engaged. The estate had not originally belonged to Gil's family, and hadn't been passed down to him through the generations. His roots here weren't like those of the Renshaw family at Foxwood Hall.

Gil hadn't been in the china business, but had purchased controlling shares in several of the region's coal mines. As they had learned today, it was the combination of coal and water that had made this area perfect for china production, as well as powering other industries. Gil had acquired Lyndale Park when he became a viscount after the Boer Wars, and apparently a bit of a fortune had come with the property. To be fair, though, he had amassed a fortune of his own in industry, first from the production of industrial steam engines, then motorcar engines. He had prospered even more during the Great War by diversifying into airplane engines.

Phoebe didn't begrudge him that. Perhaps there had been a time when Gil Townsend, Viscount Annondale, contributed honestly to the changing world, helping to usher in new technology that would make life easier for subsequent generations. But somewhere along the way, he had lost his sense of honor and fair play, done regrettable things, and paid with his life.

And now the fate of Lyndale Park hinged on the life of Julia's unborn child. If a boy, he would be the new Viscount Annondale and inherit the property, the manufacturing plants, and the bulk of Gil's fortune, leaving Julia overseeing all of it until the child came of age. A girl, on the other hand, would have an annuity, no doubt a generous one, but limited nonetheless, and Julia would gain control over nothing.

Fenton brought the Rolls-Royce to a stop in front of the pedimented entryway. He'd given Julia no further reason to complain about his driving, to the vast relief of them all. Yet, as he opened the rear door for them, a chill traveled up Phoebe's spine. The quiet, the closed front door, and the lack of anyone outside to welcome them reminded her of another arrival, well over a year ago, to their cousin Regina's home. That visit had ended in a manner Phoebe cared never to see repeated.

When still no one stepped out to greet them, a look from Julia sent Fenton to the front door. He raised the knocker and let it fall several times, until finally the front door creaked open. The butler, as Phoebe remembered from her previous visit, peeked out. A ridge of annoyance stood out across his brow. "Yes?"

Phoebe and her siblings traded mystified looks. Phoebe went to Julia's side. "Are you sure you let them know we were coming?"

"Of course I did. I wrote to Veronica last month." Her gaze darted over the front of the house, as still as a tomb. Then she strode to the entrance and nudged Fenton out of the way. "Let us in, Carmichael."

The butler's dark eyes went wide. "Lady Annondale? Good heavens, my lady, do come in. All of you, come in." He thrust the door open and stood aside to allow them to file into the vestibule. Once he'd closed the door behind them, he stuttered an apology. "We h-had no notice of your coming, m-my lady. I assure you, had we known we'd have m-made ready."

"What on earth are you saying, Carmichael?" Julia slipped her cashmere cape from her shoulders. Carmichael scrambled behind her to catch it before it fell to the floor. "As I just told my sister, I sent advance notice a month ago."

"I wasn't informed, my lady."

Julia pushed out a sigh. "I can't imagine my letter going so far astray. Something is fishy about this, Carmichael. But very well. Please ready enough rooms for us and let the cook know we're here."

"Yes, my lady, right away. I'll . . . er . . . escort you to the drawing room and have tea sent up immediately."

"No need to escort us." Julia stepped into the colonnaded front hall, tiled in marble, furnished in gilt, and presided over by a Baccarat crystal chandelier that hung from two stories above their heads. Julia breezed by these surroundings and proceeded toward a pair of open doors. "I know the way."

"I'll let the others know you're here, my lady."

Julia stopped short and pivoted back around to face the butler. "The others? Who is here besides Miss Townsend?"

It had been agreed, upon Gil's death, that his sister, Veronica, would be allowed to continue living here, especially since Julia had elected to remain at Foxwood Hall with her family during her pregnancy. The butler's suddenly cagey expression gave Phoebe an uneasy sensation . . .

"Miss Blair and Mr. Shelton have been . . . That is to say, my lady . . ."

"They're living here, too?" The shock on Julia's face was entirely genuine. "In the main house?"

"They are, my lady." The man compressed his lips, an entreaty forming in the lines of his taut features.

But it was the look on Julia's face or, more properly speaking, the anger that set Phoebe's feet in motion. She hurried over and slipped her hand around Julia's upper arm. "It's all right, we'll deal with it. They haven't been hurting anything by being here, and it's certainly not Carmichael's fault." She felt the draining of Julia's tension against her palm.

"No, it's not Carmichael's fault. Though as to whether Mildred and Ernest have been hurting anything or anyone by being here . . . we'll see, won't we?" To the butler Julia said, "Please let them all know we're here, and that we'll be staying a few days at least, if not longer," she added in a murmur. "And do tell them we're presently in the drawing room until the bedrooms are made ready for us. And then, good heavens, I'll need a lie-down."

"Yes, my lady." Looking immensely relieved that he wasn't going to be held to blame, Carmichael turned away to climb the stairs.

"Oh, and, Carmichael," Julia called to him. Slowly he turned back. "I expect to stay in the master bedroom."

The corner of his mouth twitched downward, the only sign he gave that Julia's wishes might cause a bit of a problem. With a nod Carmichael made short work of the stairs.

A quarter of an hour later Phoebe and the others were enjoying the tea and sandwiches the cook had sent up for them. "What a grueling day," she commented, selecting a crustless smoked salmon sandwich from the platter. "It's good to finally be able to relax."

"I thought we accomplished quite a lot." Teacup in hand, Julia leaned back in her chair. She smoothed the fingertips of her left hand around the smooth porcelain, perhaps unconsciously, just as Phoebe caught herself doing. She had already gauged the thinness of the china, judging it not nearly as delicate as the china they'd seen today at Crown Lily. In fact, the cup seemed almost unwieldy in its thickness, something she knew she would not have thought before today's tour. She raised her cup higher to read the mark on the bottom: *Henslow Potteries*, it read.

Julia went on, "I'm especially impressed with Mr. Mercer's suggestions and initial design. I think he's our man."

Amelia looked up from her deviled ham. "I thought Mr. Bateman captured exactly what Grams and Grampapa would like. His designs weren't nearly as outlandish as Mr. Mercer tried to make out."

Julia shrugged. "They're both working hard tonight to impress us tomorrow."

"I just hope we can come to an amicable agreement by then," Phoebe murmured behind her teacup. "But it's looking doubtful."

"What was that?" Julia pinned her with a sharp stare.

She assumed an innocent expression. "Nothing."

Fox sent a smirk in Phoebe's direction, not aimed at her, she thought, but at the situation.

Approaching footsteps echoed in the main hall. Moments later Julia's three in-laws sauntered in. Veronica Townsend, Gil's middle-aged, unmarried sister, looked defiant, her square face set and determined. Ernest Shelton, Gil's cousin once removed, frowned at them from behind his spectacles and bit his bottom lip apprehensively. Phoebe wasn't fooled. Though he might appear a mild-mannered veterinarian, Ernie knew how to be downright devious when he wanted something. Julia's third relative by marriage, Mildred Blair, Gil's illegitimate daughter, spared a cool smile for Phoebe and her siblings, tossed her bobbed black hair, and dropped into the nearest armchair.

Julia surveyed them with a bored expression, then made a gesture with the hand holding a corner of a cucumber sandwich. "Veronica, Ernie, won't you both sit down? Mildred certainly has no problem making herself comfortable."

Mildred only curled her lips, which had seen a liberal application of lip rouge. Veronica made a convulsive motion that set her bulky middle jiggling. "I do not need to be invited to sit in my own home."

"Nor do I," Ernie parroted, though a good deal less impressively.

"To my knowledge, Ernie . . ." Julia paused to take a dainty bite of her sandwich. She took her time in swallowing, then continued. "This has never been your home. Or am I mistaken?"

"No, you're not mistaken." Mildred Blair crossed one leg over the other and swung her pump-clad foot up and down. A dark-haired beauty with translucent skin and striking features, Mildred had been Gil's personal secretary for nearly ten years, and no one during that time had ever guessed the true nature of her relationship to her employer. "It's lovely to see you all. How have you been? When are you due, Julia?"

"In two months," Julia replied succinctly, and raised her teacup to her lips. She lowered it with a pensive click against the saucer. "Now that I think of it, Mildred, this has never been your home, either. At least, not this part of it. Didn't Gil allocate you a room on the third floor while you worked for him? And do you find it appropriate to be living here now?"

A ruddy tinge entered the raven-haired woman's cheeks and something in her eyes hardened. Even Phoebe stiffened slightly against the back of the settee. She, Mildred, and indeed everyone else in the room understood Julia's implication. Mildred might have resided at Lyndale Park previously, but essentially she had done so as a servant. Yes, an upper servant and a highly skilled one, but a servant, all the same. A sense of chagrin swept over Phoebe. She thought it mean of Julia to bring attention to this now.

"Julia, why don't we—" Phoebe had been about to suggest they come to an agreement wherein all of them would share the house for as long as needed, but Veronica interrupted her.

"Who are you to decide who comes and goes?" She aimed her venomous tone at Julia. "This has never been your home, either, and God willing it never will be." Her gaze flicked to Julia's belly and back up to her face.

"That's unkind," Amelia said with a gasp. And no wonder. Veronica's pronouncement amounted to wishing ill on the unborn child. Phoebe believed circumstances were about to spin out of control. Yet, it wasn't Veronica's outburst that most concerned her, but Ernie's sinister little giggle. She met his gaze and stared him down, wondering how she ever found anything in this man to admire.

And as for Julia . . . she merely sipped her tea and again gently placed the cup on its saucer. "As Gil's widow I am his closest living relative. I'm sorry, Veronica, but that's the truth. As such, I have every right to be here, and every right to occupy the master bedroom. Am I to understand one of you has moved into it?"

No one said anything, but both Veronica and Mildred darted looks at Ernie from beneath their lashes—Veronica churlishly and Mildred coyly, with yet another little smile playing about her mouth. It seemed she had recovered from Julia's slight and was ready to enjoy watching the others experience similar discomfort. Her behavior didn't surprise Phoebe at all, for she had previously shown herself to be a shrewd and grasping young woman.

"So it's you, Ernie." Julia gave a laugh. "It makes perfect sense, I suppose. Veronica has the room she has always occupied here—why move? And I very much doubt Mildred would find her father's former suite to her liking."

Mildred nodded in agreement. "I find the colors overbearing and the furnishings heavy and old-fashioned," she said without rancor.

"So that leaves you, Ernie, thinking that as Gil's only male heir, you have the right to take what was his?" Julia tilted her head as if in genuine interest. Phoebe knew better. She was baiting Ernie, as he would soon discover.

Like Veronica, he had remained standing. Now he moved onto the hearth rug, where he could look directly down on Julia. "I am not taking anything that isn't mine by rights. I have lived on this estate, seeing to the livestock, Gil's horses, his dogs, and those of the tenants and villagers, for nearly twenty years now. I've endured Gil's insults, his offensive behavior, and his absolute delight in making my life a misery." He fell silent, heaving, his nostrils flaring. He turned away from Julia, walked several strides, pushed his glasses higher on his nose, and then turned around and retraced his steps.

"And then you come along, with your flirting and cajoling and your promises to make Gil happy, and *everything* I suffered for, waited for, counted on—gone . . . in a moment." He snapped his fingers. "You made my entire life here a waste of time, and now you begrudge me the master bedroom? How dare you? How dare you even—"

Phoebe was on her feet in an instant. "That's enough, Ernie!" Amelia also hopped up and ran to Julia's side as if to shield her from harm. Phoebe seized Ernie's arm. He tried to yank it free, but she held on, and then Fox was there, too, standing toe-to-toe with Ernie, his face pressed close. It forced Ernie to back up a step.

"If your life is a waste, Ernie, it's your own fault," Fox said with more controlled anger than Phoebe had ever heard from him. "I'm sorry if you put all your eggs into Gil's basket. That's not Julia's fault. I'll thank you to vacate the master bedroom and leave my sister alone."

Ernie's expression crumpled into one of sheer incredulity. "You're a child. You know nothing of life, of what it is to have your hopes crushed. Who are you to tell me anything?"

Fox pressed closer still. "I'm the next Earl of Wroxly, that's who."

Eva stood behind Amelia at the dressing table that night, brushing out her honey-blond hair, which fell in soft waves to her shoulders. Of necessity, Amelia and Phoebe were sharing a bedroom, as they often did when away from home. Eva enjoyed seeing how well they got on with one another, and having them together in the same room certainly made her job easier.

"Eva, you should have seen Ernie's face." Amelia leaned her head back, her eyes falling closed; she always had enjoyed having her hair brushed. Eva took long, slow strokes, just as Amelia liked. "He was positively livid. I believe the exact color is magenta. And though I hate to admit it, Fox was magnificent. Wasn't he, Phoebe?"

"Fox surprised us all." Phoebe had already crawled under the covers of the wide bed she would share with Amelia. She, too, closed her eyes. "He's grown up quite a lot these past months. Since Julia's wedding, really." Her eyes came open, and she stared hard at the ceiling. "But I tell you, what happened downstairs has left me unsettled. I wish we were all staying at a hotel. I'd feel safer."

Alarmed, Eva stopped brushing, her hand hovering in midair. "You can't mean Mr. Shelton could become violent? Surely, his talk was merely that?"

"I hope so," Phoebe replied distractedly.

Amelia peered over her shoulder. "Perhaps we should all leave in the morning. Go home."

Phoebe sat up, shaking her head. "No, I'm overreacting, to be sure. It just seemed so unlike Ernie. At least the Ernie we met at Gil and Julia's wedding. Of course his actions afterward did put my first impressions to the test." She paused, then smiled. "At the same time, Fox's reaction to Ernie today seemed so unlike *him*, the Fox we've known in recent years."

"That's an understatement." Amelia shook her head with a chuckle. "But I don't know if you're overreacting when it comes to Ernie's behavior. We mustn't leave Julia alone with him. None of us should be alone with him."

"If you ladies prefer, I'll sleep here tonight, rather than on the third floor."

"Would you?" Amelia looked and sounded relieved. She scanned the room. "Will the settee be roomy enough? Perhaps we can ask for a cot. What about Julia? Do you think Hetta will spend the night in her room?"

"I have no doubt of it." Eva gently nudged Amelia around to face the mirror again, so she could finish brushing her hair and plait it for sleeping.

"Tomorrow, when it's time to decide on the

china, let's let Julia have her way. Whatever she wants." Phoebe spoke to Amelia's reflection in the mirror. "That's the only way we'll be able to finish up here and go home."

Amelia scrunched her nose. "Even if Julia insists it be modern and geometric and entirely without character?"

"Whatever you decide in terms of the china, so be it," Eva said. "But perhaps you shouldn't be in such a hurry to leave Lyndale Park."

Phoebe blinked in obvious surprise. "Why on earth do you say that? Don't you long to leave as much as we do?"

"In a way, yes." Eva helped Amelia up from the dressing-table chair, then turned to face Phoebe across the room. "But part of the reason for coming here was for your sister to assert her rights as the Viscountess Annondale. She is correct that as the viscount's widow, she is his closest living relative, and if her child is a son, she'll have every right to live here with him."

"Oh, I hope she doesn't." Amelia went to the bed and kicked off her house shoes. "Better she lives with us at Foxwood Hall."

Eva shook her head. "Her son won't inherit Foxwood Hall, my lady. Your brother will. No, the next Viscount Annondale will inherit *this* property, and the sooner the rest of the viscount's family comes to terms with that, the better—for them, and for your sister."

"Do you think Julia *will* have a boy?" Phoebe tilted her head at Eva. "Do you have a feeling about it?"

"Truly, I don't. I'm no fortune-teller," she added with a laugh. Phoebe laughed, too, for only weeks ago Lady Annondale had tricked Phoebe into driving her to see a fortune-teller, a charlatan who had assured them the child would be a son. "But she has as much chance of having a boy as a girl, and it seems only wise to position herself here as her child's guardian and advocate."

"I suppose you're right," Phoebe conceded. "And you needn't sleep here. I'm sure we'll be fine. I don't think Ernie will be sneaking around on any midnight jaunts, and, at any rate, we can lock the door."

Amelia turned large eyes on her sister as she climbed into bed. "What if he has a duplicate key?"

"You're such a goose." Phoebe leaned back against the headboard. "But I still think we should let Julia decide on the china. It *was* her idea, after all."

"If she didn't want our opinions," Amelia retorted with a yawn, "why did she bring us along?"

Eva went to the bed to straighten the coverlets over her ladies. Sometimes she truly did feel like a mother to them, and it warmed her heart to see them contented and safe. "She brought you along, my lady, so you could all agree with her."

• • •

The next morning Eva was glad to see the Renshaws had all survived the night, as she knew they would. In the end she had gone to her room on the third floor, which she shared with Hetta. The Swiss woman, too, had offered to spend the night in her mistress's room, but Lady Annondale had sent her upstairs at about midnight. Eva suspected that had as much to do with Hetta's light snoring as Lady Annondale's courage.

Now Eva and Hetta poured tea and passed around fruit and toast to the family, who had gathered in Lady Annondale's room—the master bedroom, as she had insisted. It seemed Mr. Shelton had vacated immediately following yesterday's altercation in the drawing room.

"He not only moved out of this bedroom, but the house itself, and retired to the cottage he occupied during Gil's lifetime," Julia told them.

"Carmichael confided to me that Ernie couldn't seem to leave fast enough," Fox said around a bite of sliced peaches with a liberal coating of clotted cream. A sharp reprimand for speaking with his mouth full would have been forthcoming, had his grandfather been there. As it was, Eva couldn't help smiling or inwardly congratulating the boy for yesterday's triumph. Of that, she believed, Lord Wroxly would have been proud.

"So we have something to discuss this morning," Phoebe said after draining her cup and setting it aside. Dear Lady Phoebe typically needed a bit of fortification in the morning before attending to any pending matters. "The china service. Amelia and I were talking last night—"

"Ganging up against me?" Lady Annondale's blond eyebrows, artificially darkened, rose in accusation. Yet, Eva heard the laughter in her voice and was glad of it. Perhaps today's visit to Crown Lily wouldn't be a repeat of yesterday, after all.

"I still say a pair of Staffordshire bull terriers," Fox interjected.

"Not a bad idea, actually." Phoebe's pronouncement astonished them all, judging by the looks they sent her. "Perhaps we should look into a pair of pups before we leave. But as for the china"— she addressed Lady Annondale now—"we think you should have the final vote."

"Well, of course I have the final vote. I never for a moment doubted it. I'm the only one here with impeccable taste, aren't I?"

"Julia, can't you accept this gracefully?" Amelia broke her scone in half and dipped a corner of it into the jam she'd dabbed onto her plate. "We don't wish to argue anymore. Since this entire endeavor was your idea, you may have the honor of deciding what shape and pattern we choose. Only . . ."

Lady Annondale searched her youngest sister's face and narrowed her eyes. "Only what?"

"Please don't pick something hideous."

Lady Annondale's mouth fell open. She appeared to search for words, then pinched her lips together for an instant. "All right, a compromise. How about a modern shape, but we'll incorporate florals with the crest. But not overly flowery. And with a bit of gold highlighting. Will that do?"

Amelia nodded enthusiastically. They stood to ready themselves to leave for the factory. Eva lingered, then approached Lady Annondale.

"I'm proud of you, my lady. It's gracious of you to compromise this way."

Another lady's maid would have been reprimanded for having the cheek to tell her employer any such thing, but Lady Annondale broke into a grateful smile and might even have blinked away a bit of moisture in her eyes. "Thank you, Eva. Coming from you that means a lot. Perhaps I'm finally growing up." She smoothed a hand over her belly. "And not a moment too soon."

The Rolls-Royce passed under the arching Crown Lily sign. Fenton maneuvered through the main quadrangle and into the smaller enclosure that housed the administrative building they had visited yesterday. This time Jeffrey Tremaine awaited them outside, and Phoebe wondered how long he'd been standing there against the breezes that swirled between the buildings and scattered countless bits of ash from the bottle kilns.

He hurried to open the rear door for them even before Fenton had a chance to secure the brake. "Good morning, good morning. I trust you all had a pleasant night?"

Phoebe, Amelia, and Fox traded ironic glances, but said nothing. Julia, sitting on the end, was the first to slide out. She extended her gloved hand for Mr. Tremaine to assist her.

"I believe we're ready to make our decisions, Mr. Tremaine."

"I . . . er . . . there might be a s-slight delay," the man stuttered in response. It seemed his nerves had returned to plague him today.

"Is there a problem with production?" Phoebe asked as she slid out behind Amelia.

"No, no, production is running along smoothly. It's our art director, Ronald Mercer. He's . . . late in arriving this morning. I've tried telephoning his home, but his housekeeper said he left the house earlier and hasn't been back since." The man pressed a hand to his mouth, coloring as he did so. "Perhaps that was a bit too much to share. Forgive me. I'm sure he'll be along any moment. But Percy Bateman is inside, waiting for you in the conference room."

Fox ducked his way out of the motorcar. "Is Trent here?"

"That's a good question," Mr. Tremaine said.

He smoothed his hair. "I couldn't say. The general employees sign in at their entrance near the packing warehouse. It's up to our foremen and department supervisors to keep track of their arrivals. And I didn't think to ask about Trent when I telephoned over to the Mercer house."

"Very well." Julia set off toward the building. "Let's go in and see what Mr. Bateman has to show us." Mr. Tremaine stumbled to reach the door ahead of her and swung it open.

They found a delighted-looking Percy Bateman in the conference room. The teacups and other china had been moved aside, some of it now occupying the tops of the cupboards that filled one wall. Mr. Bateman had spread out several sheets of design ideas. Phoebe saw that he had built upon what he had shown them yesterday by incorporating elements of what he'd heard expressed by each of them.

"Good heavens," she exclaimed upon studying one of them. She lifted the paper from the table and held it up. The Wroxly coat of arms occupied one side, surrounded by a scenic view of rolling Cotswold Hills, and . . . "Is that a bull terrier peeking out from behind the crest?"

The young man burst out in a grin. "Nothing to be taken seriously, my lady, but, yes, I couldn't resist." He aimed his grin at Fox. "Just so you know someone was listening yesterday."

Fox took the paper from Phoebe. "This is it. Julia, here's our design."

"Very funny." Shrugging out of her coat, she turned her attention to another of the examples. But then she just as quickly turned back to Fox and held out her hand. "Let me see that one."

Mr. Tremaine held out a chair for her. She sank into it, her gaze never wandering from the paper that showed both the front and back of the teacup design. She let out a few *hmms* and *hahs,* and tilted the paper to view the design from different angles. Finally she lifted her face. "This is it. Minus the dog, of course, but this landscape around the crest—it's marvelous. And so unique. It captures the heart of Foxwood Hall perfectly. Amelia, don't you think so?"

Amelia went to gaze over Julia's shoulder. "Oh, I think Grams and Grampapa will love this. Phoebe, don't you agree?"

Could they actually have landed upon the perfect compromise? Phoebe hesitated to believe it, and who knew what would happen when Mr. Mercer finally arrived? He might present something Julia found equally tantalizing, and indecision would set in again. If only Mr. Mercer *didn't* come to work today . . .

She was leaning over Julia's other shoulder, admiring the scene of flower-carpeted hills and a brook spanned by a creamy Cotswold stone bridge. And in the middle of it all, the Wroxly coat of arms, somehow seeming part of the rest while neither overshadowing nor becoming lost in the surrounding details. She opened her mouth to add her consensus when a high-pitched wailing filled the air, barely muffled by the closed windows.

"What on earth?" Julia's question was immediately answered by Mr. Tremaine, who'd gone pale.

"The siren. There's been an accident."

CHAPTER 4

"Please, all of you, wait here." Without another word Mr. Tremaine hurried out of the conference room, with Percy Bateman hard on his heels. Phoebe heard the outside door opening and slamming shut. The siren's continued wailing set her nerves on edge.

Apparently, Julia agreed. "I wish they'd stop that deplorable racket."

"I'm going to see what happened." Fox began to trace the other two men's footsteps.

"Fox, we were told to stay here," Amelia admonished him. She stood behind their sister, one hand on Julia's shoulder.

Fox hesitated. "I won't get in the way." Then he was off.

"I'm going, too." Phoebe didn't wait to be told not to, nor did she look back to see if Amelia followed her. She knew her younger sister wouldn't leave Julia's side, and Julia certainly wasn't going to run across the factory's precincts in her condition.

When she reached the enclosure, she was glad she hadn't had time to shed her coat inside, as a steely cloud cover had put a bite into the wind. The bitterness of smoke and ash from the bottle kilns stung her nose. She turned several corners and came upon the first building they'd visited yesterday, where the clay was mixed, ground, and purified. An image formed in her mind of the grinding pans, like giant dough kneaders. Good heavens—but, no, surely not that. She spotted Fox's dusky blond hair among the sea of flat caps and kerchiefs the workers wore. More people were streaming out from the various buildings—mixers, throwers, painters—as the siren summoned them all.

"Have you heard what happened yet?" she asked Fox when she reached his side. He glanced at her briefly and shook his head before returning his attention to the clay-processing building.

After a moment he turned back to her. "I got here just in time to see Mr. Tremaine running inside. Two workers were standing just outside that door." He pointed. "They were distraught, Phoebe. Whatever happened in there, it's bad."

She wished Eva were here. The thought ran round and round in her brain. Eva had managed to set both her and Amelia at ease last night, and she had said something to their sister this morning that had Julia smiling as they piled into the Rolls-Royce.

The siren cut off abruptly, the resulting silence equally jarring. Little by little, voices filled the hush as workers speculated on what might have happened. Phoebe heard the word *accident* repeated many times, but no one seemed to know any details.

Fox startled her as he suddenly blurted out a name. "Trent! Over here!"

The boy they had met yesterday changed direction and weaved his way across the yard, dodging around workers. He stopped a few feet away, kicking up dust, and heaved for breath. "Have you seen Jester? I can't find him anywhere."

"No," Fox said, "but we haven't been here long. Came to give Mr. Tremaine our order when the siren sounded. Come to think of it, your father wasn't there to greet us. Maybe he has Jester."

"Do you know where your father is, Trent?" Phoebe felt a deepening concern. "He wants this commission badly. It seems unlikely he'd miss this morning's meeting."

"I can't say." Trent searched the faces around them, frowning. "We were both here early today, before sunup. Jester too. Mr. Tremaine doesn't mind him being here, so I bring him most days. Father said he wanted to speak with the head clay mixer about a new formula he'd calculated. Something that would make an even thinner cup without sacrificing strength. I think he wants it for your grandparents' china."

"Well, he must be here somewhere." Fox tapped his friend's shoulder when Trent's attention appeared to wander. "Let's try and find out what's going on. Have you heard anything at all?"

A clanging bell drowned out Trent's reply. Moments later a motor ambulance clattered around a corner and entered the enclosure. It pulled up near the entrance to the clay-processing building. The bell quieted as the doors swung open and four men in dark blue St. John's Ambulance Brigade uniforms scrambled out. Two of them went around to the back of the vehicle, opened the rear door, and dragged out a stretcher. Then all four hurried into the building.

"Someone's hurt. Badly," Trent said, unnecessarily. The tension among the crowd heightened. Phoebe could all but hear their collective intake of breath as they waited to see who among them had been injured . . . and how.

Before the door to the building had fully closed, it jerked partway open again. Those nearest the door eased away as if allowing someone through; yet, at first, Phoebe saw no one. An instant later Trent's dog, Jester, emerged from between a knot of people in a streak of brown and white.

"Jester," Trent called to him. The animal spotted him and altered his course without missing a step. Trent fell to a crouch, his arms encircling Jester as the dog crashed into his chest. "What is it, boy? What happened?"

Fox and Phoebe moved closer, and Trent turned a worried face up to them. "He's trembling all over. I can't imagine what he was doing in there, or how he got in." He turned his attention back to the panting animal, who continued pressing against his master.

A sickening sensation went through Phoebe. A missing dog. A missing father. An accident.

Minutes later the ambulance crew reemerged into the enclosure, two of them carrying the stretcher. Now, instead of being a light burden between them, something clearly weighed it down. Something draped in a plain gray sheet, unmoving but for a minuscule sliding this way and that with the motion of the stretcher. A body. Phoebe sucked in a breath. She went several paces closer and saw ruddy stains just beginning to penetrate the sheet. Trent rose and started forward, but instinct sent her hand out. She clutched his shoulder and held him back.

Mr. Tremaine exited the building next, the wind blowing his silvering hair until thick tufts of it stood up nearly straight. His suit coat, too, blew out around him. He took no notice of either, but kept on as if driven by an unseen hand, his gaze pinned on Trent.

"What's going on?" Fox's question came as a whisper, little more than an exhalation. Trent stood frozen in place, while Jester cowered against his leg and shivered, as if both boy and animal already knew the truth.

"Trent," Mr. Tremaine said as he came to a halt in front of the boy.

Phoebe needed no more than that—no more

that the weight of dread hanging on that one word. *Trent.*

The color leached from the boy's face. Fox went to his side, standing shoulder to shoulder, but Trent didn't acknowledge him. He frowned at Mr. Tremaine, and then suddenly turned about and started to walk away.

"Trent," the pottery's owner said. "Wait. There's something—"

Trent took off running, Jester loping at his side. Fox and Phoebe exchanged startled glances, and then set off together in the direction the boy had taken. Phoebe wondered if he even knew where he was going. When he turned a corner and disappeared, Fox shot ahead of Phoebe in a burst of speed. She hefted her skirts higher and tried to meet their pace, but she was no match in her pumps, especially on the cobblestones.

She found them at the base of a bottle kiln. The doorway of the structure was sealed tight, its chimney puffing black smoke to mingle with the clouds. Ash drifted gently down. Fox had his hand on his friend's shoulder. Jester's large eyes glistened as he gazed up at them.

"Come back with me. Hear what Mr. Tremaine has to say."

Trent shook his head. "I already know what he has to say. My father . . . He . . ." Trent pinched his lips together.

To Fox's credit, he didn't try to dissuade Trent

of that conclusion. It had been all too obvious.

"Don't you wish to know what happened?" Phoebe asked Trent gently. "And your mother. We'll need to let her know."

"My mother is dead. Over a year now."

Stricken to have made such a mistake, she caught Fox's eye. "Why didn't you mention this," she mouthed, but then realized it simply hadn't come up. While last night they had discussed Fox's good fortune in coming upon a friend from school, they hadn't delved too deeply into Trent Mercer's background. Except . . .

Except to comment on his obvious resentment at having been withdrawn from Eton to work at Crown Lily. A chill traveled Phoebe's back, but she shook away the sensation. Trent's education surely had nothing to do with today's tragedy.

"I'm sorry, Trent." She groped for something more useful to say, but came up empty. A sudden gust swept the area and whistled between the bottle kilns, raising a mournful cry. Phoebe shivered in earnest now, as did the two boys. "Come. Let's go back. We'll go inside. Trent, you don't have to talk to anyone if you don't wish to."

He appeared not to hear her, or at least he appeared disinclined to respond. He stood there several seconds, until Phoebe began to wonder what else to do. Then he nodded, turned, and started walking. Fox kept pace at his side. Phoebe followed a few steps behind them. Fox and Trent knew each other, making Fox the right person to offer comfort, whether with words or with sympathetic silence.

When they returned to the main enclosure, Phoebe let Fox and Trent join a grim-faced Mr. Tremaine. They spoke quietly with one another, and Mr. Tremaine walked with them back in the direction of the administrative building. The ambulance had gone, but there were several police sedans in its place, with constables spread out among the lingering crowd. Phoebe approached one and waited until he'd finished questioning a pair of workers, men in coveralls and aprons smeared with clay, their flat caps in their hands. Both men mirrored Mr. Tremaine's bleak expression.

Phoebe had a quick change of heart, and instead of addressing the policeman, she waited until he'd walked away and spoke to the workers. "Excuse me, but can you tell me what happened?" When they hesitated, eyeing her clothing and judging her not to be one of them, she explained, "Trent Mercer is my brother's friend, and we'd like to be able to help him through this. His father is dead, isn't he?"

Both men nodded, and the heavier of the two, with a short-trimmed beard and broad, round shoulders, said, "It's none-too-pleasant a thing, miss. I daresay you don't want to know what happened."

"But you're wrong, I do. As I said, my family

will want to be able to help Trent, and we can't do that unless we know the facts. How did his father die?" Although they hadn't confirmed it, that much Phoebe was certain of.

The other man, shorter than the first and with a protruding belly, wiped a sleeve across his brow. "Gus Abbott, he's our head clay mixer that operates the grinding pans. He found 'im. Found Ron Mercer when he went in to start fillin' the pans."

Phoebe remembered the grinding pans from yesterday, those giant vats where clay, stone, and bone ash poured in through chutes and were ground down and mixed together by rotating blades. *Like Mrs. Ellison's hand-cranked dough kneader,* Fox had said. But larger. So much larger.

Large enough to crush a man's body.

An image of just that formed in her brain and her hand flew to her mouth. "You don't mean to say . . . he was found in one of the pans . . ."

The two workers simultaneously nodded. The bearded one said, "I told you, you didn't want to know, miss."

"But . . . how did he get there?"

The bearded fellow shrugged. The round-bellied one murmured, "Not by accident. I can tell you that, miss. Not by accident."

Eva was surprised when she heard the sound of a vehicle coming up the drive. She looked out of her third-floor window to see the Renshaws' Rolls-Royce approaching the house and wondered why they were back so soon. Had they reached an agreement, consulted with the designer, and placed the order so quickly? The siblings had decided to compromise and allow Julia to lead in the decisions, but this seemed much too good to be true.

The call buzzer in her room went off, surprising that she would be needed so soon after the family's return. She smoothed her frock, secured a few hairs that had come loose from the low bun at her nape, and made her way downstairs. The Renshaws had gone directly into the drawing room. She found them, along with the boy from yesterday, Fox's friend, sitting close together around the hearth. They were stony-faced and silent. Fox sat beside his friend, his hand on the boy's shoulder. Then Eva noticed Trent Mercer's dog lying on the rug at the boy's feet. The animal's eyes were open, but glassy, and as he breathed in and out, he made low, whimpering sounds.

A sense of unease immediately gripped Eva. It only increased when Lady Phoebe, having spotted her in the doorway, quickly rose and drew Eva out into the main hall.

"Something dreadful has happened."

"I already guessed, simply by looking at all of you." Eva inwardly braced herself. "What is it?"

"Trent's father. He's dead."

"How? Some kind of—"

"Accident?" Phoebe shook her head. "I wish it were, but it doesn't seem possible. He was found shortly after we arrived at the factory in one of the grinding pans."

Eva gasped, unable to stop herself. "He's a designer. Why would he be in that part of the factory?"

"He did have a reason. It was to discuss a new formula he'd devised for mixing the clay. But the man he went to speak with was in another area altogether. We learned he was at one of the warehouses at the time, helping load a shipment of stone into the railcars that would bring it to the clay-processing building. I'm told he has plenty of witnesses to vouch for him."

"So then, Mr. Mercer went to the grinding room looking for this man, and encountered someone else."

"Or someone followed him inside. But listen to this." Phoebe grasped Eva's hand and walked with her another several yards away from the drawing-room doorway, until they stood near the foot of the staircase. "Trent's dog, Jester, came barreling out of the building after the ambulance brigade went in."

"Do you think Trent had something to do with his father's death?"

"I don't know. I hope not. We saw him outside searching for Jester. At least he said he was. And when he learned of his father's death . . ." Lady Phoebe fell silent. Her brow creased. Eva waited silently, until her lady met her gaze. "He hasn't cried. Not once. He was visibly upset and went striding off, but . . ."

"That doesn't necessarily mean anything," Eva said with a shake of her head. "People react in different ways. Especially young men who have been taught not to show their feelings."

"Yes, but yesterday Trent let us see quite clearly how unhappy he was with his father's decision to withdraw him from Eton." Lady Phoebe searched Eva's face, her expression filled with hope that Eva would dissuade her of her suspicions.

None of them would wish to see Fox's friend guilty of such a horrible crime. *Patricide.* The very word chilled Eva's heart. But then she, too, remembered something from yesterday.

"I also met someone who resented Ronald Mercer. Her name is Moira . . . Moira Whitstone . . . no . . . Wickham. That was it. Moira Wickham." She pictured the sturdy-framed woman and remembered her bitterness at being stuck in a position she felt overqualified for. "She's a painter. The supervisor of the painting department, as a matter of fact. She wishes she could be a designer, which is more creative, but Ronald Mercer persuaded Mr. Tremaine not to take a chance on her, and said women should remember their proper places. Or words to that effect."

"Hmm. That does make me feel a bit better. Not because I want this Moira Wickham to be guilty, or that I believe she had enough cause to want him dead. But if both Trent and this woman resented Ronald Mercer, surely others had, too. The constables were interviewing the workers. I'm sure they all have a story to tell about Ronald Mercer, and that will lead the police to the guilty person."

"Do you think it's a worker, and not someone from outside who might have held a grudge against the man?"

"No, it had to be someone who knew their way around the factory, and who knew how the grinder works. Dear heavens, Eva, he was thrown in and . . ." Lady Phoebe bit down and pressed her lips together, as if holding back illness. But Eva knew her better than that. Phoebe Renshaw was hardier than the average aristocrat.

"You can tell me, my lady."

"The grinder was turned on."

Eva clutched the collar of her dress. "How ghastly."

"It could have been worse. Apparently, the blades hit him and jammed, so the body wasn't completely . . . well . . . you know. But this was a horrid crime, all the same."

Eva nodded her agreement. Then she thought about what Lady Phoebe had said only moments ago, about the local constabulary finding the guilty party. "So, are you saying you'll leave it to the police?" She almost added *this time*. It was on the tip of her tongue, but why bring up past incidents that had nothing to do with this one? Those other times, she and Phoebe had been drawn in because of the involvement of a friend or family member, or because the crime had disturbed the tranquility of their village, Little Barlow.

"I feel frightfully bad for Trent," Phoebe replied, "and we'll do what we can for him. You know his mother is deceased, too."

"I didn't, my lady. I'm sorry to hear it."

"Yes, Fox told me it was during the influenza epidemic. So he's an orphan now. I can only hope he has family somewhere who'll take him in."

"Phoebe? Eva?" They looked up as Amelia came across the hall to them. Her eyes were large and misty. It reminded Eva that no matter how much she had matured in the past year, the youngest Renshaw sister was still but a girl and must be reeling from today's events. "I'm sorry, but it's just so hard to be in there right now. No one is speaking, and Trent looks so very lost. Phoebe, won't you come back? I'm so afraid I'll say something wrong, and poor Julia. She looks done in." The words were no sooner out of Lady Amelia's mouth than her hand flew to her lips and her eyes spilled over. "What a beastly thing to say. I'm so sorry."

CHAPTER 5

"No, *I'm* sorry, dearest Amelia. I shouldn't have left you." Lady Phoebe hugged her sister, then squeezed her hand. "I only wished to let Eva know what happened."

"Why don't you both go back in with the others, and I'll go see about some tea and perhaps something a teensy bit stronger. I think you could all use it." Eva offered them a sympathetic look. She understood how difficult it would be not only to put on a brave face under these circumstances, but remain supportive of the young man in their midst. What did one say? How to offer reassurances, when there were none? For an instant she was grateful for her position, which would not require her to interact on any personal level with Trent Mercer. She felt immediately ashamed and repented the thought as cowardly, and hoped she could be of some comfort to him, and to her ladies.

Belowstairs the servants were already abuzz with the news. In these days of telephones, Eva shouldn't have been surprised. An industrialist like Gilbert Townsend had, of course, equipped his home with the latest gadgets and conveniences.

She came first upon the housekeeper and the head butler speaking in terse whispers about the bizarre circumstances surrounding the Crown Lily design director's death; the cook and her two assistants were speculating over the making of a rich bread pudding. A gaggle of footmen appeared to be laying odds about who the guilty party might be. And even the hall boy and scullery maid seemed able to talk of nothing else. They all quieted as Eva walked by and she could feel their gazes on her back as she passed them. She wasn't one of them, and they couldn't be certain where her loyalties lay. They couldn't afford for her to report back to Lady Annondale or Miss Townsend about how the servants had descended into gossip.

Eva asked one of the kitchen assistants to help her assemble tea, enough to include Veronica Townsend and Mildred Blair, should they happen to appear downstairs. Eva cringed slightly at the possibility. Those two ladies would have no idea what they were walking into, and she thought perhaps someone should warn them, lest they do or say something to make matters worse for young Trent Mercer.

"The tea is kept in there." Barely gazing up from the batter she was mixing, the assistant cook used her elbow to point to a dry-goods pantry that opened onto the kitchen. Eva thanked her and went to see what kinds of flavors were stored there, supposing she shouldn't expect too much assistance from the staff of Lyndale Park.

Basically, they would see her as an intruder, an attitude she had encountered at other great houses when traveling with her ladies.

She came back into the kitchen with a rich-scented Darjeeling and noticed the assistant had put the kettle on to boil. Eva smiled and thanked her. The girl directed her to the larder for cakes and biscuits. The family had breakfasted not long ago, but experience had taught Eva that food usually helped settle nerves and soothe tensions. If nothing else, it distracted from whatever matter had arisen.

After assembling three trays, including one that held a small decanter of sherry and cordial glassware, as well as an earthenware bowl filled with water, she enlisted two footmen to help carry the lot up to the drawing room. Their expressions told her they didn't appreciate being given orders by a visiting servant, but they nonetheless hefted the heavier two trays and started up the stairs. They surprised her by discussing the matter on everyone's minds, almost as if they forgot she was there.

"Your sister works there, doesn't she? Does she have any idea who might have done it?" the one leading their small procession said. Both young men were tall, broad-shouldered, trim in the waist, and wore their livery as a gentleman wears a finely tailored suit—with pride and a dash of elegance. The only trait that distinguished one from the other was the color of their hair, and barely that, for one was a dark brunette, the other raven-haired.

Eva listened carefully. Perhaps this young man, whose sister worked at Crown Lily, had insights to share.

"She has a few notions about it. She's thinking it's the other designer. My guinea is on old Gus Abbott," the black-haired one said.

"What have you heard?" Eva posed the question in a friendly tone, hoping they would see it as no more than idle curiosity. So far, she hadn't heard anyone belowstairs talking about Trent, the victim's own son. Perhaps they didn't know he was just then sitting above their heads in the drawing room.

"My sister's a handler for Crown Lily," the darker-haired one said. "That means she sticks handles on teacups. She's heard the two designers have been quietly feuding. And sometimes not so quietly."

They reached the landing and would soon push through the baize door into the main part of the house. Once there, their banter would have to cease.

"Do you know why?" Eva asked.

That made both young men pause on the servants' side of the door. They held the trays as if they were of no weight at all. "Cammie, that's my sister, says it's because the new designer,

Bateman, is a better artist than Ron Mercer ever was or ever could be, which had Mercer burning with jealousy."

"That seems more of a reason for Mr. Mercer to wish to harm Bateman than the other way around."

"Could be, miss," the brown-haired one said, "but maybe that's exactly what it started out to be. Maybe Mercer lured Bateman into the grinding room, they fought, and Bateman won."

"But who is this Gus Abbott you mentioned?" Eva persisted.

"Cammie says he's head of clay mixing. He found the body. If anybody knows how to turn on one of those contraptions, it's him."

With that, he pushed through the door. The raven-haired fellow followed, and Eva had no choice but to continue through as well. But he'd made an astute point. Just because Ronald Mercer died, it didn't mean he was the intended victim. And it didn't mean he hadn't planned to be the killer. That could have made his death an act of self-defense on the part of the other designer.

But if that were the case, wouldn't this Mr. Bateman have admitted to the constables what had happened? Perhaps not. If they'd argued and fought, ending in a death without witnesses, would the police believe the survivor's story?

But the footman had added another name to the possibilities. Gus Abbott, who apparently had found Ronald Mercer in the grinding pan. As Phoebe had said, if one person resented the head of the design department, others might have as well. Perhaps Moira, Trent, and Percy were merely three of many individuals who would have been happy to see Ronald Mercer gone, for good.

In the drawing room Eva set the earthenware bowl on the floor near the hearth and called to Jester. The dog sent a questioning look up at his master, who nodded and whispered, "Go ahead, boy. Thank you," he added with a halfhearted smile for Eva.

To the sound of lapping water, she served the tea and cakes, along with the sherry. Trent had already receded back into himself, and when he made no move to accept either offering from Eva, Fox took the small sherry glass from her and pressed it into his friend's hand. "You might as well, old boy. It might help."

"Nothing can help," Trent murmured back, but nonetheless raised the glass to his lips.

"Trent," Lady Phoebe said, "there must be someone we can notify for you. A relative who lives nearby?"

The boy shook his head. "There's no one. Nearest relatives are in York. Aunt, uncle, two cousins. We don't talk to them."

"But, surely, they'll want to help once they understand the circumstances," Lady Phoebe pressed.

"Doubt it." Trent took another sip of his sherry and made a face. "They didn't come or even write when my mum died."

Incredulous, Eva marveled that any family could put such little value on its fellow members. She found it exceedingly tragic, on top of the tragedy that had already taken place. What would Trent do now? Where would he go? Though close to adulthood, he still had several years before he reached his majority. Who would put a roof over his head?

She noticed Amelia blinking back tears and lifting her teacup to her lips to hide them. Lady Annondale poured a tiny drop of sherry into her tea, set the rest aside, and sipped pensively. As Eva handed Phoebe a cordial glass, she communicated silently as best she could that they had much to talk about.

Phoebe knew by Eva's expression that she had something important to relate, but before she could slip away from the drawing room again, Mildred and Veronica joined them.

"Did no one think to invite the two of us down to tea?" With a wounded expression Veronica Townsend surveyed the occupants of the room. "Why are you back from Crown Lily so early? Squabbling again over the patterns?" Her gaze landed on Trent Mercer, and a slight frown formed above her snub nose. Then she noticed

Jester. "What in the world is that thing doing in here?"

Phoebe set her tea and cake aside and rose to her feet. "That is our guest's dog, Jester."

The woman's broad mouth turned down at the corners. "My brother never allowed animals in this part of the house."

"Well, here he stays for now," Phoebe said firmly. "And there are two more cups and plates here for you, if you wish to have tea. Eva thought you might come down." She gestured to the sideboard, where the extra settings had been laid.

"*Hmph.* At least someone thinks of us." Veronica crossed to the sideboard. She hummed tunelessly as she busied herself pouring her tea and examining the cakes. "My thanks to you, Huntford."

Eva bobbed her head in acknowledgment and kept her features even, allowing Veronica no hint as to her thoughts, though Phoebe could guess at them easily enough.

Mildred didn't follow Veronica to the sideboard, but studied each Renshaw in turn, then Eva, and finally Trent. "What's going on here? Something isn't right."

Both hands full, Veronica turned back to the others. "Yes, you're all rather quiet. Suspiciously so. There's probably a scheme afoot to run Mildred and me out of this house for good."

"Not everything is about you, Veronica." Julia

gave her a quelling look that would have made a less formidable opponent slink off. But not Veronica.

"Excuse me if I seem a bit distrustful, dear sister." Veronica thrust out her very round chin. "You did show up here without a *by your leave.*"

"I most certainly did not," Julia quipped back. "I sent notice a month ago. Either Carmichael is derelict in his duties when it comes to the mail, which I highly doubt, or you quite deliberately disregarded my letter. Probably tossed it in the fire. Oh, and, Veronica . . ." she added with cloying sweetness.

"What?"

". . . I am not your sister."

"Please, both of you." Amelia took on a pained expression. She darted a glance at Trent, who stared down at the crystal cordial glass that was nearly empty now. "This isn't helping anything."

Mildred took another steady glance around at all of their faces, paused briefly on Trent, and appealed to Phoebe. "Come walk with me and tell me what happened."

It was on Phoebe's tongue to decline the request, but a subtle change in the other woman's bearing hinted that perhaps Mildred's curiosity stemmed from genuine concern and not a desire to mock, as in Veronica's case. With everyone's eyes upon her, Phoebe walked out of the drawing room, with Mildred close behind her.

"That boy in there," she said when they'd put enough distance between them and the others, "lost his father today. It happened at the factory, and it looks to be deliberate."

"Good heavens, foul play seems to follow you and your family wherever you go."

Phoebe huffed in disgust and turned about to retrace her steps.

Mildred put a hand on her arm. "Sorry, that was uncalled for."

"Yes, it was. He's a child, Mildred, and now he's alone in the world. It's nothing to joke about."

"No, it isn't." She compressed her thickly rouged lips and flicked a strand of hair out of her face. "I should know. I also lost my father to murder."

Phoebe felt an easing of her anger, and with it the tension that had held her rigidly upright, as if ready for a fight. Her shoulders relaxed. "Indeed." She drew a breath. "We don't yet know what happened, but we didn't want Trent to face it alone. He's a friend of my brother's from Eton. It appears someone might have lured his father to one of the more industrial areas of the factory and dispatched him in a most inhuman way."

"Were you all there when it happened?"

"No. That is, I don't know exactly when it happened. We were there when he was found." She thought of Jester running out of the clay-processing building like a soul possessed, and how he'd pressed his shaking body up against Trent's legs. She could only conclude the dog had witnessed the crime. Yet, he could never tell a soul.

But how had he come to be in the building in the first place? He was always at Trent's side, or at least she had gotten the impression boy and dog were inseparable. When they'd arrived back in the conference room yesterday, Jester had not run to Ronald Mercer, nor had Mr. Mercer given the dog more than a cursory glance.

That insidious thought from earlier reared up again. Did Trent have something to do with his father's death?

"Phoebe, perhaps if—"

An insistent knocking at the front door startled them both and silenced Mildred. For some inexplicable reason, the sound filled Phoebe with foreboding. Without waiting for Carmichael to appear from whatever part of the house he inhabited when not needed, she went to open the door.

"Yes?" Even as she spoke, her stomach dropped.

Three men stood on the other side of the threshold. Two wore dark blue constable's uniforms and held their domed helmets in their hands. She recognized their faces from earlier that morning. The third, standing in front of them, wore a dark suit beneath an open trench coat. His features were unfamiliar. An instant of surprise at beholding Phoebe registered in his expression. Clearly, she was neither a butler nor a housemaid, nor any other servant who might answer the door.

He recovered quickly. "I'm Detective Inspector Hugh Nichols. These are Constables Walker and Dodge. Is Trent Mercer here? We'd like to speak with him."

His request didn't surprise her; she had already guessed what he would say. That didn't mean she didn't wish to shut the door in their faces and run to tell Trent to hide.

"Come in." She stepped aside to admit them. All three pulled up short when they noticed Mildred hovering a few feet away. Phoebe gestured to her. "This is Mildred Blair. She lives here."

The detective inspector pulled a notepad out of his coat pocket, along with a pencil. He jotted down Mildred's name, then regarded Phoebe again. "Are you one of the Renshaw sisters?"

Before she could reply, Constable Dodge said, "That's Lady Phoebe Renshaw, the middle sister, sir."

Detective Inspector Nichols nodded, scribbled, and glanced up. "Trent Mercer." It wasn't a question, but a command.

"This way." Phoebe led them into the drawing

room. "This is my sister, Lady Annondale, and her sister-in-law, Miss Townsend. At the moment they jointly own Lyndale Park."

"Mm-hmm." The detective inspector scanned the faces briefly. His gaze rested longer on Julia than the others. Admiration sparked in his eyes, as it typically did whenever a man encountered her. He seemed also to note Eva's presence. She stood off to one side, out of the way. The detective obviously took in her simple dark dress and deduced she was a servant. Then he shifted his attention to the two boys sitting side by side on the settee. Fox inched subtly closer to his friend. "Which one of you is Trent Mercer?"

This time it was Constable Walker who provided the information. "The one on the left, sir. With the dog. That's him."

Jester let out a low growl, while Phoebe bristled. Constable Walker spoke as if Trent's guilt had already been established.

Amelia apparently heard the derisiveness in the constable's voice, too. "Master Trent is a guest here. Please treat him accordingly."

The detective inspector treated her to a blank expression, but directed his next question to Phoebe. "Where can we speak privately?"

"Detective, is there some reason you thought it necessary to come here as a force of three to question a boy, the victim's own son?" Julia came to her feet with surprising agility, considering

96

how far along she was in her pregnancy. Obviously taken off guard, Detective Inspector Nichols began to sputter a response, but Julia cut him off. "I suppose you're only doing your job." She made it sound rather tawdry. "You may use the library. Come, I'll lead the way."

"That isn't necessary, Lady Annondale." Detective Inspector Nichols held up the hand holding the pencil. "These houses are all pretty much the same. Just point us in the right direction. Or maybe *she* can guide us." He pointed to Eva, who looked none-too-eager for the task.

Julia had walked past him toward the doorway. Now she stopped, half turned, and regarded him with all the haughtiness she could muster— and Julia was a master of haughtiness. "It most certainly *is* necessary, Detective Inspector . . . Nichols, is it? This is my home, and Trent is a child. He should have an adult with him. And he will." A lift of her eyebrow dared all three policemen to argue with her. None of them did.

Phoebe silently cheered her sister's actions. Julia surprised her—no, astonished her. Usually, Julia could dismiss the difficulties of another person with a simple shrug of her shoulder. Today she seemed bent on championing a boy orphaned just that morning. The instincts of a soon-to-be mother?

As all five left the room, Jester jumped up and followed, quickly reaching his master's heels.

The detective inspector stopped and whirled, his coat flapping out around him. He scowled down at Jester. "Someone take hold of this animal, please."

No one in the drawing room made a move.

"Can't he come?" Trent's voice came small and thin, making him sound very much like the child Julia had described him as.

"I'd prefer he didn't."

One of the constables, the one named Dodge, bent to grasp Jester's leather collar. Fox came to his feet with a huff. "Jester, come here, boy."

The dog stayed put, and Trent made no effort to urge him to go. Phoebe didn't think this was an intentional act of rebellion on his part, but simply an inability to be an active participant in anything happening around him. He was still too much in shock. The constable curled his fingers around the collar and gave a tug toward the drawing room. Jester whimpered.

"Leave him alone," Trent cried out. He fell to his knees and slid his arms around Jester's muscular body. Tears dribbled down the boy's cheeks. The constable backed away, clearly baffled as to what to do. Phoebe felt equally baffled. How to reassure Trent, mollify the policemen, and prevent tensions from escalating?

Fox hurried to his friend. He crouched and put one hand on Trent's shoulder, the other on Jester's collar. "Don't worry. I'll watch him for however long this takes. He'll be fine and so will you. You've got Julia going with you."

He leaned closer to Trent and whispered something in his ear. This produced in Trent a wobbly grin, and he wiped his shirtsleeve across his cheeks to dry them. The boys stood, and Fox grasped the dog's collar.

"Come on, boy. Want a treat? I'm sure we can find you something."

The dog didn't resist as Fox walked him back into the drawing room, much to Phoebe's relief.

"You won't find any dog treats in the house." Veronica spoke for the first time since the police had arrived. "Any dogs my brother kept were housed and fed in the kennels. But he didn't often keep such beasts around. It wasn't as though my brother could hunt in his condition."

She referred to Gilbert Townsend's missing leg, a result of a battle during the second Boer War. He'd worn a prosthetic, which had allowed him a certain degree of mobility, but horseback riding hadn't been possible.

"A bone, anything," Fox said with annoyance. "Just something to keep him occupied."

"I'll go below and find something for him." Eva started to leave, but hesitated. She turned to include both Phoebe and Amelia in her gaze. "That is, if you're all right and don't need me."

Phoebe smiled. "Of course we're all right. Just worried about Trent."

"Yes, and about what these policemen are thinking in coming here and questioning him." Amelia shook her head. "They were awfully rude, wouldn't you say? That doesn't seem to bode well for Trent."

Fox grimaced at her pronouncement. "Don't go thinking the worst. It's probably just their way to be grim and overbearing. It doesn't necessarily mean anything, Amelia."

Amelia shrugged, and Phoebe caught her murmuring, "We'll see."

Mildred didn't help matters when she resumed her seat, crossed her arms in front of her, and said, "Police aren't typically rude without a reason."

To distract her brother and sister from worrying, Phoebe asked Fox, "What did you say to Trent that had him smiling just before he went off with the policemen?"

Fox broke out into a smile of his own. "I told him Julia is as fierce as any bull terrier when she wants to be."

Amelia's mouth fell open on a gasp, but then the three of them fell to laughter, while Veronica and Mildred looked on with slightly bemused expressions.

CHAPTER 6

Eva went back through the baize door with a bowl of meaty soup bones in hand. The cook had been about to dump a platter of roasted beef bones into a pot of water, along with celery and onions, and Eva feared the stern-faced woman would not be willing to part with even a small amount of her broth-making ingredients. Turns out she had judged the woman unfairly, for as soon as Eva explained about Trent losing his father that morning, and the dog being all the boy had left in the world, Mrs. Wexon, as was her name, couldn't offer up the treat fast enough.

As she turned into the main hall, she heard subdued voices and footsteps coming from beyond the drawing room. Had the police finished questioning Trent? Detective Inspector Nichols came into view. The look on his face caused Eva to draw a sharp breath. Behind him came the two constables. Trent Mercer walked between them, his head down, his feet shuffling.

Last came Lady Annondale, looking none-too-pleased. "This is ridiculous. He's a boy, and we're talking about his own father." When none of the officials stopped or responded, she walked faster to catch up with them. Eva had a moment's fright when Lady Annondale's shoe slid on the gleaming marble flooring. She caught her balance and hardly missed a step. "At least let him stay here. I'll take full responsibility for him. We won't let him out of our sight."

Jester streaked into the hall and jumped up against Trent's torso. The boy absently stroked his head and said some quiet words to soothe the animal. The others hurried out of the drawing room, Lady Phoebe and Fox leading them.

"What's going on here? Detective?" When the policeman didn't answer, Lady Phoebe gazed past him. "Julia, what's happened?"

"They're arresting him." Lady Annondale circled the constables and the boy and halted in front of the detective inspector. "You're taking him on the flimsiest of evidence. Phoebe, they've got nothing against Trent except for the dog."

"The dog?" Lady Phoebe looked confused. "But that doesn't make sense."

Fox pressed forward to stand with his friend. "Trent has no idea how Jester got into that building. Didn't my sister tell you he was outside looking for Jester when we saw him this morning? He couldn't be responsible for . . . for his father."

"For his father's *murder,"* Detective Inspector Nichols said tersely. "And just because you saw him apparently searching for his dog doesn't mean he himself wasn't in that building earlier. He claims he was out strolling along the railroad tracks at the time of his father's death, but I could find no one at the factory who can corroborate that. Strolling along the tracks, indeed."

"I had a lot to think about," Trent murmured.

"They keep bringing up something called a pattern book," Lady Annondale said, "and insisting Trent stole it from his father."

"Which isn't true." Trent's chin came up. "I have no idea where he even keeps it—*kept* it—so I couldn't have taken it."

"What's a pattern book?" Amelia asked.

"It's where a designer records every pattern he's ever devised. It's both his livelihood and his legacy." Again Trent took a defensive stance. "Why would I take it? I have no desire to be a designer."

"Trent." Fox opened his eyes wide and stared hard at his friend. Eva guessed it was a caution not to say anything that could possibly incriminate him, such as admitting he resented his father's plans for him.

Too late. Detective Inspector Nichols said, "I'm sorry, but your young friend not only had opportunity, he had a motive as well."

"What motive?" Fox's gaze flicked ever so briefly to Lady Annondale, then returned to the detective inspector.

"We have it on good authority that Trent resented his father for withdrawing him from Eton and forcing him to work at Crown Lily. And I think you know it, too."

This time Fox made no effort to avoid pinning his eldest sister with an accusing glare. "Julia! How could you bring that up?"

"I didn't. Don't be daft." She clutched at the silk scarf draped over her shoulders. Her face turned florid with indignation.

Eva didn't like the looks of that blush. She turned right about, reentered the baize door, and hurried downstairs to the call-board outside the housekeeper's parlor. She set the bowl of beef bones on a nearby dresser and pressed the buzzer for Hetta's room on the third floor.

"*Ja,*" came over the speaking tube. "Hetta here."

"Hetta, please come down to the main hall. Lady Annondale may need you."

Eva heard a gasp through the tube, then a hurried, "I come now."

Then she hurried back upstairs and into the hall. Amelia stood with Lady Annondale now, and they each had an arm around the other's waist. Phoebe stood behind Fox, as if ready to reach out and stop him from . . .

From following in pursuit, which he seemed half bent on doing. He, too, had turned an angry red. A scowl knitted his brows above eyes blazing with anger. Eva suspected he was also close to tears, but masking them with his outrage. "You're making a mistake. A stupid, ignorant mistake and you'll regret it. Do you know who our grandfather is? Do you know who I am?" He started toward them, but Phoebe grasped his shoulder. He shook her off, but stayed where he was.

The policemen remained impassive as they crossed the hall. When they reached the front door, Trent stopped, tugging free when Constable Dodge tried to pull him along. With a pang, Eva realized the dog had followed along at the boy's side. Trent bent down to pet him, and reached his arms around him. Then he slowly rose to his feet.

"You'll take care of Jester, won't you?"

Fox went forward and this time Phoebe let him go. "Of course we will. But you'll be back soon. You'll see. By the end of the day, maybe. I'm not about to let them keep you at that place."

Trent shrugged. "Thanks. But there might not be much you can do about it. As long as I know Jester's being looked after, I'll be all right." He put up no further resistance when Detective Inspector Nichols opened the front door and Constable Dodge nudged him outside.

When no one made a move to close the door, Eva walked to it and gently pushed it until the lock clicked into place. The Renshaws, and even Miss Townsend and Miss Blair, stood in silence, staring at the empty place where Trent had been. Jester let out a long, low whine, prompting Fox to crouch, and then sit on the marble tiles to comfort him.

At a heavy tread on the stairs, Eva glanced up to see Hetta hurrying down. She went directly to Lady Annondale.

"Madame must rest. Come and lie down a while. *Ja?*"

Lady Annondale nodded, her features weighed with fatigue. Where her face had burned with exasperation minutes ago, she now looked wan and pale. Eva was relieved that she went docilely upstairs with Hetta.

"Well, now that the excitement is over . . ." Miss Townsend didn't bother completing her thought. She turned about and went back into the drawing room. Probably to finish her tea and cake, Eva thought.

From his inhospitable seat on the tiles, Fox looked up. "What are we going to do? We can't let Trent take the blame for a crime he didn't commit."

"Of course we won't." Amelia joined him at Jester's other side, tucking her skirts beneath her legs as she lowered herself to the floor. "Phoebe will know what to do. Won't you, Phoebe?"

Lady Phoebe met Eva's gaze. "I . . . I don't know, Amelia . . ."

She seemed about to say more, but fell silent as Fox twisted around and craned his neck to peer up at her again. "Amelia's right. You always know what to do in these circumstances. Don't pretend you don't. You might be able to fool Grams and

106

Grampapa, but we know what you and Eva have been up to these past couple of years."

"Fox, it's one thing to poke around at home in Little Barlow, where I know everyone and—"

"What about Cowes?" he challenged. "We didn't know anyone there except for the family and the wedding guests."

"Yes, but—"

Fox turned his attention back to Jester, doing a thorough job of scratching behind his ears. Eva understood this was merely a way for Fox to work off extra energy and frustration. He blinked several times, and she guessed tears once again were threatening. He was, after all, still a child despite his recent surge in height. "If you won't help," he said mournfully, "I'll do it alone."

Amelia stroked Jester from the top of his head to his tapering hindquarters. "I'll help you."

"No, you won't, Amelia. Nor you, either, Fox." Lady Phoebe went to her siblings and joined them on the floor. "All right, I'll ask some questions and see what I can find out. Eva?"

"Of course, my lady. You can count on me. Oh, I almost forgot." Hurrying back through the baize door, she returned belowstairs and retrieved Jester's treat. Back in the main hall, she set the bowl down on the marble floor between Amelia and Fox, beneath Jester's nose. After one excited snort, he happily dived in and attacked the contents with gusto. Seeing as no one seemed about to move to another location anytime soon, Eva made herself as comfortable as possible on the floor with the others.

"Ahem."

They all glanced up to see that Mildred Blair was still in the hall. She studied them with large eyes dramatically lined with kohl. Her crepe georgette hem fluttered around her ankles as she strolled closer to them.

"I hate to be the grim one here, but have any of you stopped to consider that the boy might be guilty?"

Fox started to protest, but Miss Blair didn't give him a chance.

"Yes, I understand he's your friend, and no one likes to think ill of anyone so young. But before you go trying to incriminate someone else, shouldn't you allow that perhaps the police are correct?"

Fox came to his feet, startling Jester so much he stopped gobbling and lifted his head. "You know what, Miss Blair? I didn't like you much last spring in Cowes, and I like you even less now."

"Fox," Lady Phoebe admonished, but Miss Blair waved a hand.

"That's all right, I don't require that you feel affection for me. I'd just like you all to be realistic, and fair. Because to exonerate Trent, you must incriminate someone else. Don't take that lightly."

Fox's eyes narrowed on the woman. "Come on, Jester," he said. The dog made no move to follow, but dipped his head once more into the bowl. "Jester, come." Fox glanced down, realized the problem, and stooped to slide the bowl out from under Jester's nose. "*Come,* Jester." This time the dog eagerly followed his new friend and the bowl of beef bones across the hall and up the stairs.

Amelia came to her feet. "I'll go talk to him. Miss Blair is right. We must proceed with the utmost caution."

Once Amelia reached the stairs, Lady Phoebe shook her head and sighed. "*We* are not proceeding with anything. Eva, I suppose it's up to you and me to make sure those two"— she pointed at the stairs and the two siblings just then disappearing on the upper landing—"stay out of it." She sighed again and regarded Miss Blair. "But you're right. I don't believe Trent did anything wrong, but we certainly don't want to accuse an innocent person solely for the sake of clearing another."

Eva stood and helped Lady Phoebe up.

Miss Blair came closer. "Thank you for that."

"For what?"

"For not disagreeing with me merely to put me in my place."

"That's not what my brother is doing. He's terribly upset about his friend."

"I realize that, but Veronica loves to contradict me for no honest reason, and Ernest, well, he never misses a chance to assure me that once he inherits, I'll no longer be welcome at Lyndale Park. Not up on the third floor, not even in the cottage, where he's currently residing." With a little laugh she shrugged. "I suppose I shouldn't expect anything more from your sister."

"Lady Annondale isn't like that." Eva had held her tongue during the entire encounter with the police, and the past several minutes as well. It wasn't her place to interfere. But she would not stand by and listen to anyone belittle a member of this family. Especially this woman who had plotted against Lady Annondale last spring after her husband died. "I'm sorry to speak out," Eva said to Lady Phoebe. Turning back to Miss Blair, she said, "But your judgment of Lady Annondale is entirely unfair and incorrect."

Miss Blair smiled placidly. "Is it?"

"It most certainly is." With an effort, Eva kept her features even, rather than allow Miss Blair to see what she really thought of her.

"*Hmph.* I wondered if you had a tongue, Miss Huntford. Now I see that you do. Good for you." She retreated into the drawing room, leaving Eva to wonder if she'd just been insulted or complimented. She also couldn't decide if she should feel sorry for Mildred Blair, or simply loathe her.

• • •

"Don't pay any mind to her, Eva. She likes to stir up trouble," Phoebe said. "She's also terribly arrogant."

That, Phoebe decided, was a vast understatement. Mildred Blair enjoyed nothing so much as throwing other people off balance and making them appear foolish. Phoebe didn't appreciate one bit that Mildred had chosen Eva as her target. Especially since Eva would not defend herself. She would stick up for any member of the family, but for herself, she would remain silent and endure insults as a matter of course.

"You needn't worry about me, my lady. The likes of Mildred Blair can't get the better of me."

"Good. I just wish she wouldn't try. Why don't you and I go to the library." Phoebe linked her arm through Eva's. "We'll lock ourselves in and hide from the madness that seems to have taken over this house. No, make that the entire town of Langston."

Once they'd entered the library, Eva closed the door firmly. Phoebe waved her over to a comfortable, overstuffed settee set in the alcove of a bow window.

"What a lovely place to curl up and read." Phoebe leaned back, pulled her feet up beneath her skirts, but skewed her lips. "If only this were a pleasant day where our biggest challenge had been agreeing on a china pattern for my

111

grandparents. How long ago it seems we set out to do just that. It's hard to believe it was only this morning."

"So much has happened, all of it unimaginable." Eva pulled a pillow out from behind her and held it on her lap as she settled in. "Now, how to help Master Trent?"

"I'm not sure yet. All I know is I can't allow Fox to try to catch a killer. He's my grandfather's heir and he must be kept safe."

"He wouldn't thank you for that sentiment, I'm afraid." Eva chuckled softly.

Phoebe laughed, too. "No, I don't suppose he would. It would hurt his male pride."

"You do realize, my lady, that your grandfather—and your grandmother, for that matter—would be equally devastated if anything should happen to you."

Phoebe thought about this for a moment. "Yes, that's true. But as I said, Fox is Grampapa's heir. I can never be the Earl of Wroxly. Only Fox can be that."

"So much to set upon a child's shoulders." Eva absently ran her fingertip back and forth over the velvet trim on the pillow she held. "Do you believe Fox will stay out of things?"

Phoebe heard the doubt in Eva's question and considered how much Fox had changed in recent months, how he'd matured, or, rather, had been forced to, due to events last spring. Then, within twenty-four hours he had gone from a needling, spoiled child to a young man who suddenly understood the consequences of his actions. Phoebe had wanted him out of harm's way then, but he'd insisted on helping discover who had murdered Julia's new husband. In fact, if not for Fox sneaking around and putting himself in danger, Julia might not be here now. Or Eva, either.

Phoebe shuddered to consider how life might have changed that day. "Now that I think about it," she said, "he capitulated awfully quick when I agreed to help Trent. So, no, we can't trust him to stay out of it." She reached over to put her hand on Eva's. "We'll have to act fast, won't we?"

"I fear we will, my lady."

Phoebe studied Eva's profile. "When are you going to dispense with all that wretched formality? We're alone. You're my friend— the best I've ever had. And we've been through so very much together. Can I not simply be Phoebe?"

"Such changes in our world these past years." Sounding wistful, Eva gazed across the room. Phoebe wondered if she was looking back, or ahead. "They've been easier for you than for me, you realize. You were still quite young when the war began, and the younger one is, the more readily change is accepted. I grew up during the old days, when tradition seemed eternal, a state of being that always had been and always would be. A tradition that separated people into categories with strict lines between them, and even stricter rules governing how one treated the other. We see now that tradition is as delicate as gossamer lace. In many ways change is a good thing. There are more opportunities for everyone, rich and poor alike. But change can also be . . . unsettling. Uncomfortable." Eva turned back to Phoebe with an apologetic tilt to her lips. "Difficult to get on with."

"I understand, dearest Eva." Phoebe leaned and kissed Eva's cheek. "All in good time, then. For now . . . let's consider what we've learned so far at Crown Lily. There was that Moira Wickham you mentioned."

"Yes. She's head painter, but wishes to be a designer. Ronald Mercer stood in the way of that. He didn't believe a woman could be skilled enough for the position."

"How resentful was she?"

"Quite. But not only toward Mr. Mercer. I believe she's resentful toward men in general. She mentioned being a *surplus woman,* someone who will never marry and is forced to make her own way in the world."

"A horrid term, that."

"I couldn't agree more. After serving their country during the war years by filling in for fighting men in the factories and elsewhere, and then being faced with the reality that so many men died, they'd likely never find husbands, these women are now blamed for being unmarried and having to earn their own living."

Phoebe nodded. "I've read articles suggesting these women are set to destroy the natural order of things by continuing to work. They're shredding the very fabric of family life. Can you imagine? Of course such articles were written by men. I can't blame Miss Wickham for being resentful."

"You and I are lucky."

Yes. Phoebe had Owen, an earl's second son, who, because of his brother's death in the war, found himself his father's heir, while Eva stepped out on a regular basis with Miles Brannock, a constable from Little Barlow. Both men had made it through the war relatively unscathed— at least physically. Neither talked much about his experiences, but Phoebe knew both men suffered from the memories, from nightmares born in the trenches.

"We'll want to discover where Moira Wickham was at the time of the murder," Eva pointed out.

"Yes. And the same for Percy Bateman, the other designer, who very much wanted the commission for our china pattern. Did you notice how Mr. Mercer tried to disparage Mr. Bateman's talents, calling him *overly bold* in his designs and saying he needed *reining in?*"

"I did overhear that. So then, like Moira Wickham, Percy Bateman might have seen Mr. Mercer as an obstacle to his career, as well as to his self-respect."

"You're right to put it that way, Eva. Self-respect might be more of a motive to kill someone than money. At least in some instances. It's not easy being criticized and humiliated time and again."

"Indeed, it is not." Eva glanced toward the door.

Phoebe wondered if she was thinking about Mildred again. Mildred's comments today were merely the tip of it. Last spring, during Julia's wedding, Mildred had treated Eva as though she were little better than the lowest scullery maid.

Eva turned back to Phoebe. "Your sister mentioned a missing pattern book, if I'm not mistaken. It seems to me the person who would most benefit from such an item would be Percy Bateman."

"Perhaps." Still, Phoebe wasn't so sure. "I wonder if Mr. Bateman would care about Mr. Mercer's patterns. Perhaps he didn't need or want the ideas of an older man. But Moira Wickham might. Or she might have wished to erase all traces of Mr. Mercer's influence on Crown Lily entirely."

"She might," Eva agreed. "I heard something else before the police arrived when I was

116

belowstairs preparing tea. One of the footmen mentioned he thought Gus Abbott might be guilty."

"Gus Abbott?"

"He's the head clay mixer, and he's not only the man who found Ronald Mercer in the grinding pan, but the very person Mr. Mercer went there to speak with."

"Goodness. That certainly gives him opportunity. But motive?"

Eva shrugged. "That, I don't yet know."

"And then there is Trent," Phoebe said with a sigh. "We can only find answers by returning to Crown Lily and asking questions. Where to start?" Phoebe sat back as a plan took shape in her mind. "Julia and I must meet with Mr. Tremaine and Mr. Bateman to continue with our order. They'll be only too happy that we're still willing to patronize Crown Lily, so they shouldn't suspect we're there for any other purpose."

"Are you still thinking of giving them your business?"

Phoebe held up her hands. "I don't see why not. Why punish an entire company for the horrible act of one? I'll talk to Julia. I'm sure she'll agree."

CHAPTER 7

Phoebe and Julia went to Crown Lily the next afternoon. Eva and Hetta accompanied them, but Fox and Amelia hadn't even suggested they come along. Rather, they had expressed their trust in Julia when it came to selecting the right china. Poor things, all they could think of was Trent; they'd lost their heart for the endeavor that had brought them to Langston.

Which was fortunate. Phoebe didn't want either of them involved in searching for Mr. Mercer's killer, especially if it turned out that Trent had committed the act. Strictly speaking, Eva and Hetta needn't have gone, either, but Phoebe had had a good reason for wishing Eva to accompany them. Hetta, on the other hand, had resolutely refused to stay behind. "Where Madame goes, Hetta goes," she had stated with a bullish look on her face. When Phoebe reminded her that they had gone to Crown Lily yesterday morning without her, she had crossed her arms in front of her and stubbornly replied, "That was then, *ja*? Things have changed. I go."

The motorcar brought them beneath the arching Crown Lily sign and into the main quadrangle. Here, the driver stopped as planned and allowed Eva to get out. As she stepped onto the cobblestones, Phoebe slid closer to the open door. "Be careful."

"Don't worry, I will be. If anyone asks what I'm doing wandering about, I'll tell them I'm interested in a career change." Eva tightened her coat around her and set off across the quadrangle, toward the building where she had met Moira Wickham.

The motorcar continued into the smaller enclosure that housed the administrative building. Julia had telephoned earlier, and Mr. Tremaine must have had someone watching for them, as the door immediately opened. He stepped out, all smiles, as if his factory hadn't suffered a tragedy only the day before.

"Lady Annondale, Lady Phoebe. Thank you for returning." Nudging Fenton aside after the chauffeur had opened the rear door, Mr. Tremaine reached in to help them out. "I'd feared we'd lost your patronage after yesterday's fiasco."

Phoebe winced. She didn't think the word *fiasco* suited the occasion. Mr. Mercer had worked here many years, and she would have expected his employer to have taken a more somber tone.

"Let's get you ladies inside and attend to business, shall we?" He held the door to the building open for them. He paid no attention to Hetta after an initial nod in her direction, but Hetta preferred that to having attention on her. The Swiss woman had become adept at blending into the scenery until Julia needed her. And then let anyone try to stand in her way.

They walked through the showroom again, and Phoebe's eyes were dazzled anew from the glossy displays. She had been glad on their first visit that Mr. Tremaine had sorted through the dozens and dozens of patterns and shapes and selected the ones he believed best fit the qualities Julia had articulated to him. That had narrowed down the assortment considerably, even though there had still seemed to be a vast array of possibilities covering the conference room table.

He led them not to that room again, but to his office, a large corner space with windows overlooking two separate enclosures. In one, three bottle kilns puffed their black smoke into a sharp November sky. In the other, men loaded those open train carriages, which Phoebe had seen last time, with what appeared to be packed and sealed barrels. The way the men carefully hefted them, she could only surmise they were filled with china orders ready to be shipped out to patrons all over England, and beyond.

He must have noticed her gazing out the window, for he said, "From here I can see my china entering the kilns that make it strong and lasting, and I can also see it leave on its way to become part of people's homes and their families' lives." He assisted them in shedding their coats, and held a chair for each of them, Julia first, of course. Hetta backed against the wall beside the office door, folded her hands at her waist, and stared straight ahead, like a soldier. Julia's army of one. The thought made Phoebe smile.

"Now, I believe this is what you want, Lady Annondale." Mr. Tremaine circled his desk and sat. He gestured toward a plain white cup and saucer sitting on the blotter in front of him.

It was one Julia had admired on their first trip here. It had a simple trumpet shape, narrow at the bottom and flaring wide at the top, and stood on a low round foot. A solid triangle formed the handle, which one would pinch to hold, rather than a loop one could hook one's finger through.

"I hope you concur, Lady Phoebe. This is our most modern shape, very new. Very innovative."

Phoebe wasn't at all sure she liked it. That triangle handle might prove less than comfortable, and she could imagine both Grams and Grampapa eyeing it askance. Of course neither would ever openly criticize. They'd say it was wonderful, no matter what they really thought. As for Julia . . .

"It's perfect. Phoebe, don't you think so? Isn't it just the thing?"

"I . . . er . . . yes. It's . . . unique. Modern, as Mr. Tremaine said."

"Good," that man said with a light clap of his hands. "Now, for the pattern. We can't send you home with blank china, now can we?"

"Perish the thought." Julia smoothed the front of her tunic, which flowed to her knees over a narrow skirt that reached just below her calves. The ensemble flowed gently over the contours of her belly. "Now, then, since we've gone quite modern with the shape, we'll be more traditional with the pattern." She turned to Phoebe. "You see, I'm willing to compromise. Both new and traditional." Turning back to Mr. Tremaine, she said, "Is Mr. Bateman available? I'd like him to be here when we announce our decision."

Here, for the first time since their arrival, Mr. Tremaine looked melancholy. "I suppose you felt that under the circumstances, you'd award the commission to a living designer."

"That isn't it at all, actually," Julia said. "When we saw Mr. Bateman's landscape design, I think we all knew it was what we wanted, that it was perfect for our grandparents. What happened to Mr. Mercer is most unfortunate, and his family has our utmost condolences, as do you, but Mr. Bateman won us over with his design."

Despite the odd cup handle, Phoebe found herself perfectly satisfied with Julia's decision. But the time had come to put her plan in motion.

"I'm in agreement with my sister . . . I think."

"What do you mean, you *think?*" Julia turned to her with a scowl that made slashes of her carefully delineated eyebrows. While Julia had known Eva would be asking questions among the women workers in the art department, Phoebe had made no mention of her plan involving Percy Bateman. She had wanted a believable reaction from her sister, and Julia didn't disappoint. "I believed we were in agreement. Why are you suddenly being difficult?"

"I'm not. I merely wish to see the design again." Phoebe appealed to Mr. Tremaine. "To be certain."

"Of course, of course." He picked up the candlestick phone on his desk and called his secretary. "Jessup? Yes, please send in Percy Bateman. And tell him to bring the patterns he designed for the Renshaws."

The young designer entered moments later, stumbling over the threshold in his haste, a portfolio beneath his left arm. He looked both delighted and disbelieving—as if he couldn't trust his good fortune. "My ladies. Have . . . you made a decision?"

Julia pursed her lips. "We thought we had."

"Oh." The man visibly sagged. He looked at Mr. Tremaine for clarification, but received only a shrug.

"It's between two," Phoebe told him. She motioned him closer to the desk. "We loved the Cotswold landscape pattern, but there's one other I'd like to see again. I hope you have it with you. It's the Art Nouveau floral, with all the twisting vines. Do you remember which one I mean?"

She held her breath as she waited for his reply, knowing quite well he'd never shown them any such pattern. Mr. Mercer had. Both Phoebe and Amelia had commented on it at the time, but neither had thought it might replace the Cotswold landscape. Now she wanted Mr. Bateman to believe it to be a serious contender.

"It's a very stylized design," she clarified, when Mr. Bateman seemed stumped, "with elongated flowers in soft blues, pinks, and yellows. I think my grandmother would adore it."

"She wouldn't, Phoebe." Julia huffed with impatience. "She would find it too abstract for her taste."

Phoebe ignored Julia and watched the young man closely. He blinked rapidly as his eyebrows gathered, and he fussed with a bit of hair hanging over his forehead.

Phoebe smiled eagerly. "If you haven't got it with you, we'll wait while you go and get it." Would he? Did he have the missing pattern book hidden in his office? Would he remove the page with the Art Nouveau pattern and present it as his own?

"Really, Phoebe, can't we simply place the order with the Cotswold pattern?" Julia crossed her legs and swung her pump-clad foot. She was becoming more impatient by the instant. Behind them, Hetta subtly shifted, becoming alert to her mistress's mood and ready, Phoebe knew, to intervene should Julia become overly agitated.

Finally Percy Bateman gave a decisive shake of his head. "I'm sorry, Lady Phoebe, but while I do have Art Nouveau designs to my credit, I'm quite certain I didn't design anything with that description for you. I believe Mr. Mercer did— may he rest in peace. If that's the design you want, I'm sure Mr. Tremaine can arrange to have it found for you. It would be in Mr. Mercer's pattern book, I'm sure—"

Mr. Tremaine coughed. "I'm afraid Ron's pattern book has gone missing."

"*Missing?*" Mr. Bateman slowly set his own pattern book on the desk. "How can that have happened? Has a search been launched?" To hear the urgency in the man's voice, one would have thought his own pattern book had been stolen.

"Of course a search is under way." The older man shrugged. "And as for how the book disappeared . . . how can his death have occurred here yesterday? It was no accident, you know, and it would seem, whoever killed him probably also has the book, and . . ."

Another cough, a forceful one, halted their conversation. Hetta came forward from her post against the wall. "That is enough. Such talk will upset Madame."

The men looked chagrined. With a quick glance at Julia, Mr. Tremaine said, "Right you are. Forgive us. Shall we get back to the business at hand? Now, which pattern will it be?"

"The Cotswold one," Phoebe said, not sure if she should be relieved or not. She had gauged Mr. Bateman's reaction to her request carefully. If he had pretended the design had been his and, what's more, had retrieved it for them, it might have been an indication his rivalry with the other designer had extended beyond professional competition. But did his failure to do so prove he had nothing to do with Ronald Mercer's death? Or was he merely too clever to give himself away?

Julia, too, looked relieved. "Good. Let's complete the order. Where do we sign?"

Phoebe left her sister to it and drew Percy Bateman into conversation. "It's horrible, what happened. I'm having a difficult time grasping that one of the people we came to Langston specifically to see is no longer with us."

"Believe me, my lady, I understand. I've worked under the man for the past year now, and while I cannot say I knew him well, we'd certainly established a close professional rapport."

"I believe Mr. Mercer told us you haven't been here long, but only a year, you say. You're quite talented."

He colored slightly. "Thank you."

"What had you done before that?"

"The same, pattern designing, but I was assistant, without the opportunity to head up

126

my own projects. I worked for the Davenport Potteries."

"Oh, yes. I know that company. We have pieces of theirs at home. So then I take it you heard of an opening here and applied to fill the position."

He gave a nod. "That's the way of it for designers. Most of us work at several potteries before settling in at one. It's a bit of a gypsy lifestyle, moving from place to place, often town to town, but it's necessary if one wishes to be successful."

"And you did." When he nodded again, Phoebe smiled. "I'd imagine you still do."

"Of course. What man doesn't?"

"There are other designers here, aren't there? Or assistant designers?"

"There are four junior designers and several more assistants."

"Tell me, Mr. Bateman, would a designer so wish to succeed he might kill for the opportunity?"

His eyes sparked with alarm. He drew himself up straighter, his shoulders rigid. "I . . . What are you getting at, Lady Phoebe?"

"I'm merely asking a hypothetical question. It's no secret Ronald Mercer was murdered. You yourself just implied designers are willing to uproot themselves for better opportunities. It made me wonder, what else might a designer be willing to do?"

"Oh, I see. Hypothetically speaking." He

127

released a breath and relaxed, his shoulders sloping inward as he shoved his hands in his trouser pockets. "I can't see any sane man going to such lengths, not for any reason. But an insane man? Luckily, I don't believe we have anyone of that description here." He ended with a chuckle that sounded forced.

Phoebe let go a laugh. "I hope you didn't think I was accusing you."

"Goodness no." His chuckle rose in volume and pitch. "Why on earth would you?"

"Because someone did, after all, murder Mr. Mercer."

The man paled as Phoebe turned away and rejoined Julia and Mr. Tremaine.

When Eva stepped into the painting and enameling room, only a few artists glanced up from what they were doing, and then only briefly. Moira Wickham was not one of them. Eva spotted her at her worktable in the far left corner, beneath the tall windows, intent on whatever item she held in one hand while applying color with a paintbrush. From where she sat, Miss Wickham could easily keep an eye on her workforce.

Each artist had several stacks of cups and saucers, or plates, or other items, ranged around her work area. Each sat hunched, paintbrush in hand, face close to her work. She noticed today that only women filled the room. The few men here the other day were not in evidence now.

Eva stood for several moments simply observing, but also hoping Miss Wickham would notice her. She wished to appear wistful, but not seeking. Perhaps she should walk around a little, like last time. She began a slow pace, trying to muffle her footsteps. It wasn't her intention to disrupt the workers, but within moments she realized this wasn't a problem. They seemed immune to distractions, keeping their focus on their work without missing a brushstroke.

Miss Wickham, however, did finally look up. She raised her eyebrows in question, immersed her brush in a jar of liquid, and came to her feet. She met Eva partway down the first row.

"I see you're back. Couldn't keep away, could you?" The woman smiled in an offhand manner, but something in her gaze remained expectant, and Eva didn't disappoint her.

"I couldn't, actually. My mistress and her sister are placing their order, and since they didn't need me, I thought I'd come and take another look. I hope you don't mind."

"Placing their order the day after our head designer died?" The woman expressed a world of disapproval in the upward twitching of an eyebrow. "Business as usual for them, eh? Can't have their sort inconvenienced by a little thing like a man's murder. And, yes, we all know Mr. Mercer didn't die by accident."

Eva nearly burst with the urge to contest Moira Wickham's opinion of the Renshaws, but she held her tongue and nodded as if in sympathy with Miss Wickham's sentiments. Eva glanced again at the workers with an admiration that wasn't feigned. "I find this all so fascinating."

"Do you really?"

"I know you'd rather be designing, but that kind of creativity is a rare talent. I certainly couldn't do it."

"But the painting interests you as something you'd like to try?" Miss Wickham tilted her head. Her eyes narrowed. "I distinctly remember you saying you hadn't got the talent for painting."

Eva stole a glance over her shoulder, as if she were about to impart a deep secret and didn't wish Lady Phoebe finding out. "I must admit it *does* interest me. Very much. And what I said, well, it wasn't entirely true. I've got a steady hand—one must, to be a lady's maid, you see. Stitching, dressing hair, applying cosmetics—it's all a kind of artistic work. I think I could do this, if given the chance."

"You also said you loved working for your ladies." Apparently, not only did Miss Wickham possess a good memory, she was not to be easily convinced of Eva's change of heart.

"Honestly, until I walked into this room day before last, I had never considered changing situations. But now . . . I don't know. To be truly

130

independent and have a life of my own . . ." She trailed off with another sigh.

"Yes, a lady's maid isn't afforded that luxury, is she? I know that from listening to my mother's stories. Always at another woman's beck and call, at any hour of the day or night. In your case, *two* women. And how much time to yourself? Half a day on Sunday, after church?"

While that was often the case, Eva had more time to herself than most lady's maids ever dreamed of. But that was something she didn't need to share. "Besides having little time to myself," she said, "I've no sense of achievement, nothing to show for all my hard work." A lie. She derived a great sense of accomplishment from watching her young ladies, motherless for most of their lives, grow to become confident, generous, intelligent young women, and knowing she helped them achieve their potential. "Not like here, where you can point to a solid object and say, *I had a hand in creating that. That's my work.*"

Moira Wickham remained silent for several moments, studying Eva with a shrewd expression that made Eva suspect she hadn't fooled the other woman. That was, until Moira spoke next.

"Can you get away for an hour or so, come six o'clock?"

"Why?"

"Can you?"

131

Eva pretended to think it over. "I suppose I could, but only for an hour. I'll need to return and ready my ladies for dinner by a bit after seven."

"All right, after that, then."

Eva again pretended to think. "They shouldn't need me again until bedtime. So, yes, I could manage it."

"They won't object to your leaving?"

"I can't imagine they would. As I said, they won't need me." Basically, another lie. Between dressing her ladies for dinner and helping them to bed, Eva usually spent the hours tidying their wardrobes, cleaning shoes, mending anything that needed it, and readying soiled clothes for the laundress. However, Phoebe and Amelia could have no objections to her using that time to become better acquainted with Miss Wickham—and perhaps delve further into her resentment against Mr. Mercer and being denied opportunities she felt fully qualified for.

"Good. Then meet me at the Royal Oak on Dormer Street as soon after seven as you can. And then we'll see if you have the courage to leave your old life behind and become a painter, perhaps even an enameler."

"I knew what you were up to, you know." Julia's whisper darted across the small space between her chair and Phoebe's. "It felt like going to the bank in Little Barlow all over again."

Phoebe felt duly chastised. Only weeks ago she had involved Julia in a scheme to help one of Little Barlow's local farmers save his orchard. However, she had neglected to explain her plan to Julia, in effect using her sister's position as a viscountess to persuade the owner of the bank to take them seriously.

"I'm sorry," she whispered back out of the side of her mouth.

They were still in Mr. Tremaine's office, and Julia had yet to sign her name to the contract that would bind them in an agreement for a china service from Crown Lily. Mr. Tremaine and Percy Bateman had retreated to the leather couch that sat against one wall. They were ironing out a few details between themselves about production schedules and timing, and speaking in equally hushed tones.

Julia shot Phoebe an incriminating look. "You might have trusted me beforehand rather than let me figure it out for myself."

"I wanted you to act naturally, which you did. I was afraid your anger at me for tossing a cog in your plans wouldn't be believable, otherwise." Phoebe grinned. "You were splendid, by the way."

Julia relented and returned her grin. "Thank you. I pride myself that I might have been an actress under vastly different circumstances." She tipped her chin up, showing Phoebe her aristocratic profile. "But what exactly was the purpose of your little ruse?"

"I'll tell you as soon as the forms are signed and we're on our way back to Lyndale Park."

"Does it have anything to do with Eva making herself scarce?"

Phoebe smiled and nodded. At the same time, she wondered what, if anything, Eva had learned about Moira Wickham. The woman had ambitions to become a designer. Perhaps *she* had the pattern book.

Mr. Tremaine and Percy Bateman rose from the sofa and returned to the desk. Mr. Tremaine sat; Mr. Bateman remained standing, his face alight with a beaming smile.

"Now, then." Mr. Tremaine pushed several sheaves of paper across the desk to Julia.

Julia didn't glance at the paperwork. "You can promise delivery by February first?"

"I can, my lady. It says so right there." He pointed to the first page of the documents.

With a raised eyebrow Julia leaned to read, and Phoebe, likewise, pressed forward to peruse the contract. Her signature might not be needed, but she nonetheless wished to understand the terms of their commission. It took them several minutes, and then Julia turned her head to meet Phoebe's gaze. Her expression clearly asked if Phoebe found the terms and conditions satisfactory, and Phoebe nodded. Secretly, she found that small act on Julia's part heartening—her sister had cared to seek her opinion, even if silently. Julia took up the fountain pen Mr. Tremaine had provided and emblazoned her swooping signature on the bottom of the last page.

"That's it, then." She came to her feet, and Phoebe rose beside her. Julia extended her hand across the desk. "Thank you, Mr. Tremaine."

He hesitated before clasping it, taken aback, perhaps, by the familiarity. "It's been my pleasure, Lady Annondale."

"And thank *you,* Mr. Bateman. Without your design I don't know if my siblings and I ever would have agreed on anything. You apparently knew what we wanted before we did." Julia offered her hand to him as well. He took it and pumped it several times before apparently realizing he was taking a liberty, whereupon he promptly released her.

Phoebe also shook hands with both men and thanked them. They were helped on with their coats, and prepared to leave. "Come, Hetta," Julia said unnecessarily, as Hetta had already moved to the door. "Time to go home."

"Home?" Phoebe asked as they stepped outside. Her stomach sank at the thought. She wasn't ready to leave—not until they'd cleared Trent of murder, or discovered the police had the guilty party all along. Phoebe desperately hoped not, as much for Fox's sake as for Trent's. "As in Little Barlow?"

"No, goose." Julia grinned. "As in Lyndale Park. If it's all the same to the rest of you, I'm going to call Grams and Grampapa and tell them we've decided to extend our stay. I'm not at all ready to cry uncle and run away. Even if I don't have a son, Lyndale Park is my second home, and my child's rightful home, and my darling in-laws will simply have to learn to live with it."

Once reunited with Eva, and the four of them were safely in the motorcar leaving Crown Lily, Phoebe filled Julia in on her hopes of tricking Percy Bateman into revealing that he had the missing pattern book. "I thought if I feigned interest in one of Ronald Mercer's patterns," she said as Fenton turned the Rolls-Royce onto the main road, "Mr. Bateman would wish to take credit for it. But either he doesn't have Mr. Mercer's pattern book, or he's too clever to give himself away."

"My guess, he's too clever." Julia gave her gloves a tug each. "Really, Phoebe, that was a rather transparent plan. Only a fool would have fallen for it. And, besides, once he saw that I favored the Cotswold landscape, he wasn't about to defer to your wishes, was he?"

Phoebe didn't reply. Julia was right, and indeed her remarks made her feel the fool. For a moment she doubted her ability to find a killer—doubted being clever enough or having a clear enough head. But then, her gaze connected with Eva's, and with a steady nod Eva communicated her confidence in Phoebe, her belief that they would prevail. And that made Phoebe remember the two of them had done this before, and that Julia herself had benefited from their prowess.

Still, she said nothing to defend her actions regarding Mr. Bateman. He might not have admitted to anything today, and indeed he might not have anything to admit. But if he did, Phoebe would find a way to trap him into revealing his guilt.

A gleam in Eva's eye also reminded her that her lady's maid had been busy this afternoon, too. "Did you learn anything from Moira Wickham?" Phoebe asked her.

"Not yet."

Julia made a noise of impatience and tossed her head. "And you won't. The two of you are grasping at straws. I hope as much as you that Trent didn't kill his father. As a mother-to-be, I find the notion of a child murdering a parent horrific. But if you'll allow the police to do their jobs, they'll find the truth."

Phoebe gave her a significant look. Julia tossed her head again. "All right, sometimes the police get it wrong, and sometimes they're slow to see the whole picture. But you two endangering yourselves is becoming wearisome for the rest of us."

It wasn't until they reached Lyndale Park that

Phoebe continued her discussion with Eva. She could see by Eva's expression that despite not learning anything new from Miss Wickham, she nonetheless had more to say. Upon exiting the Rolls-Royce, she linked her arm through Eva's and started them walking along the grounds.

"Aren't you coming?" Julia stood framed in the open front door while Carmichael waited to take her coat. Hetta stood waiting as well, looking as though she wished nothing more than to bundle her mistress in a thick blanket before the fire and ply her with hot tea.

"Not yet," Phoebe answered with a wave.

Julia pursed her lips, shook her head at them, and went into the house.

Eva didn't waste a moment. "Can you spare me after I've readied you and Amelia for dinner? And may I make use of Douglas and the touring car?"

"Of course. Why?"

"Moira Wickham has invited me somewhere called the Royal Oak, in town, I presume. It's on Dormer Street. We're going to talk about my leaving service and becoming a painter at Crown Lily."

Phoebe brought them to a sudden halt and turned to face Eva. "Good heavens, you're not really thinking of doing that?" She found herself nearly shaking at the thought, her heart pounding and her stomach tying itself in knots. While she knew Eva would—and should—leave her someday, the notion of it happening this soon filled her with a sensation close to despair.

Eva had grasped both her gloved hands and gave reassuring squeezes. "Of course not! I merely led Miss Wickham to believe I wished to become a painter as an excuse to get to know her better and see if she's hiding anything."

"Of course." For the second time that afternoon a sense of foolishness swept over Phoebe. "That was silly of me. It's just that . . . well . . ."

"I'm not going anywhere, my lady, rest assured. Now, I agreed to join her just after seven o'clock. She wanted to meet right after work, but I wanted to be able to spend more time with her and not have to rush back here in time to help you dress for dinner."

"You know, you really don't need to help Amelia and me dress. We could manage."

"Perhaps, but I don't want to give Miss Wickham any reason to think my interest in changing situations is anything less than sincere. Better she believes I'm at your beck and call constantly, and that I'm slipping away on the sly until you need me at bedtime."

"Good thinking. In fact, if anyone asks, tell them you and Douglas contrived to sneak into town," Phoebe said, "you to meet with Miss Wickham, and Douglas to enjoy a few pints at the pub, perhaps play some rounds of darts. And if we're lucky, he might be able to engage some Crown Lily workmen in conversation."

"I'll arrange it with Douglas."

"Good. I'll feel better knowing you didn't go alone."

"Actually, so will I, my lady."

CHAPTER 8

The interior of the pub delivered on the promise of its stone and timber exterior: a several-centuries-old construction of ancient hardwoods, rough surfaces, low-beamed ceilings, and smoky gas lighting. Douglas had already entered and made his way over to the bar, crowded with flat-capped men several bodies deep. Eva wouldn't go there; no woman did, as the bar and its immediate surrounds were male-only territory.

Riding above the odors of beer and perspiration, inviting aromas from the kitchen made her stomach rumble. She'd eaten lightly upon returning to Lyndale Park; since Miss Wickham had indicated they'd be having supper together, she'd wisely saved her appetite. She was glad she did, as the savory meals she saw in front of patrons put her in mind of her mother's kitchen.

The noise of the place swarmed in her ears as dozens of conversations, laughter, and the shouting around the dartboards blended into one blurred roar. A waving hand caught her attention, and she made her way over to a table for two dimly illuminated by a sconce a few feet away. Moira Wickham grinned as Eva removed her coat, scraped back a chair, and sat. She was glad of the table's positioning, which allowed her to see over to the bar and the dartboards with only a slight turn of her head. She wished to keep track of Douglas—should she have any need of him.

That thought surprised her. Surely, in a crowded place such as this, she had no reason to fear Moira Wickham, even if she *had* killed Ronald Mercer.

"Wasn't entirely sure you'd come," the woman said as Eva settled in. She lifted the pint in front of her as if to make a toast. "Thought you might lose your nerve."

"You don't know me. When I decide something, I act upon it."

"Good for you." Moira Wickham eyed her with an amused smile.

No doubt she was taking in the plain way Eva had pulled her hair back into a bun at her nape; her black broadcloth dress, her lack of jewelry. Eva wondered, was the other woman seeing an image of her own mother, and judging that image to be courageous or lacking in fortitude?

"I hope you don't mind, but I've already taken the liberty of ordering for us. Tonight is steak and kidney pie and potatoes with onions."

"Sounds wonderful." Eva meant it. Her stomach rumbled again. Her eyes gradually adjusted to the shadows, while the general roar faded into an almost soothing background noise. Eva might reside at Foxwood Hall and eat Mrs. Ellison's fine fare, but she never forgot that folk such as these were her people, and places such as the Royal Oak were where her family felt most comfortable when they were away from home.

Miss Wickham raised her pint again. "Supper comes with a pot of tea, but do you want a pint as well? They've a good stout here."

"No, thank you. Tea will be fine."

Miss Wickham shrugged. "Suit yourself. They make a good strong brew as well."

Eva darted a gaze around neighboring tables, pretending to be nervous. "You said we'd talk and see if I've got what it takes to leave service and change my life. Exactly how did you mean we'd do that?"

"If you're asking if I'm going to have you draw something for me here, don't worry, I won't." Miss Wickham laughed, a hornlike sound that startled Eva. "No, if you've the talent to paint, we'll find it out later. For now, I want to see what kind of mettle you're made of, Miss Huntford."

The barmaid arrived at that moment and set down an earthenware teapot and two mugs. Though they were nothing fancy or costly, Eva was nonetheless impressed by the etching and colors worked into the clay.

"This is lovely." She held up one of the mugs to better see it in the dim lighting. "For something used in a pub, it shows great skill and thought."

"We're in Staffordshire, Miss Huntford. The china and earthenware capital of England. We take great pride in what we do. Even I. Yes, I'd prefer to be doing more—designing, making decisions on what is produced at Crown Lily—but I also take my work in painting and enameling seriously. Very seriously, indeed. Because when things are done properly, strangers I might never meet will hold a cup as you're doing now and admire the workmanship that went into it. And that, Miss Huntford, is as it should be."

Eva found herself admiring not only the earthenware, but Miss Wickham. Whatever she might or might not have done, she held the work she and her colleagues did in high esteem. Yet, Eva couldn't ignore one statement: *Yes, I'd prefer to be doing more . . .*

How strongly did that preference influence her sentiments, her actions, and her very life? Passion, Eva had learned, could produce great achievements, but also desperate acts. If Moira Wickham had believed Ronald Mercer to be a hindrance to the art she so obviously loved, could she have been driven to remove him and the obstacles he posed?

"My only doubt," Eva began, fingering the grain of the tabletop in front of her, "is what you said about women being held back and not allowed to advance according to their talents."

Moira Wickham harrumphed and curled her lips downward. "That is one of life's great injustices. I am every bit as skilled as Ronald Mercer, Percy

Bateman, or any other designer, but I'll likely never be given the chance to prove it."

"And that must make you so angry."

"Indeed, it does." The woman drew back, scowling. "Why shouldn't it?"

"Believe me, I'm very much on your side." Eva leaned forward in a confiding manner. "I'm faced with a similar dilemma. Even if I'm someday promoted to housekeeper, I'd still be below the butler and paid less, not to mention respected less. And, whether lady's maid or housekeeper, such a woman is expected to remain single during the whole of her career, whether or not she is lucky enough to find an available man. It might not seem as consequential as the hurdles you face, but for someone who devotes her life to service, it's rather short shrift."

"*Short shrift* is what we women get." Miss Wickham might have added more, but she fell silent when the barmaid returned with a tray laden with their pasties and potatoes. The rich aromas once again stirred Eva's appetite, and she took several moments to simply savor a bite of each portion.

"Oh, Miss Wickham, you choose your eateries well."

"I'll bet your high and mighty Renshaws never eat so fine or so heartily."

It was on Eva's tongue to admonish the woman not to speak ill of her employers. But on one hand, she didn't wish to put Miss Wickham off, and on the other hand, she was right. The Renshaws only rarely had the opportunity to eat food such as this. Eva would take a hearty farmer's meal over French delicacies any day of the week.

But that was beside the point.

Holding a morsel of beef dripping with gravy on her fork, Eva forestalled bringing it to her mouth. She raised her eyebrows, leaned forward again, and spoke barely above a whisper. "Now that Mr. Mercer is gone, might new opportunities arise for you?"

Miss Wickham didn't answer right away. She slowly chewed, her broad cheeks working, her slight frown drifting to a point somewhere over Eva's shoulder. Then she brought her gaze close again to connect with Eva's. "I've been pondering that very possibility. It's not that I wished ill on the man. Certainly, I'd never do that, not to anyone. But what's done is done, and since there's no going back, why not surge forward and take fate by the reins." She suddenly did something that seemed so out of character Eva was taken aback. Miss Wickham hunched her shoulders and giggled like a schoolgirl who just realized the boy she'd set her cap for liked her back.

"But how will you do that?"

Her amused expression faded. "By convincing

Mr. Tremaine he needs me as a designer. I've got patterns I've been working on for years. I'll show them to him and then he'll see who has talent. He'll realize the truth."

Patterns. Were they Moira Wickham's own? Or did she have Ronald Mercer's stolen pattern book? "I'd love to see them," Eva said. "Could you . . . could you show me?"

"I don't have them here." The woman spoke curtly, but then relented. "But, yes, if you're terribly interested, I suppose we could meet again tomorrow. Or will you be able to manage it?"

"Oh, I'm sure I could." Eva ate a couple of bites and pretended to be mulling over whether or not to ask her next question. "Do you have any ideas on who might have murdered Mr. Mercer, and why?"

"Why would you think I'd know?" Once more taking a curt tone, Moira Wickham seemed about to end the conversation.

Eva spoke quickly. "I simply thought someone in your position of authority at the factory might have heard rumors or if threats had been made. People often threaten without meaning it, but in this case someone obviously did." Eva leaned forward. "Thank goodness you work in an entirely separate building from the one where the clay is mixed. I cannot imagine stumbling on such a sight. I understand a worker found Mr. Mercer."

"Gus Abbott, yes. I've actually never been inside that building. Never had reason to go in. Never will do, now." Miss Wickham gave a light shudder.

"*Never?* Well, I have been, and I wish I hadn't, because I can't erase the image of those dreadful blades from my mind." Eva savored a bite, then said, "So I suppose you were safely in the painting room when . . . when it happened."

Miss Wickham eyed Eva for a long moment, making her wonder if she'd made a mistake. But the woman said, "Don't know, exactly, because no one is sure exactly when he died. I might have been at work, or I might still have been on my way in."

"I see." It was an honest enough reply, Eva conceded. If Miss Wickham had murdered Ronald Mercer, wouldn't she have an alibi at the ready? Eva paused for another bite, pretending to consider. Then she asked, "You don't think the boy did it, do you?"

"Trent?"

Eva nodded, letting her eyes grow large.

"He's always seemed a good lad to me, although it was no secret he didn't wish to follow in his father's footsteps, and that he was boiling mad when his father brought him home from Eton. But you know all about that, don't you?"

"I do. He's a schoolmate of my lady's brother. It was awful for the family when the police came to arrest him."

"I imagine it was." Miss Wickham shrugged as if the trials of the Renshaw family were of little account. "What's frightfully strange is that the dog was in the grinding room with the body. That dog is Trent Mercer's shadow. Didn't much like the father. So, why was he there?" She held up her forefinger, tapping it at an imaginary point in the air. "That's the question, Miss Huntford. If Trent didn't fight with his father and manage to dump him into the grinding pan, why was the dog there?"

Eva wasn't feeling at all reassured about Trent's innocence, however much she and the Renshaws wished to believe in the boy. Gus Abbott, the man Ronald Mercer had gone to meet in the grinding room to discuss the clay-making formula, said he hadn't been there, and there were witnesses to corroborate his whereabouts. Such had not been the case with Trent that morning, but he wasn't a true employee, not like the others. As evidenced by the first day they had encountered him in the factory yard, he often came and went as he chose and appeared to answer only to his father and Mr. Tremaine. Which meant he could very well have met his father in the grinding room. That would surely explain his dog being there at the time.

Miss Wickham refilled their mugs with tea so dark it looked nearly like coffee. The rich steam recalled Eva from her reverie. Miss Wickham said, "We haven't talked much about you, Miss

Huntford, and your sudden desire to join the china industry. It seems a bit of a whim to me, I'm sorry to say."

"No, I assure you it isn't. Perhaps this specific type of work, yes, but I've long been itching to leave service and do something more fulfilling."

"*Itching,* eh?" When Eva nodded eagerly, the woman said, "Then perhaps we'll just have to scratch that itch of yours." Miss Wickham nodded at Eva's plate. "Eat up. Tomorrow night is shepherd's pie. We could meet again for supper. But before that, could you manage to come to Crown Lily in the morning?"

"I might be able to manage it, depending on what my mistresses have planned." She didn't wish to appear as though it would be easy for her to slip away again. "Perhaps midmorning?"

"That will suit. Bring something that shows me your skills as an artist."

"Like what? I haven't any paints available to me. I have some embroidery I've been working on . . ."

"Draw something. Draw a cup and saucer and put a design on them. And be prepared to do some painting when you arrive." Miss Wickham laughed. "We'll see if we've got a designer in the making."

"I'm going and there's nothing you can do to stop me." Fox rummaged through the cloakroom in

150

the rear hall until he came upon his chesterfield coat. Phoebe and Fox had both risen earlier than the others this morning. Phoebe had believed it to be a habit he'd formed at Eton, but she soon learned he had a particular reason for wanting to slip out of the house unnoticed by his siblings today.

"Actually, Fox, I can. I can order Fenton and Douglas not to take you anywhere." Phoebe might have added that she could also call their grandfather, which would certainly stop Fox in his tracks, or at least give him pause.

Fox went still, his coat half on, one sleeve hanging empty. "You wouldn't."

Phoebe expelled a sigh; he had called her bluff. "No, I wouldn't. But I want you to think about this first. Seeing your friend in a place like that . . . it's awful, Fox. I know."

"Yes, like when you went to visit Julia at the Cowes Jail." He shoved his other arm into his sleeve and tugged the coat around him. "I'm not expecting tea and biscuits. I merely want to show my friend some support. Show him I believe he's innocent. And bring him a change of clothes."

"I could do that."

"I'm going, Phoebe. You can't talk me out of it."

"Look, Fox, I'm not referring to the reception you'll receive at the police station. I'm talking about what it's like to see someone you care about in circumstances like that. The fear and fatigue in his eyes, the reality of bars and locks, the knowledge that he can't walk out with you. He's a prisoner and there is nothing genteel or noble about having your freedom stripped away." Phoebe moved closer to her brother. "It will haunt you for longer than you think. I still have nightmares about Julia in that horrible place."

"That may be so, but I'm still going. Unless you intend blocking the door or brandishing a gun at me."

Phoebe quickly scanned the garments hanging along the rack until she spotted her own fur-trimmed topcoat. Her deep-crowned tan felt hat sat on the shelf above it. She whisked it down and crammed it on her head. "I'm going with you."

"I'm not a child, Phoebe." Fox strode briskly through to the main hall and headed for the front door. Phoebe followed along at a trot.

"Legally, you are, and Julia and I are responsible for you. And since a jail is the last place she needs to be, especially now, it's up to me to make sure you don't come away traumatized."

The touring car sat ready on the drive. Fox had apparently arranged for Douglas to take him, rather than ask Fenton to drive him in the Rolls-Royce. Sneaky. Fox knew Fenton would have checked first with Julia or Phoebe, in case

152

either of them needed the motorcar this morning. Douglas, on the other hand, would only have to worry about Eva and Hetta, who rarely went anywhere without their mistresses.

Phoebe had been relieved when Eva and Douglas had arrived home last night. Not that she had believed much harm could come to them in a public place, but Eva had asked Moira Wickham some pointed questions, and Douglas had got some of the Crown Lily workmen talking as well. If one of them happened to be Ronald Mercer's killer, he or she could take issue with Eva's and Douglas's probing.

Eva had paved the way for a friendship with Miss Wickham; the woman was gradually opening up. She planned to return to Crown Lily today to continue her ruse of wishing to work there, but not until later this morning. Phoebe and Fox should be back by then, or Eva could go in the Rolls-Royce with Fenton.

But Phoebe preferred she go with Douglas. Apparently, he had learned two quite significant things last night. According to Eva, one of the warehouse clerks had hinted that someone had been stealing finished china—whole cases of it. Mr. Tremaine was aware of the problem, but had admonished the clerk to say nothing; he hadn't wished to tip off the thief that anyone suspected him. The clerk had only wagged his tongue last night due to excessive ale and Douglas's assurances that since he was only visiting Langston and knew no one in town, there was no one he could tell. She hoped if Douglas returned later with Eva, he might discover more about it.

The other item of consequence had been a certain name that popped up several times: Gus Abbott. While it didn't surprise Phoebe that the workers would have discussed the very man who had discovered Ronald Mercer's body, they had raised a doubt about his alibi. Douglas related that one man had said, and others had agreed, that Crown Lily workers protected their own. Had they fabricated an alibi for a well-liked coworker? Phoebe wondered if this Gus Abbott could be Crown Lily's thief, and Ronald Mercer had discovered his perfidy and confronted him.

She let the matter go for the moment, as she could do nothing about it presently. Fox slouched at the other end of the bench seat, his arms crossed, his chin tucked into the velvet collar of his coat. He resented Phoebe coming—that much was obvious.

"I'm sorry, Fox. Grams would have my head if she discovered I let you go alone."

"I'm so tired of being treated as a child."

"Yes, I understand. But really, I'd like to see Trent, too. Can't you look at it that way?"

"Do you believe he's innocent?" he asked in a challenging tone, as if to test Phoebe's loyalty.

"I do. Perhaps for no other reason than that you

believe in him. You know him better than anyone else here, I'd wager. Probably better than his own father did."

"You'd win that wager. His father not only didn't know his own son, he didn't care to learn anything about him. Didn't care what was important to him."

Phoebe studied her brother's profile, wondering. Then she voiced her thoughts. "You're Grampapa's heir. You've been raised to run Foxwood Hall someday and oversee Little Barlow as its chief patron. It's what is expected of you. But is it what you *want?*"

His brows drew inward. "What do you mean?"

"I mean exactly what Trent was facing before his father died. He was expected to enter the china industry, whether he wished to or not. And we all know he didn't. You've never said what *you* want."

His frown tightened. "Of course I want to be the Earl of Wroxly."

"Do you, Fox? Truthfully?"

"I don't know . . ." He slouched down farther, sliding lower on the leather seat. "Yes. Yes, I do. I want . . ."

"What?"

"To make Grampapa proud, I suppose."

Phoebe smiled, reached across, and laid her hand on his forearm. "You will. You *do,* Fox. Grampapa's terribly proud of you. If he doesn't always say it—"

"He *never* says it."

"That's not true. But I realize it's a rarity, and that's because men of his generation are simply like that. They have expectations for their sons and grandsons, but that doesn't mean they take them for granted. I assure you, Grampapa does *not* take you for granted."

He shrugged, but his features softened as the perplexity faded from them. "It's one thing for Grampapa to expect me to live up to his expectations and follow him as earl. There are generations of tradition to uphold. But I can't imagine why it was so important to Mr. Mercer that Trent enter the china industry. Why *not* let him choose his profession?"

Phoebe sat back, but kept her gaze on her brother. "I suppose in this part of the country, china also has its long traditions. It must have been very important to Mr. Mercer that those traditions continued."

"I don't know . . ." Fox shook his head. "It's really not the same thing at all. It's not as if Mr. Mercer owned Crown Lily. I could understand it then."

A possible reason occurred to her. Although she supposed a head designer at a china factory earned a substantial salary, since without him Crown Lily could not successfully compete with other companies, Mr. Mercer could have hit a financial stumbling block. "Could money have been the issue? Tuition at Eton is no small matter. Unless Trent was on scholarship."

"I suppose it's possible, but, then again, no. Trent wasn't on scholarship, but he surely would have applied for one if money had suddenly become scarce." He was silent a moment, obviously pondering. Then he asked, "Does Mr. Tremaine have sons? Someone to inherit the factory?"

"That's a very good question." So good, in fact, Phoebe's pulse jumped. Had anyone thought to ask Mr. Tremaine about his heirs, and whether there could have been a problem between one of them and Ronald Mercer? Or had Ronald Mercer hoped to take over the business upon Mr. Tremaine's retirement? Could that be why he wanted his son to learn every facet of Crown Lily's operations?

If so, it wouldn't happen now.

The police station occupied one end of a busy road lined with businesses and shops. With a steep slate roof, stone block trim around the windows and main entrance, and flanked by two narrow towers at either end, the redbrick structure might have been a school or even a small manor house. Douglas pulled up to the pavement. Fox gathered up the portmanteau of clothing and other small luxuries he'd brought for Trent. They let themselves out of the motorcar and climbed the two stone steps. Before entering, Phoebe glanced up at the scrolled pediments on either side of the door and the eagles carved in stone above it. She hadn't thought to enter a police station again so soon after the one in Cowes. A sense of despondency settled over her.

Holding the portmanteau by its handle, Fox opened the door and glanced at her expectantly. She sighed and went in before she changed her mind.

She soon found herself settling onto a wooden bench in the foyer, as Trent could only have one visitor at a time. Fox had taken in the portmanteau, and Phoebe could only imagine some dour-faced bobby rummaging through it, checking pockets and unwrapping the scones, nutty Dundee cake, and crunchy toffee they'd brought. Did he sniff at the ingredients of each? He'd find neither chisels nor poison hidden within their gifts to Trent.

Fox returned to her about half an hour later, the empty portmanteau hanging lightly at his side. He looked weary and grim. "It's your turn, if you still want to." He gestured over his shoulder to the policeman waiting in a doorway. "He'll take you back."

Phoebe came to her feet. "How are you?"

He shrugged. "All right, I suppose. Glad I went in, if *glad* is a word you can use in circumstances like these. Trent *isn't* all right." He lowered his voice. "I told him you'd help him."

Phoebe glanced at the policeman waiting by the

door, then at the one behind the reception counter. Neither seemed to have heard Fox's comment. Good. She didn't need them threatening her to leave matters alone, as the detective in charge of Julia's case in Cowes had. She'd very nearly landed in a jail cell of her own. Placing her hand on Fox's shoulder, she nodded.

Trent awaited her in a room very much like the one in the Cowes Police Station when she had visited Julia: sparse, utilitarian, illuminated too brightly, yet not sufficiently heated. Trent sat hunched before a table facing her; no restraints held him in place, Phoebe was glad to see. The policeman who had led her there did not leave, but closed the door and took up his position beside it. He crossed his arms and assumed a wide stance, as if ready to block an escaping Trent with his own body.

"How are you, Trent?" Phoebe pulled out the chair opposite him and sat. She folded her hands on the tabletop. "I'm sure Fox told you we brought some things for you, but if there's anything else you need, you're to let us know. Can you leave messages with the policeman at the front counter?"

"I suppose if I asked. I won't need anything, though." He kept his hazel eyes on her as he ran a forefinger absently down the length of his curving nose, so like his father's. "Thanks for what you brought, Lady Phoebe."

"Just Phoebe will do, please. Trent, I want to ask you a couple of questions, if I might." She resisted glancing over her shoulder at the bobby, though she wondered how closely he was listening. Trent half shrugged and nodded his permission. "Do you know why it was so important to your father that you start at Crown Lily rather than finish your studies at Eton? Was there a financial difficulty?"

His features went taut as he considered. Then, "Not that I know of. We live in a good-sized house on the edge of town, the house Father and Mother bought when he became a china designer, and he had no plans that I knew of to sell it, although it would have brought a goodly sum."

"Your mother died a couple of years ago, I understand."

"In '18, from the influenza," he mumbled.

"I'm very sorry about that. Are you sure we shouldn't contact your aunt and uncle? Where did you say they lived?"

He didn't look at her. "York. I've another uncle, gone to America. We were never close with any of them. All my grandparents are dead."

Despondency gripped Phoebe again, like a hand on her throat, another around her heart. What would happen to Trent? Once he left here, where would he go?

"You said you had a couple of questions," he prompted her.

"Oh, yes. I've wondered whether Mr. Tremaine has heirs, and if you happen to know them."

"He had two sons."

Trent's emphasis on *had* told Phoebe all she needed to know. Still, she asked, "The war?"

He nodded. "Both at the Battle of the Somme. If he has other heirs, I've never met them."

"So I wonder who will take over the factory when he retires," Phoebe mused out loud. "Had your father any ambitions in that direction?"

Once more, Trent answered with a shrug. "He never said anything about it. But I think he was talking to a couple of the other china works."

"What do you mean?"

"Seeing if they wanted to hire him away from Crown Lily. It's all competitive, you know. Designers move around depending on how much they're offered. Crown Lily wasn't the first company my father worked for."

"Yes, I have learned that much since being here." Had he agreed to a move, made promises, only to go back on his word, prompting the owner of another company to murder him? That seemed a far stretch. Besides, why do it at Crown Lily, in a grinding room? She shook her head at the notion, eliciting a puzzled look from Trent. No, she believed whoever killed Ronald Mercer worked at Crown Lily. Then there was another perplexing matter to be solved. "Trent, do you know what happened to your father's pattern book?"

The boy shoved back his chair and came to his feet. "I already told you I didn't know. Why don't you ask Mr. Bateman?"

From behind her, she heard the shuffle of the policeman's feet as he came to attention and started to intervene. Phoebe held up a hand and glanced over her shoulder. "It's all right." Then, to Trent, she said, "I have asked Mr. Bateman." In a manner, at least, she acknowledged silently.

"And I suppose he denied it. But the man's a liar. He lies all the time. It's his fault my father's dead."

CHAPTER 9

Lady Phoebe's trip to the jail to visit Trent
Mercer had obviously upset her, but there hadn't
been time to talk about it. Eva didn't like leaving
her lady in such an agitated state, but she had her
brother and sisters to comfort her, and Eva had
promised to be at Crown Lily by midmorning.
Disappointing Miss Wickham could result in
a loss of the woman's regard, and with it her
confidence. Eva had climbed into the touring car
with Douglas, practically as Phoebe and Fox slid
out, with promises to compare what they each
learned later.

When they arrived in the factory's main yard,
Douglas sauntered off in the direction of the
packing warehouse. Eva steeled herself with a
deep breath. She carried a folder with several
teacups she had sketched the night before, and
found herself fretting over whether she would
pass muster with Miss Wickham. She tried
reminding herself that her interest in becoming
a painter was nothing more than a deception, a
means to acquire information. Yet her sense of
pride and her belief in always doing one's best
had her fingers quivering as she let herself into
the building. Her legs trembled slightly as she
climbed the stairs to the second-floor studio.

Her qualms were forgotten as shouting reached her ears, and she hurried through the doorway. In the second aisle, about two thirds of the way back, Miss Wickham stood with her hands on her hips, her back to Eva. Another woman, younger, shorter, and more slender, with blond hair and childlike features, looked up at the other woman from her seat at one of the worktables.

"You'll pack your things, such as they are, and leave immediately." Miss Wickham's voice filled the silent space. None of the workers even pretended to be concentrating on their painting. All gazes converged on the confrontation.

"You're making a mistake," the blonde protested. "I've done nothing wrong. This isn't fair."

What had she done to warrant dismissal? Eva wondered if she should back her way out of the room and pretend she hadn't seen or heard the matter, but just then, a graying redhead in the front of the room noticed her.

The woman scowled. "Ahem, Miss Wickham, we appear to have company."

Miss Wickham turned, looking very much annoyed at the interruption. Yet, when she spotted Eva, whose face turned fiery, her features softened. She motioned for Eva to come farther into the room. She turned back to the blonde.

"It so happens, I might have a ready replacement for you, Lydia. So hurry up, off with you."

Lydia stood her ground. "Mr. Tremaine is going to hear about this."

"Mr. Tremaine has no time for your nonsense, my dear, now does he?"

"He'll listen." Lydia's face darkened. "He has to. You're being unfair. You decided I'm a spy for Royal Wiltshire for no good reason."

"No reason? You've been seen with one of their assistant engravers. That's reason enough to incriminate you."

"We haven't been stepping out together for weeks now. There's been no sneaking around, never was."

Miss Wickham harrumphed. "Lies. The thefts began several months ago, when you first started seeing that young man. Obviously, the pair of you plotted to increase your fortunes by stealing patterns and bringing them to Royal Wiltshire. Otherwise, how did Royal Wiltshire suddenly release a pattern almost identical to our Violets and Vines?" The girl started to protest again, but Miss Wickham thrust her chin in the air and made a chopping motion with her hand. "That will be all, Lydia. Collect your things, and out with you."

Eva expected tears, but when Lydia brushed past her on her way out the door, her meager possessions stuffed into her bulging handbag and her coat tossed over her arm, Eva saw nothing but defiance on the young woman's face. Defiance, and a square-chinned dignity that made Eva wonder if indeed Miss Wickham had unjustly accused her.

She wasn't afforded much time to ponder the matter, for Moira Wickham waved her over.

"Come in, come in. Don't mind them." Miss Wickham referred to the many faces now turned in Eva's direction, their curiosity evident. They'd seen her here before; now they must be burning to know why she had returned, and if she might be the ready replacement their supervisor had spoken of moments ago. Eva wondered that, too. "Back to work, the lot of you."

Miss Wickham returned to her workspace and Eva met her there. The woman sat, but allowed Eva to remain standing. After moving aside paints and the china she had been embellishing, she held out the flat of one broad palm. "Well, let's see what you've got for me."

Eva handed over the folder and held her breath as the other woman opened it and slid out its contents. That earlier sense of wanting to do well, to prove herself, gripped her again, despite the fact that she would never work here—not for any price. Miss Wickham spread out Eva's four drawings and leaned over them.

"Mm-hmm. Ah. Yes, I see why you did that. Mmm . . ." Her brow creased, her lips skewed, her head tilted this way and that. "Well, then . . ."

And yet she gave no opinion, but continued to stare down at Eva's handiwork. She hadn't rushed

166

these drawings last night. She'd first made rough sketches, pondered over them, showed them to Ladies Phoebe and Amelia, who had declared them splendid and engaging. Well, Eva knew better than to take their opinions to heart, as they were quite certainly prejudiced in her favor. Still . . .

Miss Wickham suddenly raised her chin and pinned Eva with her gaze. "They're awful. Entirely predictable, the work of an amateur."

"Oh . . ." Something inside Eva deflated painfully. "I'm terribly sorry." She bent to gather up her wasted efforts.

Miss Wickham's hand came down on the drawings with a thwack that made Eva jump. She snatched back her hand as if Miss Wickham had slapped it. "Not so fast. I didn't expect any different. In fact, I expected far worse. These surely aren't acceptable as they are, but they show promise, Miss Huntford, real promise. You've got a raw talent. What you need now is training. Lots of it."

Briskly the woman rose from her chair and strode into an adjoining room, perhaps a storage room, for she returned with a white plate bearing a simple transfer design in one hand and a sheet of paper in the other. "Follow me."

She just as briskly led Eva to the second row and to the worktable so recently vacated by Lydia. "You may sit here and use Lydia's paints and brushes. Here is your canvas, Miss

Huntford." She set the plate down on the table. "And here are your instructions." She slapped the paper down beside the plate. "Show me what you're capable of. Don't worry about ruining the finished product. This is one of our least expensive shapes to produce—very plain, as you can see—and no great loss should we end up tossing it in the bin. It's what we use in training all new painters."

With that, she walked back to her corner station and left Eva to work out the instructions. They seemed a jumble of numbers and indecipherable diagrams at first, but as she perused them several times over, they began to take shape in her mind as coherent directions of where to apply which colors on the transferred design. The instructions even indicated which size brushes to use for each part of the design. Eva set to work.

Phoebe looked up as Eva entered the doorway of the drawing room, her coat hanging over her arm. Phoebe had left a message belowstairs for her to come up to the drawing room as soon as she arrived back at the house.

"I have a position, my lady. A china painter-in-training."

Her pronouncement sent a shiver of dread through Phoebe; she clasped her hands in her lap and tried her best not to show it. Seated across from her, Veronica Townsend made no secret of her disapproval as she turned her mouth down at the corners and *hmphed.*

"The only servants who ever enter this room are the footmen to bring us tea, or the housemaid to clean—and she only comes in early in the morning, before anyone else is awake. Really, Phoebe, this is not a place to entertain your lady's maid." She hefted her bulk out of her chair and stalked out, practically knocking her shoulder into Eva's in the doorway.

Phoebe chuckled and motioned for Eva to join her. Though she had initially intended for the two of them to retreat elsewhere for their talk, in light of Veronica Townsend's indignation, she decided the drawing room was as good a place as any. Eva took the seat so recently vacated by the other woman and tossed her coat over its arm.

"Heavens," Phoebe said in response to Eva's startling news, "does Miss Wickham expect you to be there first thing every morning?" She realized how the question sounded—or, rather, made *her* sound. Like a helpless, spoiled aristocrat who couldn't get by without someone to bring her tea and toast and dress her each morning. Quickly she added, "If she does, of course, we'll manage it."

But it hadn't been the thought of beginning each day without Eva's help that had made her shudder. It was the thought of Eva leaving her, of losing the closest friend she had ever known.

"I've worked it out that my training will be on a part-time basis, whenever I can find time to be there. I explained that I didn't wish you to discover my new ambitions until the proper time came to inform you, preferably right before you and the others return to Little Barlow."

"And Miss Wickham accepted that?"

"She seemed to believe me entirely. I think she's so gratified to be *saving* me from a life of service that she'll make whatever allowances are necessary for the time being. It's on account of her mother, who was a lady's maid until she married. Apparently, Mrs. Wickham never spoke well of being in service, nor of the woman she worked for." Eva smiled. "Unlike me, my lady. But then, I'm uncommonly fortunate. Much more fortunate than a poor girl who was sacked today."

Phoebe listened as Eva went on about what had occurred in the painting room when she had first arrived. "Do you think Miss Wickham was justified in dismissing her?"

"I'm not sure. Her name is Lydia Travers, and I intend to ask the other workers what they thought of her. I didn't have a chance this morning, as Miss Wickham kept me far too busy until it was time for me to leave. But there was something in the girl's countenance, a wounded dignity and an utter lack of shame that prod me to suspect she may be innocent."

Phoebe crossed one leg over the other, well

aware her grandmother would frown at her doing so. "I would think Percy Bateman is the likeliest culprit when it comes to selling patterns. If he felt he couldn't advance at Crown Lily because of Mr. Mercer's strict hold on the design department, he might well have decided to help a competitor in exchange for an eventual position there."

"Or it's Miss Wickham selling patterns, and using Lydia as a scapegoat."

Phoebe nodded at this possibility. "Which would also mean it's likely she has the missing pattern book."

"The next question is whether the pattern thefts are connected to the china thefts."

"Good heavens, Crown Lily is rife with crime."

"It seems that way. Did you learn anything useful this morning from Trent Mercer, my lady?"

The question jolted Phoebe back three hours earlier, to Trent's blurted accusation. "There was one startling moment when he claimed it was Percy Bateman's fault his father was dead."

Eva's dark eyebrows climbed in her forehead. "Was he accusing Mr. Bateman of murder?"

"That's exactly what I thought at first, but once I'd calmed him down again, he admitted he'd only said that because of the competition between the two designers. You see, Ronald Mercer reigned supreme at Crown Lily for years, until Mr. Tremaine hired Percy Bateman.

Suddenly Mr. Mercer faced a whole new level of competition, and from a much younger man. Hence his hubris when we first arrived, when he attempted to belittle Mr. Bateman's talents. Anyway, the rivalry between them prompted Mr. Mercer to try to best Mr. Bateman in whatever ways he could, his latest attempt being to experiment with new formulas to make the china even stronger. That explains why he was in the grinding room that morning, looking for the head clay mixer to discuss his latest formulation."

"So Trent's accusation is really one of circumstance, rather than actual guilt."

"Yes, that's it exactly. The accusation doesn't amount to anything legally, but Trent's anger and his belief that his father would still be alive if not for Percy Bateman are quite real."

"Then, although Trent resented his father for withdrawing him from Eton, he wouldn't have wished him dead," Eva said.

"I don't believe he did. More than ever, I believe him to be innocent."

"I do hope it's true, my lady."

"Hope what's true?" Mildred Blair came into the drawing room, looking chic with a silk scarf wrapped as a headband around her bobbed ebony hair. She had donned a dress Phoebe suspected had been designed to mimic the new flowing Chanel fashions Julia favored.

"That Trent Mercer is innocent," Phoebe

172

informed her, glad Mildred apparently hadn't overheard more of their conversation.

"Oh, that." Mildred took a moment to stare Eva down, a silent but just-as-thorough disapproval as the vocal one Veronica Townsend had expressed. "Yes, he seemed a nice boy, and one pities him for the position he's in. It would be a shame for him to swing."

At such bluntness Phoebe exchanged a disgusted look with Eva, but decided not to dignify the comment with a response.

"Where's his hound got to?" Mildred swung herself into the easy chair across the little table from Eva's, facing Phoebe on the settee.

"I suppose Fox has him somewhere," Phoebe said.

"Actually, I saw the two of them on the grounds as Douglas and I drove in." Eva curled her lips at Mildred with a disdain only Phoebe could detect. Since their very first meeting last spring on Gilbert Townsend's yacht, the two of them had taken a dislike to each other, which no amount of time or, Phoebe suspected, civilized encounters would overcome. "Fox was tossing a ball for him. Jester seemed rather exuberant about bounding after it."

"What fun." Mildred's tone and expression said she considered such an outing anything but. She dismissed Eva with a toss of her hair, and said to Phoebe, "By the way, I've just been to visit Ernie."

"That hardly interests me, I'm afraid." No,

Ernie had lost Phoebe's regard and wasn't likely ever to win it back. She made no effort to hide her sentiments about him.

"He's hired a solicitor." Mildred's tone held a hint of merriment that raised Phoebe's apprehensions.

She narrowed her eyes at the other woman. "Why?"

"Well, I don't know if I should say . . ." She gave another toss of her hair, letting it fall coyly around her chin.

"Then you shouldn't have mentioned it, should you?" Eva took a tone she would never ordinarily use with someone she considered her social superior. Mildred blinked in surprise.

"*Hmph.* If you must know, he's exploring his options about this house. Seeing if there is any way of dislodging your sister until the child is born."

"How dare he?" Phoebe surged to her feet. "He's going to regret this."

She cut a determined path to the cloakroom to retrieve her coat. Not bothering with a hat, she let herself out the front door.

"My lady, wait for me."

A glance over her shoulder confirmed that Eva hurried after her, swinging her coat around her. Near the driveway Fox was running with Jester, but he came to a halt when he spotted Phoebe walking in such a hurry. She didn't stop to explain, but a voice from the house brought a pause to her steps.

"Phoebe, where are you rushing off to?" It was

Julia, calling out from the library window she had swung open. "Has something happened?"

"Not yet, it hasn't, but it will if someone doesn't do something."

Julia wrinkled her nose. "What *are* you talking about?"

"I haven't time, Julia. Suffice it to say, I'm off to defend your rights as a Townsend."

The window swung shut. Good. Julia was apparently content to let Phoebe handle matters. Eva caught up to her on the path and fell into stride as Phoebe resumed her trek around the house and across the gardens.

"My lady, are you sure it's a good idea for you to confront Mr. Shelton?"

"Someone has to, Eva." She skirted a dormant flowerbed and clambered over an ornamental footbridge with a Japanese design.

Eva's footsteps matched hers. "Yes, but he isn't the mild-mannered gentleman we once thought. He can be reckless and spiteful, not a good combination. You could be putting yourself in harm's way."

"I can handle Ernie Shelton." A cold breeze slapped Phoebe's cheeks and reached down her nape, making her wish she'd taken time to don a hat and scarf. Too late now. Jester's barking drew her attention once more behind her, past Eva to where Fox and the Staffordshire terrier scrambled after her.

"What's going on, Phoebe? Why are you racing across the grounds?"

Phoebe didn't stop, not even when another voice beckoned. "Phoebe, I can see you're headed toward Ernie's cottage. I demand you tell me what's going on." It was Julia, who hadn't been content to stay in the house, after all. Next it would be Amelia hot on Phoebe's trail.

At the south edge of the garden, she trudged through a stand of trees and onto a graveled road wide enough to allow the passage of vehicles. She heard the crunching of the others over dried leaves and foliage. She wished Julia would go back before she tripped over the uneven terrain.

"Eva, convince Julia to return to the house. Go with her, please."

"I'm not going back to the house, Phoebe," Julia declared before Eva could respond. "Not until you tell me what you're up to."

With a corner of Ernie's cottage with its thatched roof now in view, Phoebe finally came to a stop. She turned to her sister, and Fox as well, who had kept pace along with Jester. "Ernie hired a solicitor to see how to dislodge you from Lyndale Park until your child is born. In other words, he's trying to throw you out."

Julia blinked and tightened her coat about her. "Is he?"

"Yes, Julia, he is. But I'm not going to let him."

"I won't, either." Fox came to stand, shoulder

to shoulder, with Phoebe. Jester stood at his side, looking happy to be included. "Ernie's a greedy blighter and he won't get away with this." He glanced down at the dog. "Isn't that right, Jester?"

Jester let go an eager bark.

"Get away with what?" Julia laughed. "Just because he's hired a solicitor doesn't mean he'll have me out. I've already talked with Grampapa's solicitor, and there's really nothing Ernie can do at this point. So leave him alone and let's all go back to the house."

The ire that carried Phoebe all this way receded like rainwater down a gully. "Are you sure? Don't you want to at least put him in his place?"

"Why? He'll still be the same greedy blighter as before, as Fox so eloquently put it. Besides, I don't need you or anyone else to protect me, Phoebe. The only person who needs to hover over me is Hetta, and that's more for her own sake than mine. The dear thing is frightfully protective, and I haven't the heart to dissuade her. Now come along, let's all go back to the house."

Julia didn't waste a moment, but turned around and started back through the trees. That left Phoebe, Eva, and Fox lingering and looking to one another for a hint as to what to do. Phoebe didn't like leaving Ernie to his shiftless devices, and she could see by their expressions that Eva and Fox liked it no better. Even Jester seemed to expect some sort of action from them, given his tensed, ready stance to be off and doing something.

"Well?" Fox said for all of them. Jester released an impatient whine. "What now?"

Phoebe turned and cast a long stare at Ernie's cottage, where he'd been living since obtaining his degree in veterinary medicine. The home had been provided free of charge by Gil Townsend in exchange for Ernie's tending to the estate animals. The two-story cottage contained a room that served as Ernie's surgery, and he had made a good living administering to the pets and livestock of Langston and the surrounding area. But that apparently hadn't been enough for Ernest Shelton, who had these many years yearned after Gil's title and estate. Julia and her child certainly posed an inconvenience to his plans.

She very clearly made out a hand behind a pane of glass, holding back the lace curtain. She raised her gaze to behold Ernie's face staring back at her. Had he overheard the commotion? What about their words? Did he know she had come to give him a thorough dressing-down?

Eva's hand came down lightly on her shoulder. "I suppose we should all go back. My lady?"

Yes, Phoebe supposed they should, and yet she couldn't. "You two go back. I'll just be a few moments." With that, she trudged to the cottage.

CHAPTER 10

Phoebe pretended not to notice that Eva and Fox waited near the trees, rather than go with Julia back to the main house. Jester, however, had sprung forward to follow her, and now trotted alongside her. Fox had admonished him to stay put, but the dog apparently had other ideas.

She reached the paneled front door, painted pale blue to match the trim around the windows. The cottage walls were beige stucco, painted fairly recently, and smoke curled from one of two chimneys. Tidy rock borders defined two small flowerbeds, merely mounds of dirt now, on either side of the front door. The place had an aspect of calm respectability, the home of a country professional who was content with his life. If only that were so.

Phoebe knocked on the door. Upon receiving no answer, she called out, "Ernie, I know you're here. I saw you looking out the window. Open the door, please."

After a pause she heard the bolt slide back and the door opened a few inches. "What do you want, Phoebe?"

Jester barked. Not a threatening sound, just a friendly hello, but it prompted Ernie to slam the door in Phoebe's face. She knocked again. "He's friendly, Ernie. You needn't be afraid of Jester. Besides, you're a veterinarian. You should be used to all manner of animals." She waited a moment, received no response, then called out again. "How do you know I didn't come because he needs medical care?"

The door opened, once again only a few inches. "Have you?"

"No. Let me in." Phoebe shoved with both hands, forcing Ernie to step aside or be struck by the door. Jester followed her into the vestibule. Ernie tried to block the way through into the parlor, but she simply strode around him and kept going until she stood before the cheery fire crackling away in the stone hearth. She unbuttoned her coat and let the heat pour over her. "Thank goodness. It's really quite cold out."

"Phoebe, what can I do for you?" Ernie's tone implied no desire to do anything for her, but rather a grudging courtesy he felt obliged to offer. Jester ambled into the room, and Ernie nearly lost his balance when the dog nosed the backs of his legs. "Will you control this mutt, please!"

"He's not a mutt, he's a Staffordshire bull terrier, and I've already told you, he's completely friendly. And, besides, why would a veterinarian shy away from any dog? It positively makes no sense, Ernie."

"It's not the dog," he said with a sigh. "It's you. Mildred's been telling tales, I suppose."

"They're not tales if they're true, Ernie." Phoebe glanced down at the dog. "Jester, come here." When the dog complied, wagging his stub of a tail as he did, she asked, "How dare you attempt to toss a pregnant woman out of her rightful home? What's got into you? And what happened to the sensitive, kindly man we met in Cowes? Did he ever exist, or was he merely an illusion?"

He neither sat nor invited her to do so. Instead he paced past her to the fireplace and rested a hand beside the rosewood mantel clock. "Yes, he existed. Long ago, before he had dealings with Gilbert Townsend." He turned, his face gripped by sadness. "Even for a while after that. But Gil's constant insults and offenses had a way of wearing a body down. Lucky Julia. Your sister escaped a fate like mine. She won't become jaded and callous as I have."

Phoebe studied him a moment, taking in his rolled-up shirtsleeves, his wrinkled trousers and waistcoat, his mussed hair. Had he been sleeping in his clothes? Yes, he'd had to endure a good deal of abuse from his second cousin over the years, had been the butt of many of Gil's jokes—mean ones. But did that give him license to treat others in kind? She shook her head. "I'm sorry, Ernie, but you've failed to rouse my sympathies."

"You saw how he treated me at the wedding. Do you think it was ever any different with him?"

"No, I don't. I believe Gil treated you badly. Unfairly. But I don't believe that's what changed you—or that you were ever different from the way you are now. Had you been that kindly young gentleman you suggest you were, you'd have carved out a life for yourself where you could find contentment. Your profession, for instance. But I understand you're barely practicing anymore." She waited for him to correct her on that. When he didn't, she said, "The moment Gil died, you moved in for the weighty handout you expected from his will. You and Mildred. Do you deserve a share of Gil's fortune? Assuredly so. Do you deserve to inherit everything?" She shook her head again.

"Easy for you to say, Phoebe. You're the granddaughter of an earl, one who dotes unabashedly on all of you. He'll do right by you, you've no fears about that. Try putting yourself in someone else's place for a change. Imagine believing for years in an inheritance that would eventually come to you, only to find out at the eleventh hour that you're cut off, left out in the cold. And this after years of service to the estate you'd pinned your hopes on, and to the man you detested but tolerated because it would one day pay off. Only then, it doesn't."

Hunching as if he'd be ill, he turned away, set his hands on the mantel, and ducked his head. He stood there for several seconds, making Phoebe wonder if she'd been summarily dismissed. But then he turned back, avarice and anger glittering in his eyes in equal measure. "No, it doesn't, because some chit of a woman—oh, yes, admittedly a beauty—flirts her way into his life and his bed. So easily she works her charms on him—without a thought to whom she was cheating."

"Julia didn't cheat anyone," Phoebe said low, barely maintaining a hold on her temper. "And she did not flirt her way into Gil's bed. That was something they saved for their wedding night. It was done honestly, and Gil was as much a willing participant as Julia."

Ernie laughed, a snide little sound. "We'll see, won't we, if your sister gives birth to an eight-month baby."

The implication made Phoebe want to fly at him. Instead she gritted her teeth. "She won't."

He held her gaze, unblinking. "But if she does, it will only strengthen my case that the inheritance is rightfully mine, not her illegitimate whelp's."

"You have no case, Ernie. You never will. Come, Jester." She retraced her steps to the door, but once there, her hand on the latch, she turned, still able to see Ernie through the parlor doorway. "I'm sorry I came here. I should have known there would be no reasoning with you. Do what you must. And Julia and the rest of us will do what we must."

● ● ●

Eva sat on the floor of the master bedroom, her legs tucked under her skirts, Jester stretched out against her as she administered a thorough petting. He seemed to be systematically getting to know the whole group of them, from Fox to Lady Phoebe to Amelia, and now her. He had even spent a few minutes sniffing in friendship at Hetta, but Hetta had been too busy tending to her mistress to give him more than a perfunctory pat on the head. Jester had yet to cozy up to Lady Annondale, but perhaps he sensed that she carried a new life inside and felt particularly vulnerable now.

Not that she'd ever admit to it. No, Julia Renshaw Townsend would rather go through life with her teeth clenched than reveal anything she viewed as a weakness. Thank heavens, then, for Hetta, who watched over her mistress like a she-wolf and anticipated her needs almost before Lady Annondale herself did.

The siblings were ranged about the bedroom: Fox on the Aubusson rug near Eva, where he could lean over and stroke Jester's back; Phoebe and Amelia on the dark burgundy leather settee, both sitting cross-legged; and Lady Annondale half reclined on the gigantic bed, with its massive mahogany posts, her legs hanging over the side and dangling several inches from the floor, like a child's.

Phoebe had described her encounter with Ernest Shelton in great detail, which elicited anger in Fox, indignation in Amelia, and silent if intense anger in Eva. Her blood boiled at the suggestion that Lady Annondale carried an illegitimate child. *Illegitimate?* How dare he? She knew for a fact, Lady Annondale had gone to her marriage bed a virgin. If not for Jester's warm coat beneath her palms, her fingers might have curled into fists.

But the revelation produced only a shrug from Lady Annondale herself. "What did I tell you, Phoebe? There was no point in confronting him."

"At least now we know exactly where he stands," Lady Phoebe pointed out.

Lady Annondale treated her to another shrug. "I believe we knew where he stood when we learned he'd hired a solicitor."

"I don't understand how a man with an affinity for animals can be so selfish." Lady Amelia put out her hand. "Animals aren't selfish, are they, Jester?"

The animal lifted his head, seemed to debate a moment, and hefted himself to his feet. He trotted over to Amelia and submitted his head to her gentle touch. Eva recognized a natural amiability in the terrier, a deep-rooted desire to both please and trust. Poor dear, he had no notion of what his master faced. No doubt he believed Trent had temporarily gone away, as he habitually did when returning to school, for instance, and viewed his stay at Lyndale Park as a kind of holiday.

"Animals can certainly be selfish," Fox countered. He sat up straighter, then leaned back on his hands for support. "Not to mention vicious if they're treated badly. I suppose Ernie was treated badly all those years." He darted a sheepish glance at Lady Annondale, who didn't like hearing anyone speak ill of her husband. She had worked through much of her guilt concerning Lord Annondale's untimely death, but there lingered in her a deep sense of remaining a loyal and, yes, dutiful wife to him.

But Lady Annondale made no comment. She cocked her head to one side as though deep in thought. Her silence continued as a little shadow deepened between her brows.

"Well, badly treated or not, he had no right to insult Julia as he did." Lady Phoebe also reached down to pet Jester, who accepted her overture with a lap of his tongue. "There's no excuse for his boorish behavior, and if I—"

"Whose *boorish behavior?* Are you speaking about Ernie?"

They had left the bedroom door open, and Eva looked over to see Miss Townsend filling the doorway.

"He's hired a solicitor to try to press his rights over Julia's when it comes to this house," Phoebe explained.

Much like Julia herself, Miss Townsend shrugged her shoulders. "He can try, one supposes." She took a couple of steps into the room and paused. When no one protested, she ventured farther in. "I suppose I don't care who inherits this old pile. It's nothing to me, is it?"

"Nothing?" Lady Annondale slid her feet to the floor and stood. "Why would you say that, Veronica? This is your home. It has been your entire life."

"You needn't remind me." The dour statement reminded Eva that Miss Townsend had once been engaged to marry, but her brother had refused his permission. Miss Townsend had never had another opportunity to become a wife. "I suppose no matter who inherits—your child or Ernie, or even Mildred, I'll be sent packing. Ernie, at least, has made that abundantly clear."

"Has he?" Lady Phoebe's voice rose in outrage.

"How beastly," Amelia put in.

Lady Annondale approached her sister-in-law. "I'm sure the terms of your brother's will make allowances for you to remain here as long as you wish."

"I don't know. Perhaps. But even so, would I wish to remain among people who don't want me?"

Lady Annondale's expression revealed sincere perplexity. "Actually, I have no intention of asking you to leave. As Amelia said, that would be beastly. It's true you and I have not become friends, and perhaps we never will. We're very different, you and I. But we can be civilized, can't we." It wasn't a question; it was a statement of intent. And it sent a furious blush to Miss Townsend's countenance. Obvious confusion garbled her next words.

"I . . . s-so unexpected . . . really? N-not a joke? You're sure . . . I h-hardly deserve it after . . ."

There was no embrace, no words of sisterhood or newly forged friendship. There was merely one woman recognizing the needs and fears of another, and putting her mind to rest. Today showed that despite her sometimes icy if beautiful exterior, Julia Renshaw had grown a compassionate heart, the heart of a woman born to look after others, as the lady of a great estate was meant to do. Eva felt a surge of pride in her.

"I've been thinking about what you and Ernie discussed today," Eva said later as she laid out Phoebe's and Amelia's clothes for dinner. "Ambition and, yes, greed drove him to do some reprehensible things. I don't know that I agree with you that there was never a time when honesty and honor drove his actions."

Lady Phoebe took a necklace from her jewelry box and held it up to the light. "You believe he wasn't always the wheedling man we see today?"

"I'd like to think Eva is right about that." Lady Amelia stood before the full-length mirror, holding up her hair this way and that in an attempt to devise a new style for herself. "I still believe a man who sets his life course for the benefit of animals can't be all bad."

Eva laid a rose chiffon dinner gown across the bed. "His comments put me in mind of Moira Wickham. When I listen to her talk about her own ambitions, I believe there are noble ideals and worthwhile intentions. She is right that whoever possesses talent should move ahead in their field, regardless of their gender. But when I hear the anger and resentment running through her argument, I feel"—she inhaled deeply—"a kind of dread. It's a sense that she is indeed capable of a dishonest or even underhanded deed to achieve her goals."

Phoebe studied her intently. "Which is how Ernie makes me feel. And why I could never trust him again."

"Part of me wishes to trust Miss Wickham," Eva said, "while another part echoes that same warning that she isn't to be trusted."

"She frightened me a little when we toured the painting room." Amelia turned away from the mirror, allowing her hair to tumble down her back. "Perhaps *frightened* is too strong a word. I sensed it would be difficult to work under her supervision, that she could be excessively critical and exacting."

"That's true," Eva confirmed. "But it's her responsibility to uphold the standards of perfection so vital to Crown Lily. Without them, they couldn't compete."

"Yes, but need she be so very stern?" Amelia gave a little shudder, and Eva smiled. Undoubtedly, tenderhearted Amelia would not fare well in such an environment as the painting room at Crown Lily. Then she switched back to her original train of thought. "Mr. Shelton's revelations have me thinking. Perhaps Miss Wickham is more than ambitious."

"Are you thinking about Lydia . . . what was her last name?" Lady Phoebe gazed at her from across the room; Eva had her full attention now.

"Travers, and, yes, the possibility that Miss Wickham fired her for supposedly doing exactly what Miss Wickham herself has been doing all along—selling patterns to the competition."

"If so, would she stop at that?" Lady Phoebe's voice deepened with speculation.

"Your talk with Mr. Shelton convinces me more than ever that Miss Wickham might *not* stop at murder if she felt cornered. Not that Mr. Shelton is a murderer, but it's a lesson in the extremes an individual will go to when they believe it's necessary. I need to become friendlier with Miss Wickham and gain her confidence. Perhaps even lead her to believe I share her views and feel sometimes women must resort to cheating if we are ever to advance beyond our secondary roles."

Phoebe moved beside her at the bed and laid the necklace she held on the dress Eva had placed there. She nodded briefly in approval of the match and turned to Eva. "That could be dangerous. She might at some point realize what you're doing, and if she *is* a murderer—"

"You mustn't do it, Eva." Amelia hurried over to them. "We forbid it, Phoebe and I."

Eva laughed softly. "If I don't do this, we certainly can't rely on the police to expand their investigation to include Miss Wickham. They'll say they see no reason for it."

After a hesitation Lady Phoebe nodded. "You're right. But you must be very careful. Avoid being alone with her, if you can."

"I will. In all honesty I hope to exonerate her, rather than the opposite. She can be rather brusque, but she's also talented and has been treated unfairly."

"That would leave us with Percy Bateman and Trent himself, at least at this point." Lady Phoebe tapped her chin.

"Don't forget about Gus Abbott, in the clay-mixing department," Eva reminded her.

"Yes, Crown Lily's possible china thief." Phoebe began pacing and thinking out loud. "See what more you can find out about him, Eva. But I also need a reason to return to Crown Lily. Now that the contract for our china service has been signed . . ." She stopped pacing and faced Eva and her sister. "Julia signed that contract."

"Yes?" Lady Amelia held out her hands. "So?"

"So I might consider signing another. I just had

the most splendid idea. And it would kill two birds with one stone."

Eva winced at the reference to *killing,* as did Lady Amelia.

"Sorry, a poor choice of words." Lady Phoebe smiled ruefully. "What about another set of china . . . for Julia's child? I've seen tea sets made exclusively for children, to be used at their birthday parties and other special occasions. They have bright colors, animals, elves, that sort of thing. I'll return to Crown Lily and tell them I'd like a pattern that would suit either a boy or a girl, and order a set for perhaps six. Or make it twelve. Any child of Julia's is sure to be very popular among his or her peers."

Lady Amelia clapped her hands together. "A marvelous idea! Even if we weren't investigating Mr. Mercer's death—"

"The only *we* here are Eva and I," Lady Phoebe corrected her.

Amelia made a face that dismissed the comment. "You'll need me to go back with you if we're to make a new commission look real. Oh, but it will be real, won't it? It's a darling idea, such a lovely thing to do for Julia. And her child. Yes, we must go tomorrow. We'll telephone over, first thing in the morning."

"No, actually, we won't." Lady Phoebe tapped a finger to her chin. "Let's catch Mr. Tremaine and Mr. Bateman unaware."

"But what if they're too busy to see us?" Amelia asked.

"They'll see us." Lady Phoebe smiled. "They'll make time for us because of who our grandfather is, and because of the amount of money we've already spent at their establishment. There's no better advertisement than that, and they won't wish to lose it."

CHAPTER 11

Phoebe and Amelia arrived at Crown Lily at half past nine the next morning. They had decided Eva would go later, to preserve the illusion that she was sneaking away from Lyndale Park when her employers wouldn't be needing her. Since they hadn't called ahead first, no one met them as they drove into the enclosure. However, upon seeing them enter the building, Mr. Tremaine's secretary jumped up from his seat and ran to inform his superior.

"Lady Phoebe, Lady Amelia." Mr. Tremaine hurried out of his office; he looked flushed and worried. "Is there a problem with the order? Something you'd like to change before production begins?"

"No, nothing like that." Phoebe began unbuttoning her coat, and Amelia did likewise. "Actually, we'd like to place another order."

"Another order?" His demeanor instantly changed to one of delight. "How splendid! Please come into my office and we'll discuss it." To his secretary he said, "Tea and cake, Jessup, in my office."

"Right away, sir."

Mr. Tremaine gestured for them to precede him into the room, but then he moved past them to reposition the chairs facing his own across the desk just so. Next he helped each off with her coat. "Now then, tell me what it is you'd like."

"A child's tea set," Amelia said eagerly. "Can you do something like that for us? It's a secret, of course. You mustn't say a word to our sister. It's for her child."

"Lovely, lovely," the man intoned. He started to go on, but Phoebe cut him off.

"I do have one concern, however. The thefts I've heard about."

"The . . . thefts?"

"Yes, Mr. Tremaine. Our footman supped at one of your local pubs the other night and heard about it from several of your employees."

His eyes sparked. "Which ones?"

"Oh, I really couldn't say. He didn't mention names. He said shipments of china were being stolen in transit, and that has me worried. What is our guarantee that our china won't go awry on its way to us in Gloucestershire?"

"Lady Phoebe, you realize I can't control what happens once our china leaves the factory." The man tented his fingers beneath his chin. "However, all of our shipments are fully insured, and then some. At worst there could be a delay while the set is being duplicated, but I promise it would be replaced at no cost to you. Or to Crown Lily, for that matter."

"We certainly can't ask for more than that,

Phoebe." Amelia beamed at Mr. Tremaine. "That puts our minds to rest, sir. Thank you."

"But it has happened, then," Phoebe pressed.

"A few isolated incidents," he replied. "Nothing more."

"And you've no idea how it's done or who is doing the stealing? A warehouse worker? Perhaps one of your clay mixers?" Phoebe suggested, thinking about Gus Abbott.

"A clay mixer? I can't imagine. But rest assured I've got my eyes and ears open. Should I find out anyone here at Crown Lily is involved, the police will know about it immediately."

Phoebe nodded, doing her best to assume a thoughtful look. "You don't suppose, do you . . ."

"Suppose what, Lady Phoebe?"

"Well, I don't like to say, but . . . do you suppose Trent Mercer had anything to do with it? In light of the fact that he didn't wish to be working here, as we all well know."

Mr. Tremaine let out a long, regretful sigh. "That's very true. If only his father hadn't forced him. The boy was much happier studying at Eton. I can't help but think . . ." He left off, shaking his head.

Phoebe pretended to study him, and at length she asked, "Mr. Tremaine, are you thinking Trent Mercer might have had a hand in his father's death? Do you believe him capable of such an act?"

Just as she had hesitated in asking, he took his time in replying, emitting another sigh. "In the past I'd never have thought so, but now? But what am I saying? No, no, Trent wouldn't commit murder, much less kill his own father. But . . ."

"Yes?"

He compressed his lips, then said in a confidential tone, "I only tell you this because of your brother's friendship with Trent. He's been a virtual powder keg since leaving school. I only agreed to allow him to bring that dog of his here because it seemed to mollify him a bit, make him more amenable to his circumstances. I also agreed because Staffordshire bull terriers are popular around here and the dog is good for morale generally. I'm a connoisseur of the breed myself. But I also realized it was one way for Trent to irritate his father, which he'd seemed bent on doing at every turn. Murder? No. But ill will toward his father? Yes, I'm afraid so. In abundance."

"Goodness." It was Phoebe's turn to sigh. Should the police become privy to this information, it wouldn't go well for Trent. Or had Mr. Tremaine already shared his opinion of Trent's state of mind with them? And could it be possible Phoebe and her siblings were putting too much trust in the boy?

"I'm sure you didn't come here to discuss such dismal matters." Mr. Tremaine's expression brightened. "Children's china isn't our main business, mind you, but I'm certain we can accommodate your needs with something perfectly charming. Let me just go and get Mr. Bateman . . ."

Phoebe and Amelia both came to their feet. "No need," Phoebe told him. "We know the way."

"But I've ordered tea . . ."

"We'll come back." Phoebe waved a hand. She and Amelia left the office and went along the corridor until they came to the designer's office. The door was partly open, Mr. Bateman sitting at his drawing table. Phoebe knocked, startling him. He looked up, saw them, and after a hesitation, he shoved some papers together and stood.

"I do hope we aren't disturbing you," Phoebe said as she and Amelia sauntered into his office. Unlike Mr. Tremaine's, furnished in fine leathers and mahogany, Percy Bateman's office projected a much more utilitarian air, with chairs, table, and desk made of inexpensive metal and wood.

"On the contrary, it's a pleasure." The young man dragged a second chair next to the one already positioned in front of his desk. He bade them both sit. "Now, what can I do for you? Does Mr. Tremaine know you're here?"

"We just saw him," Amelia said. "But you're the man we need to speak with. We'd like to commission another china service, for our sister's child."

The man's eyebrows went up.

"Yes, a child's tea set, on a smaller scale, of course, than a typical adult set," Phoebe explained, "but not a play set. We want this to be functional for when our little niece or nephew has birthdays and that sort of thing. Can you come up with a suitable design, do you think?"

"I'm sure I can . . ." Something in his countenance suggested he was less than confident in his abilities when it came to children's designs.

"We would hate to have to go elsewhere," Phoebe said as incentive.

"No, indeed. We can certainly work with you." He thought a moment, his fingers tapping on the desk. "Do you have certain preferences for the design?" Perplexity flashed in his eyes. Phoebe guessed he was remembering all the bickering that went on concerning her grandparents' china.

"Bright colors," she said. "And something adorable, like bears."

"Or kittens," Amelia suggested. "Or what about fairies? Oh, Phoebe, wouldn't that make an enchanting theme?"

"Well, yes . . . if it's a girl," Phoebe said slowly. "Fairies might not suit a little boy." She said to Mr. Bateman, "I think it's best we go with animals. Puppies, I should think. Amelia, what do you say about that?"

Amelia pondered that a moment, then nodded. "Yes, you're right. Puppies." Her nose wrinkled. "But what kind?"

The lines across Mr. Bateman's brow deepened. With no small amount of foreboding, he asked, "Tell me, is your brother in on this decision as well?"

"No, this was Phoebe's idea." Amelia showed her brightest smile. "And it's splendid, isn't it?"

He nodded, appearing relieved. Then he took out a sheet of paper and a charcoal pencil and began to sketch. "How about hounds?" he asked as he worked. "Foxhound pups?"

"Hmm." Amelia pondered a moment. "Foxhounds might not be squiggly enough."

Mr. Bateman glanced up. *"Squiggly?"*

"You know, the way puppies are." Amelia looked to Phoebe for affirmation, but Phoebe felt as puzzled as Mr. Bateman looked. Amelia let go an impatient sigh. "All warm and squirmy and soft. Foxhounds, even as puppies, might be too adult-looking, if you see what I mean."

Phoebe didn't. She rolled her eyes. "Of course. Squiggly. Any suggestions, Mr. Bateman?"

"Ah . . . Mmm . . ." Absently he scratched behind his ear with the end of his pencil. "Beagles? Also a hunting dog, but perhaps a bit more, um, squiggly?"

"I think beagles will do." Phoebe decided to end the matter before Amelia had any more suggestions. "Hunting dogs happen to tie in with our own history at Foxwood Hall, before the war, when our father and grandfather used to host foxhunts every fall. We haven't any dogs anymore." To her surprise and dismay, her eyes began to burn and she found herself blinking back tears.

"Exactly what I was thinking." The man's lower lip crept between his teeth as his pencil swished across the paper. "So many dogs were lost to the war." His pencil stopped and he sat back, shaking his head. "No, this won't do. May I have a day or two to experiment?"

"Certainly, Mr. Bateman." Phoebe turned to consult with Amelia after the fact; her sister agreed with a nod. Amelia started to rise, but Phoebe stopped her with a flick of her gaze. She turned back to Mr. Bateman. "Tell me, has Ronald Mercer's design book been found?"

He seemed startled by the question, then shook his head. "I'm afraid not. Perhaps whoever . . . took his life . . . took the book as well."

"Yes, that's what we were thinking," Phoebe agreed. "Yet, aren't your books kept locked away when you're not using them? I can't imagine something as important as a pattern book simply being left lying about."

"Typically, they're kept locked in our desks." Percy Bateman absently ran the back of his hand across his chin. "But perhaps Mr. Mercer had been using it when he decided to go and see our head clay mixer. He might have forgotten to replace the book in his desk. Or he did, but neglected to lock the drawer."

"Would the head of this department do something so careless?" Phoebe didn't think so. Ronald Mercer didn't get to be head of Crown Lily's design department by forgetting to secure his very livelihood—his design bible. It also seemed to her that whoever took the book knew exactly where to find it, and understood the routine in this part of the factory, to have been able to be in and out of Ronald Mercer's office without being seen. And she knew from her experiences with Eva that negotiating a lock wasn't all that difficult; a few deft turns with a hairpin, and voila! That all made it less likely the thief had been a general factory worker, and far likelier he or she had worked in this building, or was at least a department supervisor who came here for meetings and was familiar with the layout of the administrative offices.

Moira Wickham, Phoebe remembered, was just such a supervisor. Was Gus Abbott? Somehow she doubted the head of clay mixing had the same entree into this part of the factory.

"Tell me, Mr. Bateman, had you and Mr. Mercer gotten on well?"

The point of the young man's pencil snapped from the sudden pressure of his hand. The point flew off and sailed across the desk.

When Lady Phoebe returned to Lyndale Park, Eva had only a few minutes to speak with her before she herself hopped in the sedan with Douglas for the drive to Crown Lily. But in those few minutes, she had learned that Trent Mercer might have a shorter fuse than any of them had previously suspected. Or had Jeffrey Tremaine exaggerated? Many adults had little tolerance for the vagaries of youth and despaired of their behavior when it deviated even slightly from the norm. Thus, the boy's moodiness upon his retrieval from Eton could have been misinterpreted as rebellious hostility. If only his dog could tell them what had happened in the grinding room that morning, and whom Ronald Mercer had met there.

As the car maneuvered first the country lanes and then the crowded city streets of Langston, she wondered, too, about Percy Bateman's reaction to the question about how he had got on with Ronald Mercer. Had his broken pencil point signified a sudden bout of nerves? According to Lady Phoebe, Jeffrey Tremaine had appeared in the doorway a moment later, beckoning the sisters to take tea with him in his office, effectively cutting the discussion short.

And the thefts . . . according to Lady Phoebe, Mr. Tremaine had seemed about to dismiss these as false, but only when she referenced Douglas as having spoken with workers at the pub did he admit there had been a problem. True, a factory owner wouldn't want to worry his customers that their goods might never arrive at their door, and Eva supposed she couldn't blame him for that. But she also wondered if he might know more than he was willing to discuss, and for some reason he didn't wish it becoming common knowledge. A shocking betrayal by one of his trusted employees? Something that might make him appear the fool for not having noticed it sooner? At least he had assured Lady Phoebe that he would fully guarantee the Renshaws' orders.

The motorcar passed under the arching Crown Lily sign. The watchman at the gate, by now familiar with both of the Renshaws' vehicles, waved them in. Eva stepped out in the main quadrangle, tipped a nod at Douglas, and started for the art department building. Commotion at the open doors of the main warehouse, however, sent her on a detour.

A delivery of crates and barrels was being unloaded from a rail carriage, the items handed from man to man in a snaking line that disappeared into the dimmer lighting of the warehouse. Eva knew these containers could be full of supplies, or simply empty, to be filled later with finished products and shipped out. The men, dressed in denim work trousers and heavy woolen shirts, eyed her as she approached, some of them showing grins of a rather leering nature that almost made her regret venturing in this direction.

In the next instant a whistle blew and those unloading the carriage stopped what they were doing. Soon the entire line went still as the last of the containers was handed into the warehouse. Some of the men lit up cigarettes. Others hurried inside, probably to retrieve lunch pails brought from home. Eva's timing had proven perfect.

She stopped a few feet from one worker who had unabashedly watched her every step across the quadrangle. He flicked the ash of his cigarette as she reached him.

"Hullo there," she said in her friendliest manner. "May I have a peek inside? I saw it when my employers were given a tour, but I wondered if I might have another look around."

"Just a warehouse, miss." He drew on the cigarette and exhaled the smoke through his nose. "Nothing fancy."

"Yes, I know, but it's so vast, and for someone born and raised in a country village, this is all so exciting." Would he believe her round-eyed naivete?

With a shrug he stamped out his cigarette beneath the heel of his boot. "Follow me, then. But if you don't mind my asking, what are you doing here today?"

She had a ready answer. "Learning. Training, I suppose you could say. I'm considering signing on here in your art department as a painter. Do you like working here?" Again, she allowed herself to sound like a raw girl from the country.

"It puts food on the table and keeps me out

of my missus's hair. She doesn't like when I'm underfoot."

"No, I don't suppose she does." Eva chuckled. "So, what do you do here?"

"You were watching it. Packing, unpacking, storing, arranging, rearranging." He swept his hand in a wide arc, encompassing endless rows of shelving crammed with all manner of containers, in many shapes and sizes. Men moved about like worker ants. Little by little, they scattered, probably to have their lunch. "This is where we take materials in and prepare them to go to whatever department they're meant for."

"What about the finished products?"

"That's all in the adjoining warehouse, through there." He pointed toward a gaping doorway far to their left. It was so large, Eva guessed a lorry could drive through it.

"And do you work in both warehouses?"

"If need be, when there's more going out than coming in. But, generally, I'm in here. I supervise the first shift." He shoved his hands in his trouser pockets and gave her an assessing look. "Why all the questions?"

"I told you. To me this is all fascinating."

He continued to eye her quizzically, as if trying to decide whether or not to believe her. He shook his head, his earlier grin reappearing. "I know why you're poking about. You heard all about it, didn't you?"

"About what?"

"Don't play coy with me, miss. The murder. Mr. Mercer. Had you met him? You did come in that day with your betters, those Renshaws. My guess is you want to know what happened."

A spark of panic heated Eva's cheeks; she'd been caught and wouldn't learn another thing from anyone. Not only that, but she'd be exposed to Miss Wickham, who wouldn't take at all kindly to having been taken in. But then the man set her fears to rest when he said, "I'll bet murder never happens where you're from."

She shook her head eagerly and told a blatant lie. "Never. We're a sleepy little hamlet in the Cotswolds. Nothing extraordinary ever happens there. And while murder is a ghastly and detestable act, I can't help but admit that . . . well . . . it's an intriguing subject. Does anyone know what happened yet?"

"They arrested Mr. Mercer's son, Trent. A deuced shame, that."

Eva opened her eyes wide again. "Yes, I'd heard that, but do you really believe the boy killed his own father? I heard something from one of our footmen, who's here in Langston with us. He said . . ." Eva trailed off and made a show of looking about her. Then she lowered her voice. "He said he'd heard down at one of the pubs that a lot of people here didn't like Mr. Mercer. Is that true?"

The man shrugged. "I suppose. Sometimes that's how it is between laborers and the blokes in charge."

Eva nodded. "They also told him they were only too happy to protect their own, meaning some of them were willing to give Gus Abbott an alibi."

His eyes narrowed and his silence stretched. Then he said in a tone resembling a low growl, "Meaning?"

Eva should have recognized the warning in his voice, and should have gone on her way immediately. Ill advisedly, she said, "Meaning perhaps they lied when they claimed he was here in the warehouse the morning of the murder."

Abruptly, the man took her arm, albeit gently, turned her around and started her forward, out of the warehouse. "Come with me, miss."

"Where? Let me go." Taken completely off guard, she failed to put up much resistance.

In the next instant he did indeed release her, but kept walking. Over his shoulder he said, "You want to know what happened, don't you?"

Had she only imagined his abruptness, his less than gentlemanly demeanor when he'd grasped her arm? "Yes, but—"

"Then follow me. I can introduce you to someone who might be able to answer your questions."

"Oh. Are you sure this person won't mind?"

He replied with a raised hand that beckoned her to continue following him. They crossed the quadrangle, heading in a direction that made Eva drag her feet. "Are you taking me into the clay-mixing building? Because I'd really rather not." What she had rather not do was confront Gus Abbott, if that was what this man had in mind.

He stopped outside the heavy metal door that led inside. "If you have questions for Gus, I suggest you ask him yourself."

"I didn't mean—"

"No? It seems to me, then, that you'd rather spread rumors and play with a man's reputation." He tugged the door open and stood aside to let her cross the threshold. "If you're going to toss around words about someone, you should do it to his face and not behind his back." He raised his eyebrows at her, waiting.

She was backed into a corner of her own making. If she'd been more careful with her questions, she wouldn't be standing here now. But if she backed away, she'd be a coward, and what was more, this man would be right about her. She entered the building.

He followed her in and bustled her down the corridor. At the same time he called out for Gus Abbott. A man in gray coveralls, smeared with dried clay, shuffled out through a doorway. He wasn't what Eva would have expected of someone who worked in these rough, industrial surroundings. He was neither large nor particularly muscular, and a good two decades past his youth.

When he saw her, he removed the flat cap he wore and gave a little bob of his head. "Floyd," he said in greeting to Eva's companion. His gaze shifted back to her, his puzzlement clear. "Can I do something for you, miss?"

"I . . . er . . ."

"This young lady has a question or two for you, Gus." Floyd, as Eva now knew he was called, didn't exactly speak kindly, and she flinched.

"I'm sorry about this," she said to Mr. Abbott. "I have no desire to disturb you."

Floyd spoke for her. "She's wondering if you might have killed Ron Mercer—instead of Mercer's boy doing it. What have you got to say about that, Gus?"

CHAPTER 12

Gus Abbott raised a callused, clay-soiled hand to his breastbone. "Me, a murderer?"

Eva couldn't decide if he looked outraged or simply baffled. "I never said any such thing," she protested. Indignation and, yes, mortification made her face burn. "It's just that . . . well . . . you see . . ." While both men watched her expectantly, she drew a deep breath and started again. "The other night my employer's footman was at a pub in town and he heard people—workers from Crown Lily—say they were only too happy to protect their own, the implication being that perhaps they'd create an alibi for someone when none actually existed."

There. She had said it. Except . . . Mr. Abbott didn't appear any more enlightened than he had a moment ago. If anything, he looked thoroughly confused.

"What she means, Gus, is that they were lying when they claimed you were in the warehouse, and that you were most likely right here the morning Ron Mercer died. And that the murderer was probably none other than you."

Eva whirled on Floyd. "I'll thank you to stop putting words in my mouth."

It wasn't Floyd who replied, but Mr. Abbott. "If

you don't believe I was in the warehouse, ask Mr. Tremaine. He knows."

"Oh, I suppose he saw you there," she said weakly.

"I don't think I need to explain myself to the likes of you." He regarded her with disdain. "Call me a *murderer,* will you?"

Eva hadn't actually called him anything, but then again, what else should he think? "I was only trying to get at the truth. Trent Mercer is a schoolmate of my lady's brother, and—"

"And anyone else will do, so long as it's not the boy, is that it?" Gus Abbott pivoted on his heel and ducked back inside the room he had been in, but not before issuing a curt order. "Come in here."

Eva glanced at Floyd, who shrugged and pointed through the doorway. "I think you owe him that much, miss."

Did she? Exactly what did she owe him that required her to go deeper into this building? Before the lunch whistle blew, the premises would have been filled with men, the sounds of their voices filling the corridor, along with the whir and grind of machinery. Now all lay quiet, and Eva felt only too aware of being very much alone with these men. And yet . . .

With another breath to steel her nerves, she proceeded into the next room, aware of Floyd following on her heels. She stopped short just inside the doorway, forcing him to back up a step or bump into her. Though she hadn't been in this specific room before, it was very much like the one she had seen on the tour of the factory, with its chutes and conveyors and several grinding vats. She didn't have to look inside to know those vats contained vicious blades that turned raw materials into malleable clay.

And yet Gus Abbott waved her closer to the nearest contraption. "Have a look."

"I've already seen—"

"I said *have a look,* miss."

Eva went forward to join him at the vat. He pointed over the edge, and she had to rise onto her toes to see inside. This particular vat stood empty, the blades on full, unsettling display. Eva's breath caught. She let it out unevenly, wishing she were anywhere but here. Gus Abbott's hostility rolled over her in waves.

"Do you realize what kind of death Ron Mercer met in that vat in the other room?" he asked.

Eva hesitated, her fingertips shaking at the mere thought of it. She said in a half whisper, "It must have been horrific."

He nodded. "Yes, it must have been. The vat he was dumped into was filled with stones and the rest, which would only have added to his terror and his suffering."

Eva gulped, her heart fluttering. The pulses pattered in her wrists and her temples, making her dizzy and queasy.

"I'm an artisan, miss. Do you know what that means?"

She turned her head and met Gus Abbott's gaze. "It means you're a craftsman. An artist."

"It means I've worked my entire life to learn my trade and do it properly. It means I care about what I do, that it's important to me. These vats may be ugly to you. There's nothing pretty about them, but to me they're beautiful. Can you understand that?"

Actually, she could. Farming could be brutal. Cows became ill, died, or needed someone to put them out of their misery. Both the milking and the mucking were backbreaking, grimy labors. Some years weren't good ones, and money ran short. It was always a struggle. Still, her father, who had been a farmer all his life, found it satisfying, at times beautiful, and never once wished for anything else. Neither had her mother.

She raised her chin and answered steadily, "I believe I can understand, Mr. Abbott."

"Then you'll also understand that I could never defile something so important to me with anything as foul as murder. And so violent a murder, at that. It would be like sacrilege, like desecrating a church."

She wanted to believe him, and for the most part she did. Yet a tiny voice reminded her that not so very long ago, someone she loved very much had nearly lost her life inside a chapel,

214

and the person responsible, who should have respected the sanctity of the church above all else, had shown no regard for it whatsoever. So, where did that leave Gus Abbott, standing before her in a decidedly convincing aspect of wounded self-righteousness?

"I'm very sorry I said what I did, Mr. Abbott. I listened to hearsay and rumor, and spoke out of turn. It won't happen again."

She moved to leave, and they allowed her to go. She hurried blindly across the quadrangle. Once she was upstairs in the painting room, her hands continued to tremble and she despaired of producing any results that would pass Miss Wickham's scrutiny. Making matters worse, she found herself once again seated at the worktable so recently vacated by Lydia Travers. Whereas the first time she had worked here, the others had paid her little attention, now she felt their stares burning into her. She braved several glances in their directions and did not believe she was mistaken in detecting resentment and accusation glaring back at her. They obviously blamed her for Lydia getting the sack.

The very notion got Eva's dander up, until she realized that Lydia's dismissal and her being hired happened simultaneously. Perhaps these workers believed Eva had been instrumental in Lydia losing her position. She must find a way to talk to them and convince them one had nothing to do with the other. And then see what she could find out about Lydia Travers and where she lived. She still had questions about why the girl had been let go.

Phoebe paused in the upstairs gallery to view the portraits ranged along the wall between bedroom doorways. Studying the attire, hairstyles, and symbolic objects in each composition, she judged that the paintings spanned recent times—a picture of Gilbert Townsend and his first wife, Georgiana—all the way back to the 1600s. A man and a woman hung side by side, looking grim. She wore a long-waisted gown, open to show the petticoats beneath, with voluminous sleeves and a square neckline edged in lace, the style reminiscent of both the Stuart and Georgian eras. The man wore a long velvet coat edged in fox fur, wide knee-length trousers with stockings, and a cascade of lace that began at his collar. Something in his eyes struck Phoebe as defiant, challenging, and she guessed he had hailed from the merchant class and had only recently, at the time of the portrait, been raised to the nobility.

The pair looked nothing whatsoever like Gil, yet he had often conveyed that same look of defiant self-entitlement she saw on their faces. She smiled. Though she couldn't say how directly related the couple in the portraits were to Gil, they certainly appeared to be kindred spirits, if nothing else.

Fox appeared at the top of the staircase, Jester lumbering along beside him, and the pair crossed the gallery to join her. Jester sniffed affectionately at Phoebe's hand until she obliged him with a pat on the head. He sat beside her, leaning against her leg. Fox, meanwhile, stared up at the man in the picture for all of a second or two, gave the jacket of his Norfolk suit a tug, and murmured, "Glad I didn't have to live back then. By the way, Phoebe, I want to talk to you. What have you learned about Ronald Mercer's death? If you can't find a way to clear Trent soon, I'll start digging around myself."

"No, you won't."

He leaned in closer. "Try me."

"Fine." She let out a huff of frustration. "But let's wait until Eva gets back from the factory."

"Why is she there alone? Why didn't she go with you and Amelia this morning? And why the blazes is Amelia allowed to sneak around, but not me?" His combative tone brought Jester to his feet again, and he stared up at them with questions glistening in his eyes.

Phoebe held up her hands. "One question at a time."

"Fine. The last one first."

"You know why. You're Grampapa's heir, and you're also the youngest of all of us. And Amelia is not sneaking around. She merely accompanied me to place a new order."

"An order for what?" His voice bounced off the gallery walls.

"Shh!" Phoebe glanced toward the staircase, and then Julia's bedroom. "It's a surprise for Julia and her baby. Do not say a word to her. And would you really have wanted to come and pick out more china today?"

"Since you put it that way . . ." He recoiled with a comically disgusted look. "No, thank you all the same."

"Well, then. As regarding Eva, she and I didn't go together because she's pretending to have an interest in working there."

"Eva, working at a factory? Leaving you and Amelia? That's preposterous."

"Of course it's preposterous, but the people at Crown Lily don't know that. She's been training for a position in the painting department, and she needs to make it look as though she's sneaking off on her own time, with me none the wiser. The whole point is to see what we can find out about the department supervisor, Moira Wickham. Mr. Mercer wasn't very nice to her, so that may have given her a motive to want him out of the way. So you see, we are working to clear Trent."

He raised his chin and stared at her down the length of his slightly aquiline nose. "All right, then. Thank you. Come, Jester."

She shook her head at him as he and Jester turned away. Fox may have matured in recent months, but at times he could be as infuriating as ever. The pair headed for his bedroom, while she continued to the stairs. All three of them were stopped in their tracks by a cry that came surging from below. Jester let out a whine. Phoebe and Fox traded looks of alarm. He said, "That sounded like Julia."

Phoebe's eyes were wide as she nodded her agreement. "Yes, it did. It does." The yelling continued, and Phoebe heard her name being called out. She started down the stairs when her bedroom door banged open and Amelia came running out.

"Is that Julia?"

"It is." Phoebe's fingers curled tight around the bannister as she continued her descent. Her siblings' footsteps thudded on the steps above her, along with Jester's thumping ones. Mildred Blair's calm countenance appeared below her, at the foot of the staircase. "Mildred, what's happening? Is Julia all right?"

"I believe she might be having the baby," Mildred replied, sounding as if it were no greater matter than what Julia had chosen for lunch that day. She tucked a cropped strand of midnight-black hair behind her ear.

"Baby?" That brought Phoebe up short. "She can't be. She has another two months to go."

Mildred's lips curled in an ironic smile. "Tell that to her baby."

"Goodness!" Phoebe skipped over the last two steps and landed with a shuddering jolt on the marble tiles of the hall. Her teeth clattered painfully but she kept going, turning to cross the hall to the drawing room just as Julia stumbled her way into the wide doorway, leaning over and clutching her stomach. Phoebe ran to her. Julia all but collapsed against her.

"Get me into the library, Phoebe."

"Why the library? Why didn't you stay where you were in the drawing room?"

"Because the furniture in the drawing room is all silk brocade, whereas there's a leather sofa in the library. Now get me to it before something happens."

Amelia came to Julia's other side and, together, she and Phoebe helped her make the painstaking trip to the library. From the corner of her vision Phoebe spied Fox hovering near the stairs with Jester, a frightened look on his face. She felt frightened herself. Craning to glance over her shoulder, she said as calmly as she could, "Mildred, have you telephoned for a doctor?"

Mildred had the audacity to shrug. "I hadn't time yet. Shall I now?"

"Of course you *shall now.*" Phoebe didn't add *you idiot,* but she certainly thought it. "And please ring for Hetta to come down. Where is Veronica?"

"Out shopping, I believe. Or visiting someone."

Mildred gave another light shrug, so like one of Julia's. "I don't remember."

"It doesn't matter," Julia half shouted, and ended with a yelp. "Oh, it hurts."

Phoebe heard Mildred's footsteps clattering across the floor as she apparently went to use the telephone. Before she disappeared into the rear section of the house, Phoebe had a frightening thought. "Mildred, how far is the nearest doctor?"

"I couldn't say," she called back, and kept going.

"What difference does it make?" Julia asked between gritted teeth and let out a moan.

Phoebe thought it could make a great deal of difference, but thought better of explaining that to Julia. As Julia doubled over again, Phoebe met Amelia's gaze. Amelia nodded, apparently reading her mind. "As soon as we get her settled, I'll tell Fox to run and get Ernie."

"*Ernie?* Are you mad?" With an effort Julia straightened as they reached the library. They walked her to the long sofa, upholstered in tufted green leather, which took up the greater portion of the wall beside the doorway.

"Ernie's a veterinarian, Julia," Phoebe explained. "And if the real doctor doesn't get here in time . . ." She didn't finish. She couldn't. The notion formed a leaden ball of dread in the pit of her stomach. Though she knew the basics about pregnancy and the birth process, the notion of presiding over the birth of Julia's child filled her with terror.

"What do I look like to you? A cow? A horse?" Julia paused to clamp her teeth; she pushed a groan out between them. "What do I need with a veterinarian? Especially Ernie?"

Phoebe mouthed to Amelia, "Go." Then she said to Julia, "He's still a doctor and he understands the process. He's better than nothing."

Eva knew something was wrong the moment she stepped into the house. She could feel the tension in the air surrounding the kitchen, the kind of urgency that typically signifies unexpected company—much as the Renshaws had been unexpected company earlier in the week. She had also noticed Ernest Shelton's motorcar in front of the house. Why would he be here? Had he come to reconcile with Lady Annondale? Or to confront her with his insistence that she vacate the property until her child was born? There had been another vehicle beside his, one she hadn't recognized. His solicitor's? Her blood sizzled at the thought.

She seized the attention of a passing footman. He held a copper pot of water—hot water, judging by the rising steam. "What's going on? Who's come to visit? And where are you going with that?"

His frown revealed his impatience at being detained from his errand. "Doctor's here. Lady Annondale is having her baby." He hurried up

222

the back staircase, somehow without spilling a drop. A housemaid followed, carrying a bundle of linens.

Eva's heart clogged her throat. She rushed up the steps behind them, nearly tripping in her haste. Her temples pounded, her breath came in short bursts. It was much too soon for the baby. This could only mean something was terribly, dreadfully wrong. Bursting through the baize door into the main hall, she called out to Lady Annondale's sister-in-law, Veronica Townsend, who was pacing back and forth in front of the drawing-room doorway. "Is Lady Annondale all right? The baby?"

Miss Townsend, wearing a fox-trimmed coat, as if she were going out or had only just arrived home, met Eva's gaze with a troubled countenance, one that did little to reassure her that Lady Annondale was in no peril. "Library," came her succinct reply. She pointed as well, unnecessarily, since Eva could see the footman and housemaid turn into that very room.

As Eva reached the doorway, voices drifted out to her—a calm, soothing male voice and one indignant female one. But none to signify fear or alarm or grief. And then, Eva distinctly heard Lady Annondale say, "Are you sure you know what you're doing, Doctor?"

Baffled, Eva moved to step across the threshold, only to be forced back into the hall by the same footman and housemaid she'd followed up the stairs. Both carried the same items they had brought from downstairs; those items appeared unused. Then came Lady Phoebe's voice from inside.

"Julia, I'm sure Dr. Wright knows his business."

Eva entered the room to find Lady Phoebe and Lady Amelia flanking the sofa upon which Lady Annondale reclined, her feet up and several pillows stacked behind her. Poor Amelia stood wringing her hands and biting her lower lip, while Phoebe kept a sharp gaze pinned on the doctor. Hetta hovered like an avenging angel at the man's shoulder, undoubtedly ready to haul him away at a word from her mistress. And Ernest Shelton, the most unexpected occupant of the room, perched at the edge of the very solid-looking mahogany desk, his face pale except for the dark shadows around his eyes and mouth, as though he might, at any moment, be ill.

As for the attending physician himself, he stood over Lady Annondale, holding an instrument Eva knew to be a fetal stethoscope, for she had seen such a device used on livestock on her parents' farm. Shaped like an elongated earpiece to a candlestick phone, the wider end could be placed on the stomach of a pregnant woman—or animal, for that matter—and allow a doctor to hear the baby's heartbeat.

Eva could almost understand Lady Annondale's doubts when it came to this young man, who could be little more than thirty, she judged. Though he spoke with authority, his physical appearance simply didn't match his confident tone. Small of stature, with bland, youthful features and mild blue eyes, he appeared as if he couldn't have been practicing medicine for more than a few years.

Lady Annondale waved a hand at him. "*Pish.* I tell you, I've been having labor pains for over an hour and a half now. This baby is coming."

The doctor contradicted her. "False labor, Lady Annondale. It's actually quite common, and nothing to worry about."

The eldest Renshaw sibling rejected this pronouncement with a scowl and another wave of her hand. "Ridiculous. I've never heard of such a thing. What in the world could be false about the dreadful pains I've been experiencing?"

"For one," the doctor said patiently, "I've been here for nearly twenty minutes. You had a pain when I first arrived, but not one since, although you say they had been coming with great frequency before that."

Lady Annondale treated him to one of her cavalier shrugs. "So?"

"So true labor doesn't proceed that way. The pains increase in severity and frequency. They do not diminish. And there are other symptoms you haven't exhibited."

If Eva had expected Lady Annondale to question what those other symptoms were, she'd have been mistaken. Lady Annondale shot a look at Ernest Shelton, pinched her lips together, and scowled all the more.

Dr. Wright placed his stethoscope in his leather bag and snapped the bag shut. Ernest Shelton slipped off the desk and, giving Lady Annondale a wide berth, made his way to the door. "I don't suppose you'll be needing me anymore."

"Never needed you in the first place," Lady Annondale grumbled.

Lady Amelia went to him. "Thank you for coming, Ernie. Sorry for the false alarm."

Lady Annondale rolled her eyes to that.

The doctor, too, took his leave with a slight bob of his head. "You know how to reach me, Lady Annondale. If you experience anything alarming, even slightly so, don't hesitate to ring me up."

He'd already reached the threshold when Lady Annondale murmured, "Why? You'll only treat me like a hysterical female again."

"He did no such thing, Julia." Lady Phoebe came around the sofa and perched on its edge, facing her sister. "And he said it was a common thing. So you see, you're not the first expectant mother to be fooled."

Hetta also approached the sofa. She took a folded blanket off one of the arms and spread it over her mistress, with a little help from Lady Phoebe. She offered her mistress a gentle smile. "I bring tea, *ja*?"

Lady Annondale leaned back against her

pillows, letting herself sink into them. "Please. And make it strong." Hetta turned to go, but Lady Annondale hadn't finished. "With cinnamon. And a bit of clove."

"*Ja*, right away." Hetta disappeared into the hall. She was replaced in the doorway by Fox.

"Is Julia all right?"

Jester circled his legs and trotted into the room, going to the sofa and staring up at Julia with solemn eyes, as if sensing her ordeal.

Julia absently patted his head and leaned a bit to one side to better see Fox. "Come in," she beckoned. "It's safe now. And, yes, I'm fine. So is the baby. I was just being foolish, apparently."

Lady Phoebe shook her head. "Oh, Julia, no one thinks that." She leaned forward to give her sister a kiss on the cheek, which Lady Annondale accepted rather than pull away, as she sometimes did. It heartened Eva to see even that infinitesimal acceptance between them.

Lady Amelia had drifted back to the sofa, and Lady Phoebe rose to allow her younger sister to take her place beside their elder one. If anyone could soothe Lady Annondale, it was Amelia. She had that effect on everyone in the family. Meanwhile, Eva caught Lady Phoebe's silent signal. They slipped out of the room together, only to realize Fox followed them. Jester stayed with Julia, apparently judging her need to be greater than anyone else's at that moment.

"Go away," Lady Phoebe told her brother.

He folded his arms and dug in his heels. "I want to know what you two have found out. What happened at Crown Lily today, Eva?"

Lady Phoebe shushed him. "Lower your voice. Come along. We can't talk here."

She led the way to the morning room, unlikely to be occupied at that time of day. Decorated in yellows, muted golds, and soft greens, the room was situated at the opposite end of the house from the library and guaranteed their privacy.

Once they'd seated themselves, Lady Phoebe turned to Eva. "What did you learn today, if anything?"

"I had a rather harrowing time of it, at first," Eva began, and told them what had occurred with Gus Abbott and the warehouse worker named Floyd.

"He brought you into a grinding room?" Lady Phoebe looked both outraged and fearful. "You shouldn't have gone, Eva. It was too dangerous."

"After what I'd said, I couldn't blame either man for taking me to task." Eva shrugged. "I should have been more discreet with my questions, not to mention insinuations. And, anyway, I couldn't imagine either of them doing away with me in the middle of the day like that, when anyone might come along and catch them at it. At least now we know Mr. Abbott's alibi is a valid one. I doubt he'd have mentioned Mr. Tremaine's name, otherwise. He'd know it would be too easy to check."

"Even so, promise me you'll be more careful in the future." Lady Phoebe's forceful tone and pleading expression warmed Eva's heart, and she eagerly made that promise.

"My day didn't stop being interesting after that," she went on. "I learned there's some festering resentment toward Miss Wickham for giving Lydia Travers the sack. Mostly among the younger workers."

"That's certainly understandable, especially if the reason for it doesn't seem believable to them. You said Miss Wickham accused Lydia of revealing design secrets to a rival company."

"Yes, through her beau, who works for Royal Wiltshire. Although Lydia claimed they were no longer stepping out."

"How do you know she isn't lying?" Fox wanted to know. "Maybe she's been helping the other company and Mr. Mercer found out. And she killed him to keep him silent. Maybe she stole his pattern book and is even now selling more designs to the enemy."

Lady Phoebe sighed with impatience. "Fox, please." She seemed about to order him from the room.

"No, he has a point," Eva said. "Lydia could be guilty. Meanwhile, Moira Wickham herself could be selling secrets, and she sacked Lydia as a scapegoat."

"Or it's someone else entirely," Lady Phoebe

put in, "and Miss Wickham suspected Lydia because of her beau. Or former beau. But how do we figure out which it is?"

"I intend to speak to Lydia Travers." Eva couldn't help a little grin of triumph. "I found out today where she lives. I'd like to go tonight, if that's all right. I thought if I offer to help her, perhaps with a small amount of money, or invite her for a meal, she might be willing to speak with me."

"We'll go together and have Douglas drive us in the touring car."

Eva was shaking her head before Lady Phoebe finished speaking. "You can't go, my lady. I'm supposed to be sneaking off to learn the pottery-painting business. Our being seen visiting Lydia together would look suspicious. It's better I go alone."

Lady Phoebe blew out a breath, nodding. "I don't like it, though."

"I'll go with you." Fox sat forward in his seat.

"How is that any better than my going?" Lady Phoebe challenged. "You'll be recognized." Suddenly her eyes brightened. "I've got the perfect solution. I'll go—"

"But, my lady, we just agreed—"

"I'll go and wait in the motorcar with Douglas. Meanwhile . . . I've got to speak with Julia." She jumped up from her seat and hurried out of the room, leaving Eva to wonder what on earth she might be planning.

CHAPTER 13

Douglas maneuvered the sedan through Langston's narrow lanes. The one they searched for lay a mere stone's throw from the Crown Lily factory. In fact, Eva had been told the street ended right up against one of the pottery's perimeter walls.

She couldn't imagine living so close to those belching bottle kilns. How did one breathe? How did one ever wash away the stench of the coal fires, the soot, and the ash?

Beside her, Hetta stared out the window, her expression mirroring Eva's thoughts. Eva thought once again of the Swiss woman's origins, growing up in the vast spaces and freshness of the Alps. No wonder the ridge above her eyes grew with each mile they traveled, each corner they turned, as the lanes narrowed and the sky all but disappeared behind the looming tenements, unless one looked directly straight up.

When Eva considered it, there had been times her own family had had little money to speak of, surely no more than many of the people residing in this neighborhood. Yet, growing up on a farm, she had rarely noticed being poor. Between their vegetable garden, their egg-laying hens, and their cattle, there had always been enough to eat, even if sometimes it had been only just. Before her brother Danny died, her parents had always been quick to laugh and eager to embrace their children. The farm had been safe, bright, teeming with life. Not like these grimy brick tenements, with their alleys and rickety stairways and dim gas lighting.

Beside her, Lady Phoebe gazed straight ahead, working the strap of her handbag between nervous fingers. She didn't like this—she had said as much at the house. Though why this excursion should be any different than a dozen others she and Eva had undertaken these past couple of years, Eva couldn't say. A presentiment? Eva shook her head at the notion. Lady Phoebe wasn't one for premonitions. Eva expected only to talk to Lydia Travers. Certainly, no cause for fear.

Douglas brought the motorcar to a stop and turned to speak to them. "Will this do?"

Eva nodded. Even in the fading light she could see Crown Lily's outer wall in the near distance standing as a sentinel against intruders from the neighborhood. The inhabitants might be welcome to work there during the day, but they were adamantly forbidden access at night.

There were people out, traveling to and fro along the pavement, most of them dressed in shabby woolens and drab colors. They'd passed several pubs along the way here, the most recent just there on the corner. Lit windows in the tenements provided glimpses of crowded parlors and kitchens, voices and laughter tumbling out onto the street. Even in November, those windows had been shoved open. Otherwise, flats such as these, constructed during the previous century, provided virtually no ventilation.

"The one I'm looking for is there, I believe." Eva pointed to a three-story building about a dozen yards down the street. Constructed of brick, the ground floor had been whitewashed—although even in the darkness one could see the ashen veil left behind by the kilns—while the bricks above had been left naked. "Nedra, the young woman who used to sit beside Lydia, told me she lives on the third floor." She turned to Hetta. "Ready?"

Hetta sucked in a breath. "I should not be away from Madame, *ja*, but we are here. Let us go, then I get back."

It had taken some persuasion to convince Hetta to leave Lady Annondale's side. But Lady Annondale, having had the situation explained to her, had seen the sense in Hetta coming along. She had insisted the false labor pains had ceased, and, she had added, as a mother-to-be, she wished to give Trent every opportunity to clear his name. Prison was no place for a boy.

Eva collected her handbag and the basket provided by Lyndale Park's cook. In it were pasties, scones, a few apples, and a bottle of milk. Lady Phoebe had also contributed a handful of shillings. Any more than that and Miss Travers would realize these gifts could not have come from Eva.

The building stood beside an alley, a dark, cramped passageway that prompted Eva to walk faster as they passed it. After they climbed the front steps, they entered a foyer as cold and grim as outside. They heard muffled voices from behind doors: a woman shouting, a baby crying, and, incongruously, laughter. At the very top of the wooden staircase that trembled with each step they took, a tight hallway revealed several doors. Good heavens, how many flats had been squeezed into this cramped space beneath the roof?

They knocked at the first door, both of them lurching back a step when a man with unkempt hair and several missing teeth growled out at them with a burst of foul breath. "What?"

"We . . . we're looking f-for Miss Travers," Eva stammered. She wondered if she should have come here with Douglas instead of Hetta. She pulled back another step when she noticed the fellow eyeing the basket hanging from her arm. "D-does she live here?"

"Over there." The man pointed with a none-too-clean finger and slammed the door in their faces.

They turned in the general direction of his gesture to where three more doors lined the hall before it turned. Hetta shook her head. "Which one?"

Eva made a quick judgment. "I think he meant that one." She walked to the second door down and knocked again, bracing for another rude encounter. This time, however, the door opened a crack and a single eye peered out at her.

"What?" Though the female voice spoke the same word the man had, it came as a whisper laced with fear.

"Lydia Travers?"

"Why? Who are you?"

"My name is Eva Huntford, and this is my friend Hetta Brauer. I was wondering if I might speak with you."

"What about?" The eye narrowed speculatively. "Wait, I remember you. From Crown Lily. You came with that posh family. And then . . . yes . . . you were there when Miss Wickham sent me packing." The door started to close.

Eva stuck the toe of her low-heeled oxford shoe into the gap between the door and the jamb. "Please wait."

"You stole my job."

"I feel dreadful about what happened in the painting room. Yes, I'm considering taking a permanent position there, but I assure you that I had nothing to do with your being let go. And . . . and

I've brought you some things to help, to see you through a few days until you find a new situation. I promise we mean you no harm."

Slowly the door opened wider. Lydia Travers glanced at the basket hanging from Eva's bent arm. She shrugged and turned away. "Come in. Close the door behind you."

A quick glimpse revealed this to be a one-room flat with a bed—neatly made—a small table and single chair, and a low cupboard. There was no cooker, and little room to prepare anything resembling a meal. Clothing, sparse as it was, hung on a few pegs pounded into the wall. A single window overlooked the alley and the building next door. It couldn't let in much light during the day. Eva's heart went out to Miss Travers.

She held out the basket. "This is for you. There's a little money, too. Not much, but I hope it helps."

"I don't need your charity. Besides, why are you being kind? What do you want?" Lydia went through the contents as she spoke, and then covered it again with the cloth. Lydia jerked her chin at Hetta. "Doesn't she talk?"

"Hetta doesn't speak much English. I mostly wanted to see that you were all right. Your friend Nedra told me I'd find you here."

"I'll have to have a word with Nedra, then, won't I?"

"She meant no harm. She and some of the other workers are worried about you. They feel bad about what happened. They regret not coming to your defense."

"They'd have been sacked, too. It wasn't my fault, you know. What Miss Wickham accused me of."

"Has she done this before? Accused someone and given them the sack?"

"I suppose. She's in charge, isn't she?"

"Yes, but can you remember the last person she sent packing?"

Lydia rolled her eyes, but then seemed to consider the question. "There was an incident shortly after I started at Crown Lily. A girl, she wasn't stealing patterns, but Miss Wickham said she was taking things—supplies. Sent her away. But then I heard she got married, so in the end it didn't really matter, did it?"

"I suppose not." Eva involuntarily stole another glance around the room. She decided to put Miss Wickham's accusation against Lydia to the test. "Won't your beau help you?"

"Were you deaf that day? I haven't got a beau, haven't for some time now." She pulled herself up taller. "I can take care of myself, thank you. *And* my younger sisters. They live with my grandmother, who can't work, so I've got to. And I will. I'll find a new situation soon enough. You can go back to Miss Wickham and tell her that."

"I believe you," Eva said truthfully. She couldn't help feeling a surge of pride in Lydia, in her determination to keep going when others would have despaired.

"I won't go skulking back to my parents, either." Outrage sparked in Lydia's eyes. "I'd rather starve."

The declaration explained why Lydia's sisters lived with their grandmother; the implications tugged at Eva's heartstrings. Not everyone enjoyed the happy, safe childhood she had. In good times and in lean ones, her parents had always provided a secure home for Eva and her siblings. Apparently, the same could not be said for Lydia's parents.

Hetta reached out and touched Lydia's forearm, offering her a gentle smile. It always surprised Eva how much English Hetta understood, even when she hadn't the words to express herself. Lydia blinked rapidly and turned away, pretending to busy herself with the contents of the basket.

"I can't offer you anything except what you brought," she said briskly.

"We don't need anything."

"I suppose you came here offering gifts so I'd put your mind to rest about working at Crown Lily. Tell you what a wonderful place it is and all that, and how I don't resent you for taking my position. But all I can say is, where Miss

Wickham is concerned, watch your back."

Eva decided to play along. "Yes, I suppose that's part of it. Until she sacked you, had you believed Miss Wickham to be a fair supervisor? Was she liked by the others?"

"As much as someone in her position can be liked by her inferiors. So, not much." Lydia tossed her head with a sardonic chuckle. "As for *fair*—wasn't fair what she'd done to me, was it?"

"Who do you think might have been selling patterns to the rival company, then?"

"How should I know? Maybe Miss Wickham herself."

Yes, that had occurred to Eva as well. "Do you think that's possible?"

"Look, Miss . . ."

"Huntford."

Lydia nodded. "All I know is, I didn't do it. I've no reason to lie to you, do I? And I say, I never stole nothing in my life. Now, if you're done pestering me . . ."

"I'm sorry. I didn't mean to be impertinent. But there was a murder there, after all. And the mystery of the missing pattern book, too. One worries about the future of Crown Lily."

"If you want to know what I think about that, Ronald Mercer is as likely to have stolen his own pattern book as anyone else."

This took Eva by surprise. "Why would he sabotage his own place of employment?"

Lydia laughed, a sound tinged with irony. "You still confuse the dainty china made hereabouts for the kind of industry it is. Don't be fooled. This is a ruthless business. Men like Ronald Mercer would sell their own mothers for the chance to rise to the top of their profession. He was almost there at Crown Lily, but he could have gone further. Oh, but not there. From what I've heard, Jeffrey Tremaine reigns over his designers like a king over his subjects. But Mr. Mercer could have bought his way into a partnership somewhere else. Someday the likes of your employers might have been sipping tea from Crown Mercer china. But not now."

Could china manufacturing be as cutthroat as Lydia suggested? The girl had certainly given Eva a lot to think about, and she pondered this question and more as she and Hetta made their way back out to the street.

There were few people about now, and the shadows loomed darker than when they'd arrived. Maybe Ronald Mercer had sold his pattern book to a competitor, and someone—Jeffrey Tremaine, perhaps—had found out and murdered him because of it. A king betrayed by one of his noblemen? Once upon a time . . . that would have been reason to send a man to the block.

But why kill the man, rather than offer him better recompense in exchange for his continued loyalty? And why murder him in the grinding room? Why not follow him home in the evening and dispatch him there? No, the location and circumstances surrounding the murder suggested a burst of temper combined with an unexpected opportunity.

And that, once again, pointed to someone like Gus Abbott. But what reason would Gus have had to kill Ronald Mercer? And he had sounded indignant at the mere hint he had done so—just as Lydia Travers had sounded indignant at Miss Wickham's accusations against her. Trent as well—indignant and angry. But hadn't she learned that criminals are often the best liars? At least until they'd lied themselves into a corner.

But Lydia had presented a possibility they hadn't thought of before, that of Ronald Mercer having removed his own pattern book from his office and . . . and then did what with it? Promised to sell it to a competitor for a partnership? Perhaps the deal had gone sour and Mr. Mercer paid with his life.

As they neared the motorcar, the rear passenger door opened and Lady Phoebe stepped out onto the pavement. "I was beginning to worry, you were in there so long."

"All is well," Eva assured her. "Lydia—"

She broke off at the sound of abrupt footsteps coming from the direction of Lydia's building. Instinct sent a warning shiver down her spine. She turned to see a figure swathed in nondescript dark clothing rushing toward them. A hood created shadows around his face. Pain spread through Eva's shoulder as she was knocked aside. The force of the blow sent her sprawling onto her hands and knees, the cracked pavement biting into them. Hetta, shoved aside as well, screamed. Fright gripped Eva as their attacker yanked Lady Phoebe's arm with a vicious jolt. He just as quickly released her and ran off down the street. The door of the motorcar swung open and Douglas took off after their attacker.

"Eva, are you all right?" Lady Phoebe was beside her, grasping her arm and helping her up. Hetta took her other arm, and together they brought her to her feet just in time to see the back of Douglas disappear around the corner of the next street. Lady Phoebe massaged her arm and winced.

Eva answered Lady Phoebe's urgent question with one of her own. "My lady, did he hurt you? Is your arm broken?"

"He stole my handbag, but I believe I'm all right. Quickly, then, let's get back in the motorcar." Once they'd all slid in, she held up her empty hands. "I'd been holding my bag on my lap and stupidly kept holding on to it when I got out. Serves me right, I suppose. Hetta, are you hurt?"

"*Nein*, I am good. Madame? *Fraulein*?"

"My shoulder might be sore tomorrow." Lady Phoebe gave that shoulder a roll. "Eva?"

"Mine as well. And I'm a bit scraped." Eva stared down at her palms, just able to make out the abrasions on each. Then she raised her skirts to reveal the tears in the knees of her stockings. "It's as if that scoundrel had been waiting for us, for that exact moment."

"Here comes Douglas." Lady Phoebe pointed out the window. "And look—I believe he's got my bag."

"It could have been a random occurrence. A thief hoping for a hefty prize." Phoebe curled against the pillows on one side of her bed. Eva occupied the other side, although it had taken quite a bit of coaxing, on both Phoebe's and Amelia's parts, to persuade her to take such a liberty in their bedroom. It hadn't been the first time Eva had been thrust to the ground while pursuing information regarding a crime. Thank goodness, now, as then, her injuries appeared to be minor.

Amelia sat cross-legged at the foot of the bed, her back against one of the posts, while Julia sat in a nearby armchair. Hetta fussed over the tea tray, doling out shortbread biscuits onto plates.

"Do you really think so?" This came from Julia, with a heavy dose of skepticism. "That might explain why he took your bag, and not Eva's and Hetta's. He might have seen the difference in how you were all dressed, and perhaps heard Eva address you as 'my lady.' From what you've described, it seems as though this individual pushed Eva out of the way specifically to get at you."

"It happened so quickly, I don't see how he had time to make such a deduction. Besides, he gained nothing. My purse is still inside, what little money I had in it all there. So puzzling." Phoebe shook her head before accepting the cup of tea Hetta handed her. "I should have listened to you, Eva. I shouldn't have gone along."

"Since when do you ever listen to what anyone tells you?" Julia tipped her chin up and stared down Phoebe from between her lashes.

"It was a good thing you had Douglas with you," Amelia said. "If not for him, you wouldn't have gotten your bag back, Phoebe. And who knows what else that scrounger might have done? And a good thing Douglas wasn't hurt, either."

"It was an odd thing, really," Eva mused as Hetta handed her a cup of tea and placed a plate of shortbread between her and Phoebe. "He said the thief had dropped the bag as soon as he'd rounded the corner. Without Douglas having to fight him at all for it. You'd think our perpetrator would have tried harder than that to hold on to his prize."

"Douglas isn't a small man." Phoebe chose a biscuit and took a small bite. As she chewed, she said, "Perhaps the thief caught one glimpse of him and decided to play it safe."

"I suppose." Eva spoke absently, the rim of her teacup against her lips. She sipped, frowning in speculation.

In the morning Phoebe received a telephone call from Crown Lily.

"It's Percy Bateman, Lady Phoebe," she heard from across the wire. "I'm happy to tell you, I believe I've got the perfect pattern for your children's tea set."

"That's wonderful, Mr. Bateman. If you're free today, I'll come see it."

"Anytime, I'll be here."

Eva insisted on going with her. Fenton drove them in the Rolls-Royce, and Eva assumed her proper role as Phoebe's lady's maid. However, they had decided that once Phoebe went in to speak with Mr. Bateman, Eva would use the time to "sneak away" to the painting department. Despite the ongoing deception, Phoebe couldn't help smiling at the ruse, because as Fox had astutely pointed out yesterday, the notion of Eva leaving her in this manner was preposterous.

"Wait here with Fenton until I'm safely inside," Phoebe told her outside Crown Lily's administrative building. "That way anyone who sees you leave the motorcar will think you're acting on your own." Eva agreed and Phoebe made her way inside.

Mr. Bateman seemed to have taken greater care

with his appearance today, rather than looking disheveled as he usually did. "Lady Phoebe, do come in and make yourself comfortable." He wasted no time in spreading several sheets of paper out on the desk in front of her.

She leaned forward to study them. Two bore details of a bright geometric design that would embellish the borders of the cups, saucers, and plates. Another provided an up-close depiction of two beagle pups prancing in a hilly field of yellow and purple wildflowers. Phoebe recognized the lady's bedstraw, meadow cranesbill, and greater knapweed, all commonly found in the Cotswolds. A third page showed an intertwining of those same wildflowers with a *W* and an *A,* the Wroxly and Annondale initials. The diagram indicated this would be on the inside of the cup, just below the rim, and a fourth picture comprised all of the elements into the finished design. Her mouth dropped open.

"I can make changes," he said quickly. "Anything you suggest can be incorporated, or I could start over."

She slowly glanced up, loath to take her eyes off the pages. "Don't change a thing, Mr. Bateman. This is perfect. It's wonderful. It's as though you knew exactly what I wanted, before I myself knew. If I possessed the talent to do so, this is exactly what *I* would have designed for my future niece or nephew." She stood and reached a hand across the desk. "Thank you, Mr. Bateman. Thank you very much."

His anxious expression melted into one of sheer happiness. He came to his feet and gave her hand a hearty shake. "I'm so glad. To be honest, though I've designed a small amount of children's china, mostly keepsake mug-and-plate sets for toddlers, this is my first complete tea service for a child. I found it rather a challenge, and I don't mind telling you that I'm proud of the results."

"I can understand why." She smiled as she resumed her seat, realizing what a blow it would have been if she hadn't approved the design. "What's next?"

"Had you thought about the cup shape?"

"Yes, I believe something simple would be best, suitable for a child's hands."

"My thoughts exactly, and a simple, evenly cylindrical shape will show the pattern to its best advantage." He stood and went to his drawing table. From a shelf above it he took down a book and brought it back to the desk. The title was *Crown Lily Potteries Catalogue of Shapes*. He turned pages until he found what he was looking for. "This," he said, placing his finger on the page, "is our Martine shape, and as you can see, it will allow a smooth wrapping of the pattern around the cup, so that as you turn it, the pattern tells a story. It will, of course, be scaled down to a child's size."

"That's delightful. Yes, we'll go with that."

"Very good. If you'll wait here, I'll just be a few moments." He came around his desk. "I'll just need to check the production schedule and draw up a contract. In the meantime I'll ask Jessup to bring you some refreshments."

"That poor man seems to serve a lot of tea," Phoebe joked.

"It's part of his job, along with seeing to all of Mr. Tremaine's clerical needs."

"I should think you'd have your own secretary, Mr. Bateman."

"Me?" He pointed to himself with an expression of incredulity. "Goodness no, Lady Phoebe. I'm not nearly important enough to warrant having my own secretary. Now, if you'll excuse me . . ."

"Of course. But, please, no tea this time. I had quite a hearty breakfast earlier and couldn't consume another thing until much later." She crossed her fingers where he couldn't see them as she spoke the lie. He nodded and left the room.

Phoebe sat looking into the empty space where Percy Bateman had been. He had done a splendid job of the design—that, she couldn't deny. Did he really believe he wasn't important enough at Crown Lily to warrant personal assistance of his own? Without him and the other designers, there would be no Crown Lily. And she could easily see by the two designs he had accomplished for her family that he was at the top of his profession, at least in terms of talent and creativity. But not, perhaps, in terms of seniority or appreciation. Ronald Mercer had disparaged Mr. Bateman as inexperienced, his skills raw. Mr. Bateman couldn't have been ignorant of the other designer's opinion of him. It must have rankled.

The tea set for Julia's child was only one reason why she had come here today. If Mr. Bateman had wanted to order tea for her, he must anticipate being gone for more than a few minutes. What had he said? Ah, yes. He needed to check the production schedule and draw up a contract.

Phoebe got to her feet, closed the office door most of the way, and circled the desk. She decided to start with the top drawer on the right . . .

Eva quickly covered her pigments jars and cleaned off her brushes. As the other women filed out of the painting department for their luncheon break, she stayed behind. Moira Wickham moved from her worktable to the adjoining storage room. Making certain the last woman had gone, Eva crossed the room and stood in the storeroom doorway. She absently rubbed at her shoulder, still aching from last night's frightening encounter. "I'll have to be going now. My employer will wonder where I am, otherwise. She may already be looking for me."

Miss Wickham nodded absently. "Don't get

into trouble." She moved some items around on a shelf, filling in the spaces with plain, unpainted china from a cart that had been delivered a short while ago. "Then again, let her make a fuss. It's not as though you're planning to continue in her service, is it?"

"No, I don't suppose it is."

"Suppose?" Miss Wickham stacked one last cup on the shelf and turned to face Eva. "Having second thoughts, are we?"

Eva hesitated, but only briefly. "No. I'm set on making the change, or I wouldn't be here now." Yet, she let the tiniest smidgeon of doubt enter her voice. She didn't want to appear overly confident or Miss Wickham might become suspicious. Better to let her believe Eva entertained a few qualms, not to mention fears, as most women in her position would.

That seemed to satisfy the other woman. "Good. I'd hate to think I've been training you for no good reason."

"It was a surprise when Lady Phoebe announced she wished to order another tea set, this one for her sister's child. Wouldn't it be something if it were me that applied paint to some of the pieces?"

"It would be something, indeed." A mixture of irony and disappointment in Miss Wickham's expression gave Eva the opportunity she'd hoped for.

"I can't help but wonder what sort of design Mr. Bateman has come up with. A children's theme doesn't seem the kind of subject to interest a man." She glanced down at the reddened abrasions left on her palms by her fall last night. At least the wounds had been minor and hadn't prevented her from wielding her paintbrushes today. "I wonder if he's up to the challenge."

Miss Wickham shrugged. "It's no different, really, from designing for ladies. Flowers, ribbons, and bows . . . men design those, too."

"True, but when I think of what a woman might be capable of, I can't help but wonder." Eva injected a wistfulness into her words. "Take you, for example. I'm sure you could design an enchanting child's set."

Miss Wickham didn't answer, but a sudden shimmer of tears made her blink and took Eva aback.

"Have you designed for children? That night at the pub you said you'd show me some of your patterns, but you never have. There's no one else here now, and I'd love to see."

The other woman stared hard at Eva; an obvious internal debate was taking place inside her. Finally she nodded and said, "Come with me."

She brought Eva to her workspace and unlocked a bottom drawer. Reaching in, she pulled out a leather-bound portfolio, pulled free the leather

251

cord holding it closed, and spread the cover open on the flat surface of her tabletop. Slowly she began turning pages, allowing Eva to view each drawing before showing her the next. Eva sank into the chair while Miss Wickham stood over her shoulder, continuing to turn pages. Many of the designs reminded her of those she had seen on the finished teacups in the showroom and the conference room the first day she had arrived here with the Renshaws. They were certainly as intricate and as lovely.

She saw more than common creativity here, more than mere skill with a pencil and sketchbook. Though she herself might be no expert, every instinct told her—insisted—Moira Wickham possessed artistic brilliance. Miss Wickham had told her she had, on more than one occasion, shown her designs to Ronald Mercer. Each time he had dismissed her efforts as not good enough. How could he have said such a thing? Clearly, he could not have believed it; no one looking at these designs could. Had it been his wish to prevent a woman from advancing, or something even more devious? Had he, perhaps, borrowed on her brilliance and taken the credit?

Then again, had Moira Wickham borrowed on his? That would have been easier, after all, as anyone could study Crown Lily's finished china and take ideas from that. Which was it? Eva couldn't say—not yet. But if Ronald Mercer's pattern book was found, would it reveal the answer? Or would it merely further confound the question?

Miss Wickham flipped the page again, and there, staring up at Eva, were the cherubic faces and plump, dimpled limbs of small children posed with puppies, kittens, bunny rabbits, and other furry creatures. Adorable and whimsical, these designs captured the essence of childhood innocence and roused an inexplicable yearning in Eva for . . . good heavens . . . for a child to hold and care for.

How extraordinary a reaction to mere pictures! She tried to shake the sensation away, silently calling herself a sentimental fool. But she couldn't deny that Miss Wickham had created a vision of childhood that made Eva ache both for what she had once been, long ago, and what she might someday become.

"You're quiet," Miss Wickham said, pulling Eva back to the present. "Tell me, do you like what I've done?"

"Oh, yes." Eva drew in a breath, groping for adequate words. "They're exquisite."

"Yes." Miss Wickham's agreement held cynicism rather than conceit. "I'm afraid no one will ever see them."

Eva again heard more than simple words, but rather a very real fear that Miss Wickham would never be recognized for her talents, never be given the opportunity to reach her potential. Eva twisted to look up at her. "Don't say that. Times are changing. You'll get your chance."

"Times aren't changing fast enough. At least not at Crown Lily." She shook her head sadly. "I suggested months ago we should have a dedicated children's department. People want such wares nowadays, I believe. Your employer does. Neither Mr. Mercer nor Mr. Tremaine took the idea seriously. Said there wouldn't be enough demand, but I believe sentiments have grown stronger toward the ideals of childhood. Perhaps it was the war that's done it, leaving people to harken back to a more innocent time."

Eva nodded. How often had she envisioned herself and her siblings as children, when they were still all together and so unaware of the tragedy their family would suffer? It was more than nostalgia. The image of the boy her brother Danny had been lived inside her always, and would for the rest of her life. It was all she had left of him, except for a few photographs. He had been the youngest, the baby, and having two older sisters had taught him to be patient and kind, to listen rather than always speak, to wait his turn rather than make demands. He'd have made a fine husband and father someday, but that day would never come because Danny had been one of nearly a million men who never came home from the war.

Yes, Eva could understand how the war had reshaped how people viewed childhood, how violence and loss had brought about a yearning for and a celebration of innocence.

Then she realized what Miss Wickham had said: *Times aren't changing fast enough. At least not at Crown Lily.* The implication of those words struck her. "You're thinking of moving to a new company, aren't you?"

"I didn't say that, did I? Don't worry, I won't be abandoning you anytime soon. But you mustn't tell anyone what I've shown you. I do have an eventual plan. If you mind your p's and q's, perhaps I'll include you in that plan. Until then, no more questions about it."

CHAPTER 14

Phoebe reached back to the coil of her hair and slid a hairpin free. Eva had taught her how to pick a lock some time ago and she fully intended to make use of the skill now. The top two drawers flanking each side of Mr. Bateman's desk were unlocked, and a quick search had wrought nothing but the typical items one would expect to find in an office; she had discovered nothing incriminating. The bottom two on each side, and the one long one in the middle above the kneehole, were locked. Crouching, she inserted the pin into the bottom drawer on her right. When the lock didn't give immediately, she held her breath, steadied her hand, and willed herself not to let impatience foil her plans.

After another try the lock clicked and she slid the drawer open. Still unsure what she was looking for, other than Ronald Mercer's stolen pattern book, she discovered boxes of pencils, brushes, pastels, and other art supplies. Tools of his trade, all fine quality, and she could understand why he kept them locked up. Every minute or so, she paused to scan the doorway and listen for footsteps.

The bottom drawer on the other side yielded similar results, along with sketchbooks of high-quality paper. A final drawer loomed, and after pausing to monitor activity in the corridor, she set to work once again with her hairpin.

A single item rested inside, and her heart trilled when a leather-bound book revealed itself to her. Closer scrutiny, however, disclosed this to be Percy Bateman's own pattern book. She flipped through, discovering elements, each one numbered, similar to those he had assembled to create her grandparents' china pattern, leading her to understand that he hadn't created the design from thin air, but from previous ideas he could rearrange in scores of different combinations. She turned more pages and came upon a loose sheaf of paper that had been tucked inside. It bore a floral pattern she didn't remember seeing before, surrounded by a delicate geometric design. It wasn't numbered like the others.

She almost disregarded it as an afterthought Mr. Bateman must have had, perhaps an inspiration he sketched at home and had slipped in with the rest. But something in the lines held her attention. She studied the shading, the places where he had applied more pressure to his pencil, and where he had lightened his hand. Then she compared the drawing to those on the pages of the book.

She flipped through several more, and soon found another loose page. This one presented a scene of two children seated at a garden table amid trees and flowers that bore balloons rather than foliage. A rabbit peeked at them from behind a tuft of grass. Why hadn't he shown her this sketch?

Again, something in the execution of the picture made it stand out from the others in the book, as if . . . yes, as if someone else had drawn it.

Voices from down the hallway drew a startled gasp. Quickly she closed the book, replaced it in the desk, and closed the drawer. She could not relock it or the bottom ones; her talents extended only to picking locks, not securing them. She could only hope Mr. Bateman didn't need to open either drawer when he returned. When he discovered them unlocked, would he believe he'd neglected to lock them? Probably not.

Circling the desk, she resumed her seat, and with another gasp realized she still held the sketch of the children. The voices continued, and she recognized Mr. Bateman's. Dare she attempt to return the loose page to the book? Would she have time?

Footsteps provided the answer: no. With little other choice she opened her handbag and shoved it in, burrowing it down deep beneath her purse, handkerchief, and her comb and mirror. Her fingers came in contact with another bit of paper. Puzzled, she latched onto it with two fingers and drew it out. Torn from a larger piece of paper, it unfolded to reveal words that had been hastily scrawled and half smeared, but she could make them out:

A thief, a cheat, and a murderer, rolled into one. Mischief at Crown Lily is far from done.

In the hallway the footsteps had stopped, and she could again hear voices. She re-read the words twice over. What on earth? And when had this message found its way into her bag?

The assault. Good heavens, Douglas hadn't halted a theft in progress. Thievery had never been the intention, but, instead, delivering this taunting note. But why such an elaborate ruse?

Her wrists and temples hammered with impatience. Hearing Percy Bateman and another man continuing to discuss whatever it was, for she couldn't make out what they were saying, she wished he would hurry back and let her sign the contract. She wanted to find Eva and show her the note, and then the two of them could put their heads together to divine what the devil it could mean.

There was also the matter of Mr. Bateman's unlocked desk drawers. She needed to leave before he discovered them.

Waiting for him to return, then, would be a mistake. Gathering up her things, she set off down the corridor, searching until she found him just inside the open doorway of another office, a narrow rectangular room that contained several desks positioned along the outer wall overlooking the enclosure. At each desk sat a man, absorbed in his work, some of them tapping away at typewriters. Mr. Bateman apparently heard her approach; he turned toward her with a surprised expression.

She spoke before he could question her. "I just remembered, I have an appointment . . . um . . . with my sister. I mustn't be late. If you have the contract, I'll sign it and be on my way. If not, I'll have to come back another time." Never mind that returning would be risky, once he discovered she had gone through his desk.

His puzzlement changed to alarm. A man sitting behind the nearest desk watched with interest as Mr. Bateman stammered, "P-please . . . ah . . . don't go, Lady Phoebe. We have your contract right here." He gestured at the man at the desk. "Why don't we step back into my office . . ."

"There isn't time." Phoebe stepped over the threshold, but only just. "Can't I sign it here?"

"Actually, it's not quite ready yet." He gestured again, this time at the typewriter on the man's desk. A page sat halfway down on the platen. The other occupants of the room glanced up from their work, but otherwise pretended not to notice the encounter. "This is one of our financial secretaries, Charles Hadley. He's filling out the necessary terms, pattern and shape numbers, dates, and payments. It shouldn't be another minute." He turned to the other man. "Isn't that right, Hadley?"

"Another few minutes and we'll be done." He offered Phoebe a deferential nod.

Mr. Bateman went to Phoebe and offered her his arm. "Come, let's return to my office and Hadley will bring the contract as soon as it's ready."

Phoebe thought fast. "I'd prefer to go to the showroom, actually, where you can point out more of your designs." The implied flattery brought a satisfied gleam to his countenance, telling Phoebe she'd hit upon the right ruse. "When friends admire the two sets you've created for us, I'd like to be able to tell them what other sorts of things you've created."

About half an hour later a relieved Phoebe joined Eva back at the Rolls-Royce. "And then we ended up back in his office," she said, having explained events up to that point, "where I dreaded at every moment he'd discover the drawers I'd unlocked. I nearly choked when he couldn't find a pen. Lucky for me, he found one under a folder on his desk. I signed the contract and hurried away."

"When he attempts to unlock those drawers, they won't open, because he'll have actually locked them," Eva reasoned. "Perhaps he'll simply think the mechanisms stuck, try again and think nothing of it."

"Perhaps. But there's actually no reason now for me to return to Crown Lily, so I needn't

261

encounter Percy Bateman again. He can think what he likes." She gazed out the window as Fenton maneuvered the motorcar into the largest of the quadrangles and headed for the front gate. Despite her cavalier pronouncement, a fear niggled at her. "Unless, of course, Percy Bateman is our killer, and he decides he must ensure my silence." She opened her handbag. "Eva, look at this."

Eva's blood ran cold at the implications of the note Lady Phoebe had found in her handbag. They had been purposely singled out last night in Lydia Travers's neighborhood. Watched. Waited for. The very notion sent ripples of dread through her.

She read the words again. *A thief, a cheat, and a murderer, rolled into one . . .*

"We need to bring this to the police, my lady."

"I couldn't agree more. But will that ensure our safety, or anyone's, for that matter? Why this attempt to be poetic? And why the charade of snatching my handbag? I fear there will be another murder at Crown Lily. The question remains whether the person who slipped me this note is the killer, or knows the identity of the killer. But if he meant well, why not simply approach us with information?"

"I suspect because Lydia's neighborhood lies so close to the factory. There must be quite a number

262

of workers housed there, including, possibly, the killer. Our would-be thief apparently didn't want to be seen giving us information."

"Even information as cryptic as this?" Lady Phoebe let go an ironic chuckle. "I feel more as if we're being toyed with than assisted in any way. Why didn't this person simply tell us who the murderer is? But I have more to show you." She again opened her bag and retrieved the drawing she'd inadvertently stolen from Percy Bateman's pattern book. She handed it to Eva and explained where she'd found it.

Immediate recognition left Eva speechless. The chubby faces of the children, the whimsical nature of the colorful balloon trees . . . hadn't she gazed at such designs barely half an hour ago? Yes, she felt quite sure she had.

"I recognize this. Or, not this exact sketch, but the style. Before I left the painting room, Moira Wickham showed me some of her designs. This looks very much like something she would do."

Lady Phoebe exhibited no surprise. "I thought it stood out as different from the rest of Mr. Bateman's work. I could see it immediately. He must have stolen this sketch from Miss Wickham, along with another one I saw in his book, and who knows how many more. For all I know, the very pattern I chose for Julia's child might have been designed by Miss Wickham."

Eva handed back the sketch. "I wonder how he

could have stolen it. She keeps her book under lock and key."

"As does Percy Bateman, but that didn't stop me, did it?"

"Good point. But . . ." Eva shook her head, puzzled by one inescapable fact. "Once the set has been formed and the pattern transferred onto the china, it will be sent up to the painting department. Miss Wickham is sure to see it then. Won't she realize her idea has been stolen and cry foul?"

Lady Phoebe thought this over, staring down at the pattern. "Perhaps she'll be afraid to. It would be her word against Percy Bateman's, and who is more likely to get the sack? The man or the woman?"

"Yes, once again you raise a good point. But I've gotten to know Moira Wickham a bit. She's no shrinking violet, I can tell you that. I cannot imagine her allowing anyone to take such blatant advantage of her."

"And yet it certainly appears as if Mr. Bateman is doing just that . . . unless . . ." Lady Phoebe trailed off, chewing her bottom lip. "Unless these patterns—and Moira Wickham's—are Ronald Mercer's."

The possibility startled Eva. "You mean . . . his patterns were stolen by both Moira Wickham and Percy Bateman?" That possibility led to yet another. "If that's the case, perhaps they both had a hand in Ronald Mercer's death."

"Or," Lady Phoebe began slowly, her features tight as she obviously tried to work it out, "it could be that Miss Wickham stole Ronald Mercer's pattern book, and Mr. Bateman knows and feels free to borrow from it whenever he likes. Or he's been sneaking peeks at it on the sly. And if he's been doing that, at the very least it makes him complicit in Ronald Mercer's death, doesn't it?"

"Yes, if not his murderer." Eva attempted to recall the other patterns Moira Wickham had shown her, and remembered thinking she had seen similar ones among the finished china in the showroom. "Yes, Moira Wickham might have the stolen pattern book. In fact, what she showed me today might have been Ronald Mercer's book. There were no markings to indicate who it belonged to."

"Were there pattern numbers in her book?" Lady Phoebe asked.

Eva again tried to envision the details she had seen. Numbers were not something she would have taken note of, because she'd been too engrossed in the artwork. She narrowed her eyes, considering . . . and then, "No, there weren't any. None I recall. Just the sketches."

Lady Phoebe sat back and stared out the window. "Then it's improbable that what you saw was Ronald Mercer's pattern book. In Mr. Bateman's, every pattern had a number. It's part of the process of registering the pattern to both the company and the artist's name." She returned her attention to the sketch in her lap. "Only this one, and the other like it, had no numbers."

"We should show it to the police then, when we bring the note you found in your handbag."

"Should we? What would we say? Here's a stray sketch found in Percy Bateman's pattern book, which, by the way, I stole from him. It looks like something Moira Wickham would draw. Either or both of them, therefore, must have murdered Ronald Mercer."

Eva chuckled. "I don't suppose they'd take us seriously."

"No. But they will have to take the note seriously." Lady Phoebe leaned forward. "Fenton, bring us to the Langston Police Station downtown." The motorcar turned a corner and headed away from Lyndale Park.

"Who would ever think something as unthreatening as china would turn out to be so . . . well . . . threatening." Eva sighed.

At the police station, a uniformed constable accepted the note from Lady Phoebe, took their names and preliminary statements, and had them sit in a waiting area. After nearly half an hour he returned and led them to Detective Inspector Hugh Nichols's office. The man looked distinctly annoyed by their visit, as if he had much more important matters to attend to. Still, he bid them sit down as he perused the note.

"Why didn't you report this robbery last night?" he mumbled without looking up.

"We would have done," Lady Phoebe said, "but as nothing had been taken from my bag, what was there to report? A rude encounter with someone who knocked into us."

"He did seize your handbag."

"But then he dropped it when our driver took off after him. We were shaken by the incident, but unharmed. Isn't that right, Eva?"

"It is, Detective. The first thing Lady Phoebe did upon Douglas handing her back her handbag was to check inside for her purse. Since it was there, we were only too happy to return home."

The man leaned back in his chair and regarded them from beneath hooded lids. "Can you describe the culprit?"

Eva and Lady Phoebe looked at each other and shook their heads. Eva replied for both of them. "It was dark, and it happened so fast, we didn't have time to notice his features, which was another reason we didn't report the incident right away."

Frowning, Detective Inspector Nichols turned the note over and back, studying both sides of the ragged piece of paper. "What were you doing in that neighborhood at that time of night?" The question rang with an implied accusation. Eva had a ready answer for him, even if it wasn't the entire truth.

"A young woman was given the sack from the Crown Lily painting department, and I wished to bring her some food and a small amount of money to see her through until she finds a new situation."

"Did you, now?"

Both Eva and Lady Phoebe nodded.

"And why such philanthropy in a town you don't live in, for someone you can't know at all well?"

Good heavens, he made it sound as though they were the criminals, sneaking around for no good purpose. Apparently, Lady Phoebe thought so, too, for she raised her chin and said, "Is it wrong to help another, no matter how well we may or may not know her?"

"Hmm. I suppose not. Would this individual—what is her name?"

Eva and Lady Phoebe traded glances. Eva said, "We don't wish to drag her into this. We left her at her flat and she had no involvement in what happened next. We don't want to complicate her life any further. Her circumstances are difficult enough."

That earned another *hmm*. "Are you sure she had no involvement? After all, the pair of you shows up at her door bearing gifts, and the next thing you know, someone attempts to steal Lady Phoebe's bag. Coincidence? Probably not. I certainly wouldn't put it past anyone living in that neighborhood."

"Actually, I didn't accompany Miss Huntford to the door of the flat. Another of our maids did. One who doesn't speak much English, so I don't think she could be of much help in the matter," Lady Phoebe added hastily.

Eva nodded inwardly. The last thing they needed was to upset Hetta with a trip to the police station to give evidence.

"Detective Inspector, this note is certainly a clue about who killed Ronald Mercer."

If Lady Phoebe sounded the tiniest bit condescending, Eva couldn't blame her.

"We don't understand it, nor do we have the means to attempt to trace it to its origin, which is why we brought it to you," Lady Phoebe continued.

"You brought it to me," he replied sternly, "because to do otherwise would be obstructing an official police investigation."

"Well," Lady Phoebe quipped back, "we didn't have to say a word about it, did we? And yet here we are."

"Hmm. Yes, thank you for doing your civic duty, my lady." The detective inspector opened one of many folders strewn across his desk and added the note to the assortment of papers inside. Without looking up at them he said, "Thank you, ladies. If that's all, have a good day."

Eva stifled a gasp. Did this man just summarily dismiss the Earl of Wroxly's granddaughter?

How dare he? She opened her mouth to issue a scathing reprimand when Lady Phoebe grasped her arm.

"Thank you, Detective Inspector. Eva, shall we?"

Eva found herself sputtering as she came to her feet. Lady Phoebe appealed to her with a lift of her eyebrow, then mouthed, "Not now," and guided her out the door. When they were safely in the motorcar, Lady Phoebe, with a determined look on her face, turned to Eva.

"I think we need to pay another visit to Lydia Travers. The detective inspector is correct. She might have had a hand in what happened last night. It could have been her way of telling us something she hadn't wished to say outright to our faces. Can you be sure there wasn't someone else in that flat with you, hiding somewhere?"

"It would have been quite a challenge to hide someone in so small a place." Eva thought back. "But then again, we didn't look under the bed."

"Or, for all we know, Lydia Travers herself came after you and Hetta."

"But it was a man that attacked us."

"Or did we only assume it was a man? This wouldn't be the first time we've made that misjudgment, would it?"

Eva couldn't but concede the truth of Lady Phoebe's words. It wasn't impossible that Lydia Travers owned a pair of trousers she could have slipped on, along with the hooded jacket their attacker had worn. As she had told Detective Inspector Nichols, it had happened so fast, and now that time had passed, neither she nor Lady Phoebe could conjure enough of a description of their attacker to be sure either way. A man? A woman?

Lydia Travers?

"One thing is certain," Eva said. "The good detective inspector isn't taking us seriously. So then, when do you wish to return to Lydia's flat?"

"Tonight. After dark. We'll bring Douglas again, this time right to her door."

CHAPTER 15

Phoebe and Eva returned home to a surprise. Upon entering through the front door, Phoebe expected Jester to come running to greet them, as he usually did. As Carmichael helped them off with their things, there were no happy yips, no clicking of his feet running across the tiles. Had something happened to him? Had someone opened a door, and he ran off?

"Carmichael, where is—"

And then the sound of voices reached her ears. She heard her sisters and Fox speaking, and then another male voice, which assuredly did not belong to Ernest.

"Is that . . ." Eva didn't complete the question. She didn't need to. They hurried into the drawing room.

"Trent! You're out of . . ." It was Phoebe's turn to trail off, as quite obviously the boy no longer languished in a jail cell. Jester sat at his master's feet, his chin resting on Trent's knee as he gazed up at Trent with adoring eyes. Never had she seen an animal look so blissful. "But . . . how? Have the police found . . ." She trailed off again, not wanting to say *your father's murderer.*

"Hello, Phoebe." He nodded to Eva. "Miss Huntford. Yes, I'm out, for now." Trent Mercer didn't look nearly as happy as Phoebe would have expected. She soon discovered why. "I'm still a suspect. In fact, still their main suspect, and should I go sneaking off, you'll all be in a good deal of trouble with the police."

"I don't understand." Phoebe gazed at each of her siblings in turn, hoping one of them might enlighten her.

Julia raised a hand as if answering a question in the schoolroom. "It was me, actually. I arranged it."

Incredulous, Phoebe went to the settee and sat beside Amelia, who smiled and curled her arm through Phoebe's. "How on earth did you manage it?"

"You're not the only clever member of this family, you know." Julia's eyebrows slashed inward. "So don't look so dumbfounded."

"I'm not . . ." Phoebe started to say more, but upon second thought she let it go. "Tell me how you accomplished this, please."

Julia shrugged a shoulder. "I simply applied all the pressure of a viscountess, an earl, and a marquess."

Phoebe felt no more informed than a moment ago. "I don't understand."

"It turns out there's quite a tradition of Annondale philanthropy here in Langston. In fact, throughout all of Staffordshire. A lot of people here depend on it. I assured the police and the local magistrate the tradition would continue, once my son assumed the title, provided they did me one small favor now."

Phoebe didn't state the obvious, that no one could predict whether Julia's child would be a boy or not. Apparently, her persuasive powers had been enough to sway the court. "But you said an earl and a marquess. I assume the earl is Grampapa. Did you telephone home and tell them of the situation?" If so, Phoebe thought, they could expect a summons home at any moment.

"No, I didn't have to. Using Grampapa's name was enough. As was using Theo's." Julia's lips spread in a self-satisfied grin. "I did ring Theo, however, to discuss the matter with him first. He agreed it was the best use of the Allerton title since he'd inherited it."

As Julia spoke, Phoebe could feel Amelia's arm tighten around her own. Julia's mention of Theo Leighton, Marquess of Allerton, obviously met with their younger sister's approval, not to mention her excitement. Phoebe flexed her arm slightly to encourage Amelia to loosen her hold. But Amelia had been hoping for Julia and Theo to reunite, once Julia's official period of mourning ended in the spring. Did this communication between them signify their relationship might take up where it had left off, sooner rather than later? It had astonished them all two summers ago when Julia had suddenly stopped associating

274

with Theo and encouraged Gilbert Townsend to court her.

Phoebe had known the exact reason why—they all had. Theo had inherited a nearly bankrupt estate from his brother, while the Viscount Annondale had fortune enough to sustain several estates, Foxwood Hall among them. Julia had seen marrying Gil Townsend as an obligation to the Earldom of Wroxly—to her grandparents, to the people of Little Barlow, and to Fox. But, oh, what a price Julia and all of them, Theo included, had paid for her sacrifice.

Phoebe knew better than to question her now about Theo. Instead she focused on Trent. "You know, of course, you're welcome to stay with us for as long as you like."

Trent stroked Jester's head and neck. He drew a deep breath and let it out slowly. "It's not as if my life will ever get back to normal. I won't be able to return to school. I suppose I'll ask Mr. Tremaine if I might stay on at Crown Lily." He didn't sound at all pleased about the prospect.

"That's not true, old boy." Fox sat up straighter. "There's no one to prevent you from going back to Eton now that . . ." Like Phoebe, Fox apparently realized how mentioning his father's death would impact Trent, and left off. "Well, you'll be able to go back, you'll see. The police will clear your name and you'll . . . Well, you should be able to pay your tuition with . . ."

With his inheritance, Phoebe knew he'd been about to say.

"And if not, I'll talk to our grandfather. He'll figure out a way. He was an Eton boy himself. He knows lots of people on the board of trustees."

Trent shrugged, his expression glum. "We'll see."

Phoebe's heart clenched to see the boy so dispirited. She supposed she would be, too, after spending several nights in that awful jail. She certainly remembered Julia exhibiting the same behavior after being incarcerated at the Cowes Police Station, as if all the life had simply been wrung out of her, leaving an empty shell. Phoebe clung to the notion that Julia had recovered quickly enough, once she had regained her freedom—or had she?

Perhaps that time still haunted her, which might explain some of the decisions she had made in recent months. Trent shouldn't be left alone, Phoebe decided. He needed people around him, to support him and restore his sense of well-being. To allow him to enjoy the remainder of his childhood. Fox was right. If Trent had no one else, they must talk to their grandparents and convince them to become his guardians, if it were possible.

Phoebe later knocked softly on Julia's door. Julia had gone in only minutes ago to lie down, and Phoebe was fairly certain she'd still be awake. She wasn't wrong.

"Yes, come in," came Julia's voice from inside.

Phoebe discovered Julia sitting up in bed with a book open on her lap. "Oh, good. I didn't want to wake you."

"No, I don't think I'll sleep, but an hour alone with my feet up always does me wonders."

Phoebe smiled. Though considered outgoing and sociable, Julia had always retreated to the privacy of her bedroom when feeling overwhelmed or put upon by those around her. Which was it today? Or was she merely fatigued because of her condition?

"Thank you for what you did for Trent."

Julia frowned and closed the book, using a ribbon to hold her place. "You needn't thank me. Trent already has. Several times, as a matter of fact."

"Yes, I'm sure he has, but—"

"You're surprised. You don't tend to believe I'd lift a finger to help someone, do you?"

"Julia, why do you turn everything into an argument?"

Julia laid her book aside. "Because I think you enjoy believing it's up to you to save the world, and having someone else step in, once in a while, throws you off your game."

"That's ridiculous. If I thought that, why did I come here to thank you for helping Trent?"

"To maintain the upper hand. But here's something perhaps you don't understand. As a mother-to-be, it was impossible for me to sit by and watch a child suffer, even one who is nearly grown. It could be my son someday, and if I'm not there to help him, I can only hope someone else will." Julia pinched her lips, and then said, "Oh, I forgot. He'll have you, Auntie Phoebe, to save the day."

Phoebe sighed and left her sister to her own thoughts. She'd like to think Julia didn't mean it when she said such things, that her apprehensions concerning impending motherhood and an uncertain future were to blame. But Julia's resentments were nothing new, had been apparent for years now. And, as always, they were aimed at Phoebe—not Amelia, not their grandparents, not Fox. Phoebe alone shouldered the burden of Julia's rancor, and while Julia had once explained to her the reasons for it, she had never apologized—not really—or made much of an effort to change.

And yet, Phoebe wouldn't abandon her. Because the thing Julia never said, but couldn't quite hide, was that she needed Phoebe. Even if it was merely to have someone to argue with, Julia habitually sought her out, and that said something.

Once evening had fallen, she and Eva again climbed into the touring car with Douglas, though without Hetta this time. Phoebe and Eva had also left their handbags at home, and dressed in dark clothing. They retraced their route through Langston to the neighborhood that abutted the Crown Lily precincts. The streets looked very much as they had the night before, except for a light but steady drizzle that kept most people indoors.

"I hope we'll find her at home," Eva said as they drew near the street where Lydia Travers lived. Douglas brought the motorcar closer to Lydia's building this time and accompanied them inside.

Eva led the way to the top floor, then around the corner and partway down the upstairs hall. "This one."

Douglas stepped forward and knocked. No answer came. They waited another moment, and then Phoebe nodded for Douglas to knock again. As he did, she called out, "Miss Travers? Are you at home? Miss Travers?"

Douglas resumed knocking, louder this time.

The door directly at the top of the stairs swung open. "She's not there. Stop your yammering and off with you."

Phoebe turned toward this man she assumed to be Lydia Travers's neighbor, and did her best not to show her distaste. But a more unsavory individual she could not imagine, with his hair falling in strings about his face, his dirty linen shirt stretched over an unsightly paunch, and gaping holes where teeth should have been.

Those teeth that had managed to cling to their sockets couldn't have seen a toothbrush in many a year. "I'm terribly sorry to bother you," she said. "We're looking for Miss Travers. You say she's not home? Do you know where we might find her?"

"How in the hell am I supposed to know where the hussy spends her time?"

Douglas started forward, no doubt in a temper over the man's rudeness, but Phoebe stopped him with a hand on his forearm. "As I said, we're sorry to bother you. We'll try again another time."

She hoped he'd retreat back into his flat, as she didn't relish the notion of having to pass so close to him on their way back down the stairs. Could he be the individual who snatched her handbag last night? She didn't think their attacker had been as round as this man, nor could she envision him outrunning Douglas.

He remained on his threshold, staring at them through slightly unfocused eyes. "What do the three of you want with 'er, anyway? Why's she so popular all of a sudden? Never been before."

This caught Phoebe's interest. "What do you mean, *all of a sudden?* Has someone else been here today?"

The man shrugged. "Couple o' blokes here earlier, looking for 'er."

"Did they find her?" Phoebe asked him.

He gestured at her door with his chin. "Went in for a time. Ha! Don't think I don't know what that means, the little trollop. But you three . . ." He gave a snide laugh. His eyes went small and mean. "Wouldn'ta pegged her for this sort o' thing."

Phoebe couldn't stop Douglas fast enough. He surged toward the other man, fists in the air. "I'll thank you to shut your trap. You'd better get back inside before I shove a fist down your impertinent throat."

"Douglas, no!" But Phoebe needn't have worried. The man had stepped back and slammed his door before Douglas had finished his threat. Phoebe blew out a breath and reached for Eva's hand.

Eva's fingers curled around Phoebe's. "We'd best be going, my lady."

"I'm sorry, my lady. But he pushed too far." Douglas curled his fists again, as if savoring the very thought of using them on Miss Travers's neighbor—as if such a civil term could be used to describe the insolent baggage. Douglas and Eva started for the stairs, but Phoebe lingered by Miss Travers's door another moment. She thought, perhaps . . .

She tried the latch and it moved readily. "It's open." She gave an inward push, slowly, her breath suspended and her nerves buzzing, because she knew an unlocked door, especially in this neighborhood, could only be an ill omen. "Miss Travers?"

It took her only a second or two to take in the tiny flat—and the figure lying across the bed, a leather strap wrapped around her neck so tightly the flesh bulged above and below it, her arm and one foot hanging limply over the side.

Eva hadn't expected to find herself at the police station that night, but she, Lady Phoebe, and Douglas sat together in what looked to her like an interrogation room designed to encourage cooperation with its utter lack of human comforts. Bright light poured down from bare bulbs dangling from the ceiling, hard wooden chairs sat on either side of an equally inhospitable oak table, and no one offered a beverage to help warm them. They'd been here for a quarter hour, according to the locket watch pinned to her shirtwaist. She believed she could speak for them all in saying they were exhausted, shaken, and very badly wished to go home.

Not that anyone had asked or was likely to.

"Are you sure you don't want my coat, my lady?" For the second time Douglas began to unbutton his overcoat, but Lady Phoebe shook her head.

"No, you keep it. I'm truly not cold. Only . . ." She shivered. "I've been wondering if Miss Travers's death is our fault."

"Of course not, my lady," Douglas was quick to reply. "How could it have been?"

Eva wished she could offer a similar reassurance, but she hadn't Douglas's conviction. But when another thought jolted through her, she couldn't help but speak it aloud. "I do hope there are plenty of people at Lyndale Park who can swear to Trent's whereabouts tonight—all night."

"My goodness, Eva, you're right. First he's released, and now Miss Travers is dead. Surely, the police won't think . . . but, of course, they might." Lady Phoebe shut her eyes and wrapped her arms around herself, prompting Douglas once more to look concerned about her comfort.

The door opened and Detective Inspector Nichols strode in. Without a word he circled the table and took a seat facing them. He bent forward, braced on his elbows. "Now, then."

Eva forewent chastising him for neglecting to greet Lady Phoebe properly. It would only irritate him and he already looked plenty irritated, and had been since discovering them at Lydia Travers's flat. After finding the poor girl laid out in such ghastly disregard across her bed, they'd sent Douglas to find a telephone, which he had finally located at an inn several streets away. He'd telephoned the police, while Eva and Lady Phoebe had stayed with Lydia—with the body. They'd locked the door behind him and made sure to touch nothing until he returned with the police. It had been difficult, as both Eva and Lady Phoebe had wished to cover Miss Travers and bring dignity to her death.

When the detective inspector arrived, he had treated them to disgusted looks. He had also silenced them and sent them outside as he and two constables took an account of the crime scene. When he finally exited the building, he'd ordered them to meet him here, at the station. Judging by his expression now, Eva could see that his mood hadn't changed.

"What were you all doing there?" he abruptly asked. "And don't tell me you went to deliver more charity."

They looked at each other uncertainly, and then Lady Phoebe spoke. "No. We went hoping to speak with Lydia, to find out who had accosted us last night, and why. Obviously, we were too late."

"Obviously." He studied them for several long, squirm-inducing moments. "Let me fully understand you. After being targeted the first time you went to Lydia Travers's flat, you all thought it would be a good idea to venture into the same neighborhood again. At night."

When he put it that way, Eva couldn't but agree their plan sounded daft.

Lady Phoebe explained their actions. "We would not have done it if you had taken us seriously when we came to you earlier today.

But you dismissed the note we brought you as irrelevant and—"

"I did no such thing," he interrupted. "What the h . . . er, that is . . . what gave you that idea?"

"Why, your own actions, the way you dismissed us."

Eva added her agreement with an emphatic nod.

"Even now," Lady Phoebe went on, "where is Mr. Grimes? Why haven't you brought him in?" She spoke of Lydia's neighbor, as they now knew he was called. "He saw Lydia Travers's killers. He told us he saw two men who came by her flat—"

"What Edwin Grimes saw earlier this afternoon was me and my associate. As he had nothing else to add, I saw no reason to drag him down to the station."

"You and . . . ?" Lady Phoebe shook her head. "But we never told you who we'd been to see yesterday."

The detective inspector laughed grimly. "How difficult do you think it was for me to find out who you'd visited? A few questions on the street. People remembered you. You were hardly discreet."

"Oh." The man's revelation rendered Lady Phoebe—and all of them—speechless. A sense of foolishness crawled across Eva's shoulders and prickled her arms.

Mr. Nichols quirked his eyebrows at them. "So today we questioned Miss Travers about what happened there last night, and if she had ever seen that note before. Which, by the way, she said she had not, and I tended to believe her."

"I see . . ."

"Do you, Lady Phoebe? Whoever murdered Miss Travers arrived at her flat sometime between when I was there and when you and your cohorts showed up—uninvited and unnecessarily, I might add. I was handling things, making appropriate inquiries, if you'd only have trusted me. As it is, you might have walked in on a murder and been murdered yourselves."

"Or," Lady Phoebe whispered, "we might have saved her."

Eva felt a pang in the vicinity of her heart. Yes, if they had only gone earlier, perhaps they might have prevented Lydia's death, or at the very least been able to identify the killer.

Detective Inspector Nichols's hand came down on the table with a thwack. "That is not the point I'm trying to make. Lady Phoebe, it's one thing to play with your own life, but your maid and your driver work for you and have little choice in matters such as these."

"I would never force them—"

Eva could keep silent no longer. "Indeed not. I came along because I wanted to. Because I would never let my lady do such a thing on her own."

"Nor me, neither." Douglas's face reddened with ire. "A bloke has got to have some honor in him, doesn't he? Let these ladies go alone? No, sir, not me. Even if Lady Phoebe had ordered me not to go, I would have gone."

"Settle down, all of you." The detective inspector looked bored by their protests. "We can safely assume whoever murdered Ronald Mercer most likely had a hand in Miss Travers's death. She must have known him and somehow figured out it was he who murdered Mercer."

Lady Phoebe gripped the edge of the table between them. "I hope you don't think it's . . ."

"Trent Mercer?" His eyebrows shot upward. "I telephoned over to Lyndale Park a few minutes ago. According to your sister, she and most of the household can vouch for Trent being there all night tonight. Lucky for him."

"Oh, thank goodness," Eva murmured.

"Hmph." The man leaned forward, pinning his stare on Lady Phoebe in a manner that urged Eva to administer a slap of admonishment. It was an urge she resisted. "Whether you wish to acknowledge it or not, Lady Phoebe," he said, "you might have led that individual directly to Miss Travers with your jaunt to her flat last night."

Lady Phoebe paled. Her hand rose to press her lips. Eva reached out to take hold of her free one. But she could offer little other comfort, not here, in front of this man who accused them so remorselessly.

Was Mr. Nichols correct? Could they be responsible for Lydia's death? The possibility pinched Eva's throat and stung her eyes, and a growing ache made breathing difficult. She had wished to help the girl, yes, but they had also used her in their effort to obtain information. She, Eva, had used her, for she could not forget that going there to speak with Lydia had been her idea. Not Lady Phoebe's, as the detective inspector seemed to believe. Hers. The knowledge was like a weight around her heart.

"You have very much made your point, sir." Eva felt wearier than she could remember ever being. "May we go home now?"

"No, you may not," he said without hesitation or kindness.

"Are we being held?" Lady Phoebe looked alarmed. "Are we suspected of something?"

"No, I'm not daft enough to think you murdered anyone, but I want some answers." The detective inspector folded his hands on the tabletop. He had the air of someone settling in for an extended period of time. His attention turned to Eva. "When you saw Lydia Travers last night, what did the two of you talk about?"

"Crown Lily, and some of the people there." Eva attempted to make sense of her chaotic thoughts. "Mostly Moira Wickham. I wanted to know how Lydia felt about her, as well as some of the others in the painting department."

"And?"

"And, of course, she resented Miss Wickham. She protested her innocence of the charge Miss Wickham had leveled against her, namely selling china patterns to a competitor. Miss Wickham suspected Lydia of conspiring with a young gentleman who works for another pottery. Lydia claimed they were no longer seeing each other, and I believed her." She shook her head. "No gentleman would allow a woman he cared about to live in such unfortunate circumstances."

He casually dismissed the comment. "What else?"

"I asked her about Ronald Mercer's missing pattern book, and she said something I found most curious. She thought he was as likely to have stolen it himself as anyone else. That he might have done it as part of a plan to move to another company."

"Hmm. Interesting." He said this with grudging reluctance. "If that's the case, then the book is gone and not likely to be found." He addressed his next question to Lady Phoebe. "Who else have you two harassed?"

"I'd hardly call it that," Lady Phoebe began, but Eva saw no point in concealing the truth.

"Gus Abbott," she said.

Mr. Nichols tented his fingers beneath his chin. "Head of clay mixing."

Eva nodded. "He should have been in the building the morning Ronald Mercer died."

"But he wasn't," Mr. Nichols pointed out, apparently having learned that much for himself. "Witnesses placed him in the warehouse that morning."

"Perhaps, but we have reason to believe those who claimed he was in the warehouse might have been lying," Eva said.

"Oh? Pray tell me, Miss Huntford, what reason could that be?"

"I can answer that." Douglas scowled, his face reddening again. "Down at the pub, there were Crown Lily workers saying they protected their own, even if it meant lying. They were right proud about it, too." Douglas leaned forward over the table. "I heard them myself."

"Maybe so. The point is, it's not your business to find out. All your interference is good for is getting people hurt."

At this pronouncement Lady Phoebe winced and Eva felt another stab.

Mr. Nichols sat back and regarded them with an amused smirk. "Do you know Gus Abbott lives in Lydia Travers's neighborhood?"

"No, we didn't." Lady Phoebe looked to the other two for approbation. They shook their heads. Eva certainly hadn't known.

"Yes, well, I know because contrary to what you believe, I have continued to investigate this case, even while young Mercer was still in jail. And, by the way, I don't appreciate your sister throwing her weight around to have him released."

"He's a child," Eva pointed out none-too-gently. "Or doesn't that matter to you?"

"Not if he murdered his father, it doesn't."

"He couldn't have murdered Lydia." The tension in Lady Phoebe's hands finally eased, and she released her grip on the table's edge. "As you said, my sister and the others at Lyndale Park can vouch for his being there tonight."

"Perhaps," the detective inspector murmured, "but as you've all pointed out, people sometimes lie to protect their own."

"No one is lying about Trent's whereabouts," Eva insisted. Indignation made her bold. "Certainly, Lady Annondale's word is to be trusted."

"I'm merely pointing out that nothing is settled. Nothing has been proven or disproven."

After a pause Lady Phoebe said, "If Gus Abbott lives in Lydia's neighborhood, he could have slipped that note into my purse, couldn't he?"

"Or, if guilty of Ronald Mercer's death, he could also have murdered Lydia," Eva added.

The detective inspector came to his feet. "That will be quite enough. You lot don't learn, do you? There you go again, speculating on things you've no business interfering with." He leaned, spread his arms wide, and flattened his palms on the tabletop. His booming voice filled the room. "Listen to me, and listen well. Your involvement in this case ends here and now. You will return to Lyndale Park and stay there. Better yet, leave Langston at the first opportunity and don't come back. Because if I catch the slightest hint of any of you questioning anyone, or being where you shouldn't, I'll have you apprehended and locked up for your own good, not to mention the good of this community. Have I made myself clear?"

They mumbled their replies and were only too happy when he told them they were free to go.

CHAPTER 16

After dinner that evening, Phoebe stole off alone to Gil's study, a room little used since his death. The item she sought occupied the desk, but as she sank into the leather desk chair, so large and tufted she felt like a child in comparison, she hesitated. Several times she reached for the candlestick telephone, only to ease her hand away.

It wasn't a call she wished to make, at least not for the reason that had sent her here. Detective Inspector Nichols had been brutally honest earlier, and no one, not even Eva, could silence the accusations clawing at her ever since. Through their interference they had led a killer to Lydia Travers's flat. That poor young woman's life had been snuffed out because of them. Because of her—and because of her arrogance in believing she could solve what the police could not.

It didn't matter that she had been acting on Trent's behalf, or even on Fox's. True, Fox had threatened to become involved to clear his friend's name, and she couldn't allow that. And, yes, it had appeared as though the police were satisfied with their conclusion that Trent had murdered his father and were finished investigating. But what Phoebe hadn't taken into consideration was that the detective inspector had been under no obligation to keep her informed of his activities regarding the case.

And now a girl lay dead, strangled, and she could banish neither Mr. Nichols's admonishments nor Lydia's lifeless features from her mind.

She reached again for the telephone, dragging it close. Lifting the brass earpiece, she tapped the metal switch hook twice.

"Langston Post Office," a woman's voice announced. "Do you wish to make a call?"

"Yes, please." Phoebe lifted the telephone and spoke into the mouthpiece. She gave the exchange operator the information, and waited while the proper connections were made. Finally a voice came over the wire.

"Phoebe?"

"Owen."

She hadn't asked him to come. She had only wished to unburden herself to the one person who would offer neither sympathy nor condemnation, but who would simply listen. But the next morning as Eva helped her dress, the rumble of a motorcar on the drive sent them both to the window. Phoebe immediately recognized the three-wheeled Morgan Runabout, a prewar racing vehicle that, although nearly a decade old, still had the power to outrun most other motorcars on the road. And while its canvas top obscured the interior, a glimpse through the driver's side window revealed a head of tousled black hair.

A thrill and a sense of joy rose up inside her, which she attempted to conceal behind a frown.

"I told him I'd be all right, that he didn't have to come," she said to Eva. "He never listens. Goodness, he must have driven through the night to arrive so early."

"On the contrary, my lady, he does listen. Quite well, I'd say. That's why he's here."

"Whose side are you on?" Phoebe couldn't help an ironic grin in response to Eva's shrewd smile.

"Yours, always."

Downstairs, Phoebe donned an overcoat and hurried outside, meeting Owen on the front steps as he was about to raise the knocker. His arms engulfed her, and she felt swept up in a wave of solid security she hadn't known she'd needed, not like this.

"Are you all right, my dearest Phoebe?"

"Yes, yes, I am now."

With his masculine scents swirling around her, she suddenly couldn't conceive of how on earth she would have gotten on without him. Yes, Eva had been right. Last night he had listened to her, really listened, and heard everything she hadn't spoken across the wires.

"Thank you for coming." She burrowed her

cheek against his coat front and held on beyond all sense of proper decorum.

He made no move to put space between them, but seemed as content as she to let the moments continue on. "Of course I'm here. Where else should I be? And why . . . Phoebe, *why* didn't you simply ask me to come?" When she didn't reply, he released one arm from around her and raised her chin with his fingertips until her gaze met his. "Is admitting you might need me such a regrettable sign of weakness?"

"No, it wasn't that. You've so much to worry about. The pressures from the textile union and your workers' demands . . . How could I possibly add to that, especially when I put myself in the position I'm in now? It's my own fault."

She couldn't tell him the entire truth: Yes, he was right. In some small way she didn't like admitting to needing him—not yet. Wanting him? Yes, most certainly that. But *needing* involved a host of inadequacies she'd been fighting against her entire life, and most especially in the years since Papa had died.

Before he'd gone off to war, Papa had essentially left her in charge of her siblings. Taken her aside and told her he was trusting her to look after them because she was the sensible one, the steady one. And ever since, she had fretted over making a hash of it, of disappointing him, of failing. How could she look after her brother and two sisters when she oftentimes felt inadequate to look after herself? What kind of example could she possibly set when her mistakes stretched as long as the early-morning shadows obscuring the edges of the park surrounding them?

She searched Owen's face, his dark eyes. Did he see through her, know her for what she truly was? She'd told him everything last night over the telephone. Unburdening herself across the wires, rather than face-to-face, had perhaps been cowardly, but so much easier than beneath his earnest scrutiny.

Had he reached the same conclusion as Detective Inspector Nichols, that Lydia Travers had died because of her? How could he not? Several years older than she, he must think her a silly chit of a girl, butting in where she had no business interfering. Yet, here he was, and she saw nothing of judgment staring back at her from his handsome features. She saw only kindness and concern and something that mirrored a sensation that gathered deep in the pit of her stomach. It prompted her to rise up on her tiptoes even as he lowered his face and pressed his lips to hers.

How long he kissed her, she couldn't say, or have cared. Had someone seen? At that moment the notion struck her as inconsequential, of no matter at all. When their lips parted, they smiled at each other—she somewhat ruefully, he tolerantly—linked arms, and set off around the house in an unspoken agreement that they weren't ready to go inside yet and face the others.

"So this may all be Julia's soon," he commented absently as they rounded the corner and the gardens came into view.

A scenic landscape opened before them, rolling hills and distant forests that gave no hint of the region's industrial underpinnings. The bottle kilns, the smoke and soot, the workers' poor housing, and the coal mines that fed it all—none of it was visible from here.

"Well, not Julia's, I suppose," he amended, "though it might as well be, until her child is an adult."

Phoebe only shrugged. Her arm linked through his, she leaned against his side as they walked. Julia's conundrum with the estate, once a significant issue, now seemed trivial next to a boy accused of murder and two people in their graves.

"You're quiet," he remarked as they meandered down a twisting garden path. "That detective has you riddled with guilt. But how do you know your visit to the girl had anything to do with her death? She might have been targeted much earlier. Might have known something about the murder at Crown Lily, and the guilty party decided she needed to be silenced. Or the police themselves might have led the killer to her."

"The police only went to see her because of what they learned from me, because my handbag had been snatched."

"Yes. I'm not going to say you shouldn't have gone into that neighborhood, especially at night, that it was dangerous and foolhardy and you might have been hurt." His free hand descended on hers, where it lay in the crook of his arm, and tightened around it with an urgency she understood.

And yet she also perceived his teasing and teased in return, "You just did."

"Yes, I did. I'm sorry, I won't bring it up again." His arm went around her, and hers spanned his waist beneath his open topcoat. As they reached a tall stand of rhododendrons, their leaves faded and weary-looking, he guided her around them, thus blocking their view of the house—and the house's view of them. Embracing her, he dipped her slightly back and kissed her again. Soundly, in a way that overwhelmed her. She felt absorbed by him, enveloped, elated, yet oddly calm, content. When he finally lifted away, it was only an inch or two, just enough for her to catch her breath. She wanted to sigh and at the same time let go the laughter that bubbled up inside her—delighted, wicked laughter.

"That," he said, the cool breeze catching at his words, "was to let you know I've been waiting for you, but I don't want to wait around forever."

She instantly sobered. "What does that mean? That I must make a decision and make it soon?"

He stared down at her a good long moment, fleeting thoughts darting across his face. The previous moment shattered, he helped her to straighten, released her, and shoved his hands in his coat pockets. "Damn it, Phoebe, I don't know what it means. It's not an ultimatum. It's just . . ." He shook his head briskly. "Tell me what you've learned so far since you've been here. And what did send you into that neighborhood?"

Unsure whether she was grateful, relieved, or thoroughly disappointed he had changed subjects so readily, she let him guide her back onto the garden path. "We went because of the way Miss Wickham—that's the supervisor of the painting department—dismissed Lydia Travers. Eva saw it happen, and she felt Miss Wickham might have let her go too easily, more on a hunch than any evidence Lydia had been giving away Crown Lily secrets. Designs and such."

"And did Lydia provide any new insights?"

"She denied Miss Wickham's accusations against her. But she made a curious charge of her own—that Ronald Mercer had stolen his own pattern book."

"How does one steal something one already has in one's possession?"

"The book was his, used to record his pattern designs, but in actuality it belonged to Crown

Lily. Lydia thought perhaps he sold his designs to another company for a chance to advance his career. He might have been planning to leave Crown Lily."

Their arms once again linked, Owen strolled with his free hand behind his back. "So based solely on that scenario, his killer could have been someone to whom he planned to give the book. Perhaps Mercer demanded too high a payment and this other individual decided he could have the book free and clear." When Phoebe nodded her agreement to this possibility, he went on. "Or, the owner of Crown Lily learned of or guessed his plans and killed him, and perhaps he has the pattern book somewhere."

Phoebe nodded again, but pointed out, "If either of those scenarios is true, why the clay-mixing building? He was killed in one of the vats where natural clay, bone ash, and stone are ground into a fine substance and mixed. Why would Mr. Tremaine, or even someone from another company, plan to meet with Ronald Mercer there?"

"Hmm. All right, who would ordinarily have been in that building that time of day?"

"Very few men, in fact, but a worker named Gus Abbott is in charge and was definitely on site that morning. He claims he was in the main warehouse and has several workers willing to vouch for him."

"You sound skeptical."

She sighed. "Douglas overheard some Crown Lily workers claim they protect their own, even if it means being less than honest. Although Gus Abbott did tell Eva that Mr. Tremaine saw him in the warehouse as well. I doubt he'd bring Jeffrey Tremaine's name into it if it weren't true."

"Still, any reason he might have had it in for Mercer?"

Phoebe shook her head. "None that we've discovered for certain, but someone has been stealing from Crown Lily. It could be this Mr. Abbott."

"Yes, and Mercer found out. All right, this Miss Wickham. What did she have to gain by dismissing Lydia due to what could have been imagined or invented wrongs?"

"*Invented*—Eva and I considered this. She might have been using Lydia as a scapegoat. As I said, there have been thefts at Crown Lily. Miss Wickham—or Gus Abbott—could be involved in the latter. I should think, though, that of the two of them, only Miss Wickham is in a position to sell designs to a competitor."

"All right, that's three—the factory owner, Abbott, and Miss Wickham. Who else?"

"There's the other head designer, Percy Bateman. We detected friction between the two men before Ronald Mercer's death. Although most of the resentment did seem to be on Mr.

Mercer's part. He didn't seem to relish a much younger man coming along and showing as much talent—or perhaps more—than himself."

"In that case it could have been a crime gone wrong, with this other designer defending himself and killing his attacker."

"Yes, we thought of that. And Mr. Bateman became frightened and decided not to reveal what happened for fear the police wouldn't believe his story."

They continued walking until the path looped around the late-fall foliage and brought them back toward the house. "That makes four individuals you have reason to suspect. There's someone you haven't mentioned," Owen said as he brought them to a halt. "The boy."

"Trent? None of us believe he's guilty."

"Why not? The police certainly do. Even though they've released him, according to what you told me last night, they haven't entirely ruled him out."

"Julia, Fox, Amelia, and even Mildred all swear Trent was here last night and could not have murdered Lydia Travers. It only makes sense that the same person committed both murders, doesn't it?"

"I suppose it does. But you said Trent had good cause to resent his father. Sounds like the father's and son's visions of the future were diametrically opposed. That might have made Trent desperate.

And desperate people do desperate things. Perhaps someone else murdered Lydia to protect Trent. Have you thought of that?"

People lying to protect their own. But in this case, who? Trent was basically alone in the world. His own distant relatives wanted no part in helping him. As for murdering his father . . . in her heart she simply didn't—or perhaps she couldn't—believe the boy to be capable of such a horrific act.

"If you saw the manner in which Ronald Mercer died—actually saw the grinding pan— you'd do everything in your power not to believe a child could be such a monster."

"Then let's go in, and I can meet him."

They climbed the steps to the terrace, whereupon Phoebe happened to glance over her shoulder. An approaching figure prompted her to turn full around toward the garden.

"That's Ernie."

"Ernie Shelton, Gil's cousin?" Owen peered into the distance.

"The very same. His cottage is on the grounds, through the gardens and down a lane." Her mouth slanted in distaste, yet she remembered he had rushed up to the house when they'd believed Julia to be in labor. For that, she had yet to properly thank him. "Let's wait and see what he wants."

It took him a few minutes to reach them, appearing slightly out of breath as he climbed the terrace steps. "Good morning, Phoebe. Owen, this is a surprise. What brings you to Lyndale Park?"

"Phoebe, of course." He took her hand in his, which Ernie acknowledged with a lift of an eyebrow behind his spectacles. "What brings you to the main house so early this morning?"

A twitch of that same eyebrow signaled perplexity at Owen's query, and Phoebe easily surmised Ernie didn't appreciate being questioned about entering the very grounds he felt entitled to own.

"I've come to see how Julia is doing, and to deliver a message to her."

"A message?" When Ernie offered up no further information, Phoebe said, "She's been fine. No more false contractions."

"That's good to hear, but we still must keep a very close watch on her."

Something in the way he said *we* bothered Phoebe. "*We* will, I assure you." She applied enough emphasis to drive the point home that Julia's family would take good care of her—no need for him to trouble himself.

He shivered beneath his tweed suit coat, though Phoebe herself found the morning a temperate one.

"May we go in?" Ernie asked.

"Sorry, of course."

Phoebe went to the terrace doors. Owen

reached to open one, and Phoebe preceded the men inside. The drawing room appeared deserted, until a light rustle from the far corner, beside the windows near the piano, alerted them to Mildred Blair's presence. She held a teacup in her lap.

"Ernie. What a surprise to see you here this morning. And . . ." She narrowed her eyes slightly to see across the long room. "Why, good heavens, is that Owen Seabright?" She set her teacup aside and came to her feet. Her hand extended, she strode to them looking, for all the world, like a film star greeting her audience. "How lovely of you to visit us. I do hope you'll be staying on a few days. I'll have Carmichael prepare a room for you. Have you eaten breakfast yet?"

Previously Phoebe might have burned with ire and jealousy. She knew shameless flirting when she saw it, and it wasn't the first time Mildred had practically thrown herself at Owen. Then, as now, he returned her overtures with nothing more than courtesy of a sort that wiped the grin from Mildred's face.

"How do you do, Miss Blair? I haven't decided whether I'm staying on yet, and, no, I haven't eaten. Phoebe, have you?" When Phoebe replied in the negative, he went on, "Splendid, then we can enjoy a bite together. Miss Blair, would you care to join us?"

Her lips flattening, she shook her head. "I've had my toast and jam, thank you." She immediately switched her attention to Ernie. "Did you say why you've come? I didn't hear."

"He wishes to check on Julia," Phoebe said, still curious about the message he said he must deliver. "Have you seen her up yet?"

"As far as I know, *Her Majesty* has yet to show her face downstairs." Mildred smiled without warmth and returned to her corner of the drawing room, where Phoebe now noticed she had her lap desk on the table beside her chair.

"Ernie, please show Owen into the dining room, and I'll go up and see if Julia is ready to come down. I know she'll be delighted to see you, Owen," Phoebe said.

After she parted with the men, Phoebe walked sedately to the staircase, but once she saw them enter the dining room, she took the steps at a run. Moments later she knocked quietly, but urgently, on Julia's bedroom door. Hetta opened it and Phoebe came right to the point.

"Ernie's here, and I believe he's up to something again. He says he's got a message for you, but hasn't said what it is."

Hetta returned to Julia's side before the long dressing mirror and finished buttoning the buttons up the back of the long tunic that overlaid her skirt. Then she set to work draping the fabric, just so, around Julia's belly, to charming effect.

"He did say the message was for me, didn't he?" Julia said in an offhand manner.

"Well, yes," Phoebe agreed, "but he seemed rather mysterious."

Julia tipped her head as she scanned herself in the mirror. She turned this way and that and smoothed a hand lightly over the tunic with a satisfied air. "I wonder whom this message is from . . ." Suddenly she whirled about, her expression going from disinterested to concerned in an instant. "That will be all, thank you, Hetta." To Phoebe, she said, "Let's get down there. I have a bad feeling."

The rest of the household, excepting Mildred, were all in the dining room, Fox and Trent with heaping plates of eggs, black pudding, and toast, Amelia with a light selection of fruit and sliced ham, and Veronica with scones and jam and a soft-boiled egg. Jester roamed around the table, his nose working. After darting glances to the right and left of her, Amelia slipped a hand beneath the table. Jester sauntered over to her, and Phoebe heard a quick gulp. No one else noticed, and Phoebe decided to keep their secret.

Owen and Ernie were just turning away from the buffet. Phoebe and Julia joined them there.

"Your sister was right, Julia. You're looking quite well," Ernie said.

A gleam in Ernie's gaze struck Phoebe as predatory. This could only mean troubling news, at least for Julia.

"No more pains?" he inquired.

Julia frowned. "Really, Ernie, this is hardly the place to discuss such things. And while I appreciate your coming to my aid, if I need a physician I'll ring up Dr. Wright again."

"Just remember that since I'm here on the estate, I'm infinitely closer to you than Dr. Wright, should a sudden need arise."

Her face tight with annoyance, Julia filled her plate with much more food than she typically consumed for breakfast and went to the table. Ernie hurried there ahead of her, set down his own plate, and held her chair. Julia's smile was thankful, but also suspicious.

Phoebe shared those suspicions. She whispered to Owen, still standing beside her at the buffet, "What's he playing at?"

"I expect we're about to find out."

Indeed, Julia apparently had had enough of waiting. "Phoebe tells me, Ernie, that you have a message for me. May I have it, please?"

Ernie took his time bringing a forkful of kippers and eggs to his mouth, chewed slowly, and swallowed with a sharp bob of his Adam's apple. "Oh, yes, I very nearly forgot. It's not every day I get to indulge in such a breakfast, you know. Now, Mrs. Hartman, who does for me every day, is a wonderful cook, but I don't get to enjoy such variety living alone, as I do, at my little cottage."

Phoebe and Owen went to the table; she sat across from Julia and Ernie, and Owen chose a seat near the boys. He, no doubt, wanted to become acquainted with Trent. Meanwhile, Julia appeared at about the end of her patience, while Ernie seemed intent on prolonging his enjoyment of—whatever this was.

"Ernie, the message," Phoebe shot across the table at him. She'd had quite enough of his equivocating.

"Yes, yes, quite right." He turned to Julia, his smile triumphant. "Your grandmother wishes you to call her first thing this morning."

"My grandmother?" Julia dropped her fork and exchanged alarmed looks with Phoebe, Amelia, and, farther down the table, Fox. "Is she all right? Is it about our grandfather? He isn't ill again, is he?"

Phoebe might have voiced such worries as well, except that a question surfaced above the rest. "Wait a moment. If something happened at home, Grams would have telephoned us here. Why and when did you speak with her?"

"Last night." Ernie bit into a slice of melon. "I telephoned over to Foxwood Hall."

Julia's mouth opened in shock, then closed, then opened again. "Why?"

"Because I suspected no one else had, and I thought she had a right to know her granddaughter had an emergency that required a doctor's care."

Julia pushed back her chair and came to her feet. "Ernie, you had no right. There was no

310

reason to worry my grandparents. I'm perfectly fine. Dr. Wright said what I experienced is perfectly normal for a great number of expectant mothers. Why on earth would you interfere in this way?"

"Oh, it wasn't just the medical emergency," Ernie went on amiably, unperturbed by Julia's admonishment. "It's also the danger of there being a murderer on the loose." He angled his gaze at Trent at the lower end of the table next to Fox. The boy noticed and colored to the roots of his hair. "You're all taking matters a bit too lightly, and, again, I thought for your own safety your grandparents should be apprised of the situation."

"Julia's not a child, you know." Amelia's features contorted in a rare moment of outrage.

"Nor are you the head of our family." Fox pointed his fork at Ernie, a gesture that would have gotten him sent from the table at home. "In our grandfather's absence, I am."

"Amelia, Fox, never mind." Julia had quickly recovered her poise. With a show of calm, she continued, "Ernie's ploy is an obvious one. He wants me out of the house. Obviously, his solicitor failed to come up with any sound legal grounds to make that happen, so now he's hoping Grams will order us home." With one hand on her belly, she shrugged in her most nonchalant manner, going so far as to look bored by the entire matter. "I'll go telephone her now and reassure her we're all quite safe and will be home in a matter of another few days. I'll simply explain that for now, Trent isn't allowed to leave Langston, and we can't simply abandon him."

The boy looked astonished. "Th-thank you, Lady Annondale."

"You're Fox's friend, after all. And you may call me Julia," she told him. "Now, if you'll all excuse me."

It was all Phoebe could do not to follow Julia. She longed to listen in on the conversation with Grams, and wondered how on earth Julia would manage to set their grandmother's mind to rest. If it were just Phoebe and Julia here, they might simply point out that they were both adults. But they had Fox and Amelia with them, and if Grams wished to press her point, they would have no choice but to pack up and start home. She could only hope Julia would manage to summon her most persuasive skills.

CHAPTER 17

Eva went up the back staircase, her arms piled high with freshly laundered shirtwaists, stockings, and underthings. Upon first arriving at Lyndale Park, she had gone belowstairs to inspect the laundry facilities, and had been horrified to see an electric, motor-driven washer sitting in a corner. One might as well hand one's clothing over to a petulant child with a thread cutter. However, the laundress, a competent woman who apparently knew her business, had assured Eva she never used the contraption on anything but work clothes and the like, and certainly never on delicate, tailored ladies' garments. In fact, she had raised vigorous objections to the machine when the former Lord Annondale had insisted on installing it, however much he had assured her it was the modern and more efficient method of washing clothes.

Eva would rather cut off the tip of her little finger than submit her ladies' wardrobes to the vagaries of some machine. She herself still pretreated stains with borax and gentle brushes, and often hand-washed their delicates herself.

Her deception at Crown Lily had set her back on such chores, and there were still shoes to polish and coats to brush. Ladies Phoebe and

Amelia had told her never mind, they could manage, but she found letting her duties go undone made her melancholy, as if it were proof her young mistresses no longer needed her.

Upon entering the bedroom shared by Phoebe and Amelia, she discovered only Phoebe occupied the room, sitting curled up on the settee with a book. Amelia, apparently, had gone out for a ride with Owen in his Runabout, a motorcar of which Eva thoroughly disapproved. Never mind that it had been built for speed, but three wheels—two in front and one in back? Insanity.

"What are you reading, my lady?" she asked as she opened drawers and began putting away clothes.

"*A Study in Scarlet*," she replied without looking up.

"Again?" Eva smiled. Lady Phoebe had a penchant for detective stories.

"I thought it might help me think like Sherlock Holmes."

"He's a fictional character, my lady."

"But the logic is there, isn't it? There's logic to everything, no matter how obscure it might seem. The trick is to find it. To connect the threads in just the right pattern."

A knock at the door heralded Lady Annondale's arrival. "Ernie is vanquished," she said in lieu of a greeting. "Grams isn't making us come home.

It wasn't easy convincing her, but I promised her none of us would set foot out of this house until the police apprehended the killer. And, yes, I know you'll make a liar of me, Phoebe, because no one can keep you in one place for five minutes, so I crossed my fingers and hoped Grams didn't put Grampapa on the line. You know how much harder it is to fib to him. But this gives the police a bit more time to completely clear Trent. I'm hoping once they do, we can arrange for him to return to school with Fox."

Lady Phoebe laid her book aside. "Let's hope so. Where are the boys, by the way? It's awfully quiet around here."

"I expect they've taken Jester for a run on the grounds." Lady Annondale joined her on the settee, heaving out a breath as she carefully lowered herself onto the cushions. If Eva didn't know better, she'd say Lady Annondale's belly had grown since their arrival at Lyndale Park.

"Jester's downstairs in the kitchen being fed," Eva told them, "so the boys are not with him." She felt a vague uneasiness. "Perhaps they're in the library?"

Though only just settled, Julia pushed up from the settee in that odd way expectant ladies had, belly first. "More than likely they're in Gil's billiard room. I'll go see. I want to make sure Trent knows we won't be abandoning him."

"It's awfully good of you to take an interest in

the boy, my lady." Eva smiled as she hung the last item in the wardrobe.

"I'm considering . . ."

Phoebe cocked her head and gazed up expectantly at her sister. "Considering what?"

Julia only said, "I'll go look for them." She was almost out the door when she turned back to them. "By the way, some of Trent's things from home were delivered earlier, did you see? I suggested he telephone over to his housekeeper last night and have her send anything he might need. Poor woman, she'll be out of a job soon."

"I heard the lorry," Phoebe said, "but I thought it was supplies for the household. I'm glad, though. It will help him feel more at home."

Julia nodded and left the room. In mere minutes she returned, not bothering to knock this time. "Phoebe, this may be nothing, but I can't find them anywhere, and no one has seen them since this morning."

"You know how boys have a penchant for disappearing," Eva reminded her, though she once more experienced a sinking apprehension.

"That's not all. I peeked into their room, and it looks as if it's been ransacked."

Lady Phoebe came to her feet, and both she and Eva were moving toward the door before another word was spoken. They hurried along the corridor together and turned in at Fox's room.

"Good heavens, Julia, I wouldn't say

ransacked." Lady Phoebe surveyed the scene before them.

Eva did, too, noting the room seemed no untidier than one would expect from two boys sharing a space. Despite the beds having been made, she could see they'd been sat on since, the coverlets wrinkled and the pillows indented. A few items of clothing hung over chair backs and a couple of drawers gaped an inch or two from not being pushed in all the way. What Lady Annondale referred to, Eva surmised, were the papers scattered on the rug near the fireplace, as if they'd been spread out to be perused.

Lady Phoebe sank on the hearth rug and began sweeping the papers into a neat pile.

"I'll do that, my lady." Eva went to crouch beside her.

Lady Annondale stood in the doorway, leaning against the frame. She reached up to finger the gold-and-opal necklace hanging down the front of her frock. "I find it concerning that they rustled through all that mess and are now nowhere to be found."

"So do I." Lady Phoebe sat back on her heels, papers in hand. Eva handed her the pages she'd scooped up, and Lady Phoebe began scanning them. "This appears to be random correspondence and documents that belonged to his father."

"Why send them here?" Eva rose, and then offered her hand to help Lady Phoebe up. "Why not leave them at the Mercer house? What use could Trent make of them here? And who sent them?"

"Presumably, his housekeeper at home," Lady Annondale said.

Lady Phoebe went to the foot of one of the beds and spread out the papers. "Honestly, there's nothing here that appears to be of great importance. Nothing urgent . . ."

While she fanned through the pile, Eva glanced again around the room. A brown edge peeking out from beneath a chair near the fireplace caught her attention. "What's this?" She bent to retrieve a large envelope. On her way back to Lady Phoebe, she peered inside. "Hmm. It's empty."

Lady Phoebe took it from her, holding it open with two hands. "Yes, it is. But what might have been in it?"

"Perhaps merely all those papers you two picked up off the floor," Lady Annondale suggested. She came into the room and sat at the edge of the bed, facing Eva and her sister.

Lady Phoebe shook her head. "There's too much here to have been able to fit inside that envelope."

"Then whatever was inside, they took it with them," Eva said, feeling suddenly inspired. "My guess is, it's not what's here that's important, but what isn't. What the boys have with them."

"Have with them *where?*" Lady Annondale lifted a paper, glanced at it, and set it down.

"Crown Lily," Lady Phoebe said. She held out the envelope and pointed to something on it that Eva hadn't noticed before. They turned as one and headed for the corridor.

As the touring car passed beneath the Crown Lily sign, the guard at the gate once again recognized them and waved them in. Phoebe nonetheless told Douglas to stop and opened the window. "Have you seen two boys come through here?" she asked without preamble.

The man looked puzzled and shook his head. "Boys? No. Only the night workers are coming in now. But you're welcome to enter, my lady. Here to see Mr. Tremaine about your order?"

With a nod she thanked him and told Douglas to drive on. Before leaving Lyndale Park, she and Eva had told Julia to let Owen know where they'd gone. Just in case. She would have preferred to wait for him to return from his ride with Amelia, but she had feared the boys might be walking into danger. Now, however, she wondered if she had made the right choice in returning to Crown Lily at all. Sitting back in the seat, she chewed her bottom lip.

"Perhaps we're wrong about their being here. How else could they have gotten in if not past the guardhouse?"

"Perhaps they climbed the wall," Eva suggested, "or waited until the guard was distracted and sneaked in."

"Well, I can't think where else they would have gone." No, all of Phoebe's instincts told her they'd come here to confront—someone. "Trent wasn't to leave the house at all. Only a matter of the utmost urgency could have prompted him to sneak off."

"Something in those documents spurred them to action."

"Fox has been itching to take action ever since his friend was accused." Phoebe couldn't decide if she would hug him or box his ears when she found him. "I just hope that what I took to be a hint as to their whereabouts is actually that."

A rudimentary teacup had been hastily scribbled in pencil on a corner of the envelope. Had Fox drawn it as a message, or had it been there for years, doodled by Mr. Mercer?

The motorcar entered the central quadrangle and rolled to a stop. She saw no one about and a deserted air permeated the enclosure. Still, the guard had said the night workers would be arriving, so they would not be alone here. A thought occurred to her.

"Perhaps they're not here, after all. It's late. Since most of the day employees have left, perhaps Fox and Trent went to someone's home to confront him. Or her."

"If that's the case," Eva said, "we're completely in the dark as to the direction they took. They could be anywhere in the city."

"Maybe we should have tried Lydia Travers's neighborhood. Quite a number of the workers live there."

"Yes, my lady, but not all." Eva gazed out the window at their surroundings. "No, I believe you were right that Fox tried to leave us a hint, one that wouldn't alert Trent that we might be following. Whatever the boy is planning, it must be extreme. And don't forget, Trent would know which employees tended to remain on the premises late in the day."

Phoebe met her gaze. "They would most likely be supervisors, people of importance rather than hourly workers and laborers."

Eva nodded solemnly, and apprehension swirled in Phoebe's gut. Each individual they had suspected so far occupied a position of some authority at Crown Lily: Moira Wickham, Gus Abbott, Percy Bateman. Even Mr. Tremaine.

"Right, then." The clay-mixing building sprawled to their left. Phoebe pointed to it. "Let's see if anyone is inside."

As she and Eva opened the motorcar's rear doors, Douglas opened his. "I'm coming with you."

"We won't complain." Phoebe showed him a grateful smile. Then she steeled herself with a breath and strode to the entrance of the building.

Not a sound reached her ears when she opened it. The corridor lay in darkness, but she nonetheless proceeded, peering into the first grinding room she came to, the one they had seen during their tour. Only the light through the windows illuminated the interior. "There doesn't appear to be anyone here."

Eva followed close behind her. "No, it looks as if Mr. Abbott and his crew have left for the day."

"Still, let's finish checking the building before we move on." In the silence Phoebe felt a need to muffle her footsteps, and noticed Eva and Douglas did likewise.

Eva poked her head into the next room they came to. "My lady, do you think we should check inside the grinding pans?"

That swirling apprehension became a maelstrom as Phoebe considered what had occurred in one of those pans. Before she could answer, Douglas stepped in front of them. "I'll do it. I'll have a look in these and then double back to check the ones we've already passed."

It only took some ten minutes to search through the building—until they came to the room where Ronald Mercer had met his death. There they paused, looking in, all of them hesitating. Though none of them had witnessed the crime scene, one look at those deadly blades in the grinding pan emblazoned one's mind with all manner of gruesome images.

Douglas stepped across the threshold and crept to the pan. Once he got there, he glanced back. Phoebe nodded to him and he peered into the pan. Phoebe and Eva, waiting in the doorway, clutched at each other and held their breath until spots danced before Phoebe's eyes, making her light-headed.

"All clear," Douglas said with a rush of breath. Phoebe and Eva nearly collapsed against each other in relief.

"Thank goodness." Phoebe let out a soft groan. "Although, honestly, I don't know what we expected to find. Certainly not . . . not the boys." Had she? Yes, perhaps part of her had dreaded a horrific discovery. But another part of her trusted Fox and Trent to be clever enough to outwit even a killer. "Let's move on. If they're here, we need to find them before they do something regrettable."

They crossed the enclosure to the main warehouse. The wide doors stood open, but most of the lights had been extinguished, only a few remaining on to chase away the darkness. Phoebe could just make out rows of shelving disappearing into the shadows, as well as the hulking stacks of barrels. Though the vast space appeared abandoned, they heard voices.

"I believe it's coming from the attached warehouse, where outgoing shipments are prepared. Through there."

Eva led the way to an enormous opening in one

wall. It led into an adjoining space. Here, the lights were brighter, illuminating further rows of shelves that nearly reached the ceiling and spanned the building's length. A conveyor ran along one wall, and containers of straw stood open and waiting to be used for packing. Cubbies above a workbench held a variety of items, including something that raised the hairs on Phoebe's nape.

An image of Lydia Travers filled her mind, her neck bulging around the strap that had cut off her breath. Such straps, Phoebe now saw, were used to secure the containers being readied for shipment. About a score of men were nailing lids closed, further securing them with the straps, and affixing labels. From there they hefted them onto the conveyor, which must bring them outside to the train tracks that ran the outer perimeter of the property, or to the river, where barges would carry them toward their destinations.

A worker happened to glance up. A frown instantly formed across his brow. "You there. You shouldn't be here."

Phoebe ventured closer. The man and his immediate coworkers moved in front of the crates, forming themselves into a barrier as if to protect a treasure from marauders. They eyed her up and down, with less than congenial expressions, rousing a fit of nerves she did her best to conceal and making her glad Douglas and Eva were right behind her.

"Yes, I know we shouldn't be. We're looking for a pair of boys. One of them is Trent Mercer. Have you seen him?"

"Trent?" The worker looked taken aback. The others apparently shared his mystification. "He's been taken to jail, miss. Terrible story, that."

"He's been released, actually," she told them, the news greeted with exclamations of "You don't say" and "I hope the coppers know what they're doing."

"Then none of you has seen him this evening," Phoebe persisted. "He couldn't have come through the warehouse at all?"

"Not through here, miss," another worker said. "Not while we've been here. We'd have seen him, just as we see you plain as day."

"What do you mean, *while you've been here?*" Douglas hovered protectively behind Phoebe. "You mean you haven't been here all day?"

"We're the night crew. Came in about twenty minutes ago." Turning his back, the worker dismissed Phoebe, Eva, and Douglas and said to the other men, "All right. We need to get on with it or we'll answer to the boss. Got to get these ready to load onto the evening ferry. That's less than an hour from now. Where are the rest of those shipping labels he dropped off?"

"I've got them over here . . ."

And yet, none of them moved from their defensive postures until Phoebe, Eva, and

325

Douglas made their way back into the main warehouse. Only then did Phoebe hear the sounds of packing resume.

"Not a very friendly bunch," Douglas commented.

"They've got work to do," Phoebe replied. "No time for distractions from witless fools, as we, no doubt, appeared to them."

"They did seem awfully protective of their wares." Eva kept pace beside Phoebe while Douglas walked a few steps behind them. "Did they think we were each going to snatch a place setting and run off?"

"With the recent thefts, I suppose they were just being conscientious," Phoebe said.

"Wait." Behind them, Douglas had come to an abrupt halt. "What's that?"

Phoebe turned around. "Is something wrong?"

Douglas didn't answer. He stood staring at a point hidden from her view by the shadows of the warehouse shelving. His eyes narrowed. He moved into those shadows.

"Douglas," Phoebe whispered, suddenly feeling a need for caution, "where are you going? What is it?"

"Stay back," he commanded, using a tone Phoebe had never heard from him before. "There's someone here. It's a man . . ." He trailed off. His shadow seemed to melt into the darker ones as he stooped, and then knelt on the stone floor. "I . . . I believe he's dead."

CHAPTER 18

Lady Phoebe tiptoed to Douglas's side as he pushed to his feet. She spoke in a whisper, one that trembled like a delicate breeze. "Who is it?"

"Don't know," he murmured. He dragged the cap from his head and raked his hand through his hair. "Looks like he was . . ."

"Strangled," Lady Phoebe finished for him.

Eva flanked Douglas's other side. "Just like Lydia Travers."

Eva saw a strap had been used, like those they had seen in the other warehouse. She sucked in a breath. The body lay faceup, eyes glazed and sightless, recognizable even in the dim lighting. "I know who it is," she whispered. "It's Gus Abbott."

"We've got to get help." Lady Phoebe turned and started toward the other warehouse, where the men's voices could still be heard. Eva stopped her.

"My lady, we don't know who did this. It could have been one of them."

"They were very defensive, weren't they?" Lady Phoebe replied. "Perhaps it wasn't merely because we interrupted their work."

"Let's get out of here." Douglas took the liberty of setting a hand on each of their shoulders and nudging them away from the sight of Gus Abbott lying dead on the flagstone flooring. "We might be able to telephone for help from one of the offices, if they're still open."

As they made their way outside, Eva whispered, "If it wasn't one of those men, how could this have happened and none of them heard anything?"

"It could have happened before they started working. But, good heavens, we need to find Fox and Trent." Lady Phoebe led the way to the small enclosure that housed the administrative building. No lights shone from the windows, but when they tried the main door, it opened. They came up short at the sight of a figure standing in the darkness of the corridor.

"Who's there?" the masculine voice demanded.

"Mr. Tremaine? It's Phoebe Renshaw."

"Lady Phoebe? What are you doing here at this time of day?"

When Lady Phoebe hesitated, Eva said, "We need to send for the police."

"The police? Why?" The man backed up a step as if to elude the grasp of ill fortune. "What's happened now?"

Lady Phoebe explained what they had encountered in the main warehouse.

"Please," Mr. Tremaine said. He came toward them, his face awash with heightened color. "Please come inside. We'll telephone the police immediately."

He brought them into his office and wasted no time in snatching the telephone on his desk. He clicked the cradle several times and then spoke. "Yes, it's Jeffrey Tremaine at the Crown Lily headquarters. Please connect me with the police." He continued speaking into the receiver for another minute or so and then replaced the earpiece on the base. "They're on their way. Why don't you all have a seat—"

"Mr. Tremaine, there is another emergency." Lady Phoebe spoke urgently. "We have reason to believe my brother and Trent Mercer are here. It'll take too long to explain, but we must find them as quickly as possible."

"How can that be? Isn't Trent in jail?"

"Not anymore. My sister had him released into her custody, and he wasn't to leave Lyndale Park, but the two of them have, and we think they're here. Somewhere." As she spoke, Lady Phoebe retreated into the corridor and hurried along its length.

"But what would they be doing here?" Mr. Tremaine called as he came to his feet. He circled his desk and followed Eva and Douglas in Lady Phoebe's wake. She didn't answer. She had already entered Ronald Mercer's office.

"But that room is kept locked now . . ."

Eva turned into the office to be greeted by a scene like the one in Fox's bedroom earlier. Drawers and cupboard doors had been left gaping; papers were strewn across the desk. "They've been here."

Mr. Tremaine flipped the wall switch and the overhead lights burst on. Eva went to the desk and scooped up several papers. "Order forms . . ." She glanced at the dates at the top of several. "But they appear to be old ones."

"Copies," Mr. Tremaine explained. "The original ones are kept in our records room. Ronald Mercer was a stickler and liked to keep details close on hand. But how on earth did the boys gain entry through a locked door?"

"You'd be astonished at what a determined person can do." Lady Phoebe moved beside Eva, scooped up another handful of papers, and shuffled through. "Requisition orders . . . financial records . . . more order forms . . ." She shook her head. "What could it be? What sent them here, and what did they find?"

"And where are they now?" Eva finished for her.

"I simply don't see how they could have gotten into the building without my seeing them." Mr. Tremaine suddenly frowned in thought. Then, "Wait a moment. I was out of my office, out of the building, in fact, for a short time earlier."

Eva nodded. "When you brought the shipping labels to the packing crew in the outgoing shipments warehouse." The man's eyebrows went up in surprise, and she said, "We looked in

330

the warehouse for the boys when we first arrived. That's how we discovered Mr. Abbott."

"Of course." His brows knit tightly. "It pains me to point this out, but if Trent Mercer is or was here, and another man has been . . . good heavens, has been killed . . . doesn't that tell us something? Why on earth did the police release him from jail?"

The blood drained from Eva's face, from her hands, leaving her suddenly frigid. Was Mr. Tremaine correct? Had the police made a mistake? Even Lady Phoebe went pale. Fear for the two boys, or for Fox only and what might happen to him at Trent's hands? No, Eva didn't believe it, and she knew Lady Phoebe didn't believe in Trent's guilt.

But then, where were they?

Mr. Tremaine's question again went unanswered. Lady Phoebe turned to Eva and Douglas. "I suggest we split up. Eva, you and Douglas go together and start the search on the other side of the factory. I'll keep looking through this office to see if I can discover anything. Perhaps Fox left us another clue."

"I don't like to leave you." Eva placed a hand on Lady Phoebe's wrist.

"The police should be here soon. I'll be fine."

"I don't have to tell you there are plenty of nooks and crannies where young boys can hide, should they choose to." Mr. Tremaine drew in a sudden breath. "The bottle kilns. Dear me. We're scheduled for a firing this evening."

Lady Phoebe's eyes surged open, round as saucers. "Eva, Douglas, please hurry." To Mr. Tremaine, Phoebe said, "Can you cancel the firing?"

"I can, provided the furnaces haven't been lit yet." He turned back up the corridor. Moments later his voice drifted to them as a low murmur as he again spoke into a telephone, presumably on an in-house line.

Eva and Douglas hurried back outside. Once in the main quadrangle, Douglas gestured toward the art building. "Should we try there first?"

Glancing up at the building, she saw lights on in the painting room. Someone or several people were still working. "I doubt very much that's where they are," she replied. "I think we should search the outer areas. The bottle kilns first, and let's pray they're not inside one. Then the rail carriages, and the storage sheds."

Yet as they passed the art building, a window on the second floor flew open and a voice called down to them. "Eva Huntford, I'd like a word with you."

She looked up to see Moira Wickham framed in the window, glaring down at her. After a moment the woman pulled back and disappeared, and Eva assumed she was making her way downstairs.

"She's angry," she said unnecessarily. "We

haven't time for this, Douglas. Let's keep going."

They circled the clay-mixing building, but made it no farther than the enclosure on the other side, for Miss Wickham had caught up to them.

"Miss Huntford, stop right there. I don't know what you think you're up to, being here at this time of the evening, but if you don't stop and speak with me, I'll ring up the police and inform them we have intruders."

That brought Eva to a halt. "You keep going," she said to Douglas. "Look everywhere, even if you don't think they could possibly squeeze inside."

She walked to where Moira Wickham stood, with hands on hips, an angry scowl scoring lines across her brow.

"The police are already on their way. We're having a crisis, and I really haven't time—"

"A crisis," the woman repeated, her voice snapping sharply. "I'll give you *a crisis,* Miss Huntford. You never had any intention of leaving the Renshaw household, did you?"

Eva blew out a breath. She wondered how the woman had figured it out; perhaps she had seen her with Lady Phoebe in Lydia Travers's neighborhood, or someone else had and reported back. There was no use in lying now.

"No, Miss Wickham, and I'm very sorry to have inconvenienced you. If there had been any other way—"

"*Inconvenienced me? Inconvenienced me?* Oh, you did much more than that, Miss Huntford. You came to me under false pretenses, lied to me, and tricked me into confiding in you and showing you my designs, for heaven's sake. I wasted my valuable time on you, and for what? How dare you treat me so shabbily?"

"Miss Wickham, believe me, it wasn't my intention to wrong you, and anything you told me or showed me will remain in the strictest confidence." But Eva immediately realized the lie in her own words. "That is," she amended, "provided you aren't guilty of anything."

A deepening scowl turned Moira Wickham's blunt features ugly. "Of what? Of killing Ronald Mercer?"

"You had plenty of reason to resent him. To want him out of your way."

"And ruin my own life in the bargain? You don't know me at all, Miss Huntford."

Eva narrowed her gaze on the other woman. "You said you had a plan to advance your career. Did it involve stealing patterns from the designers?"

"From Mercer? Ha! As if I couldn't come up with better designs than that old windbag."

"What about Percy Bateman?"

Before Eva could pull away, Miss Wickham advanced on her and gripped her forearm. "What's he told you?"

"Nothing. Let me go. You're hurting me."

Miss Wickham's fingers clamped like the metal teeth of a trap, making Eva feel like a hare that had been caught. She suddenly became very much aware that she could be standing in the shadow of a killer. She had grown accustomed to concurring with Miss Wickham, respecting her authority in the painting room, even admiring her; she had all but forgotten the woman remained a suspect in Ronald Mercer's death . . . along with that of Lydia Travers's and now Gus Abbott's. Broad-shouldered, large-boned, Miss Wickham could have been the person who accosted them on the street outside Lydia's flat. Had the note in Lady Phoebe's handbag been a warning, or a taunt?

One thing was certain: Eva dared not mention Gus Abbott's death. Better to pretend they knew nothing about it rather than risk Miss Wickham, if she were guilty, deciding she needed to silence yet more individuals.

"I suggest you stop asking questions," Miss Wickham said in a low, hissing tone. The pressure of her fingers eased and she released her hold. "Stop sticking your nose into other people's business. You're not from here. What happens in Langston is none of your concern."

Eva opened her mouth to speak, but Douglas appeared across the enclosure, between two bottle kilns. "Eva. Everything all right?"

"Yes. I'm coming." She turned back to Miss Wickham. "I'm sorry." Despite everything, she meant it.

"I should go outside and see if the police have arrived yet," Jeffrey Tremaine said as Phoebe continued sorting through the papers left on Ronald Mercer's desk, searching for any clue as to what had sent the boys here earlier. "You'll be all right here."

"Is that a question or a statement?" she replied absently, her attention drawn once again to the financial records of various orders and the like. While his words seemed a reassurance, something in his tone had implied uncertainty. "I'm sure I'll be fine. The police should be here any moment now."

"Exactly my thought. I'll lock you in to make certain no one else has access to the building." He rose to go, leaving the order forms he had been going through in a neat stack on the desk. "I've found nothing here that could possibly have interested Trent. He must have been looking for something altogether different, and either he found it, or it wasn't here. You know, it's quite possible they left the factory a while ago."

Phoebe sighed, her hands going still over the papers. "I realize that. But if they're not here, I have no inkling where they could be."

"Perhaps try telephoning over to Lyndale Park

to see if they've made it home by now." He pointed to the telephone on the desk.

The suggestion took her by surprise with its simple logic, and she felt foolish for not having thought of it herself. "Thank you, Mr. Tremaine, I'll do that."

He nodded. "I'll be back soon, with the police."

She felt a certain relief when she heard the echo of the outer door closing and the lock clicking into place. Being alone, she reasoned, was safer than being with anyone connected to Crown Lily, Jeffrey Tremaine included. Though she didn't seriously entertain the notion of his being guilty, until they discovered the identity of the killer, no one rose above suspicion.

She reached for the telephone and tapped the cradle, and placed the call with the operator. The butler answered, and moments later Veronica's voice came over the wire.

"Phoebe? Where are you?"

"At Crown Lily. Has my brother shown up there?"

"Fox? I haven't seen him. Not for hours now. His friend, either, come to think of it. Aren't they supposed to be in the house or on the immediate grounds? That detective inspector won't be pleased to learn they're running around somewhere, unchaperoned. I must say, if I'd had anything to say about it, I would not have allowed a suspected murderer, no matter how young, in this house. What was your sister thinking?"

"Veronica." Phoebe practically shouted into the telephone to quiet Julia's sister-in-law. "Please, if they happen to appear, keep them there. Have Owen and Amelia returned yet?"

"Phoebe, it seems everyone is deserting you today. No, they aren't back from their ride. I suspect Amelia persuaded him into letting her take the wheel. Neither man nor sheep will be safe along these roads."

"All right, I have to go. Please tell Owen I'm at Crown Lily and that he should drive over here immediately."

Veronica was still speaking when Phoebe disconnected. She glanced at the pile of papers, then down at the desk drawers, and had another thought. Slipping a hairpin free, she set to work. True, the police had already been through this office, but perhaps they missed something, or had bypassed something they'd deemed unimportant. At this moment, she reminded herself, she wasn't necessarily looking for a murderer. She was looking for her brother and his friend.

She had just managed to unlock the first drawer when she heard, from down the corridor, the main door being unlocked and opened. She quickly slid the drawer closed, not wishing Jeffrey Tremaine to see her rummaging like a thief. The footsteps approached at a rapid pace . . . lighter

338

and different, somehow, from Mr. Tremaine's. A figure rushed by the doorway.

Phoebe gasped. The footsteps halted and Percy Bateman reappeared on the threshold. He looked tousled—more so than his typical dishabille. Rather than simply rumpled, he looked as if he'd run across the factory at breakneck speed. Indeed, his chest heaved in and out and his nostrils flared as he obviously struggled to catch his breath.

His intense gaze pinned Phoebe to the chair she was sitting in. "What are you doing here?"

She swallowed and raised her chin. "I could ask you the same. Mr. Tremaine indicated there was no one else in the building but him."

"I suppose he thought I'd left for the day." She only now noticed he held a portfolio to his chest, both arms folded over it possessively. "Where is he?"

"Outside. Waiting for the police." She considered her words carefully. "It seems there has been another incident."

"What sort of incident?"

She compressed her lips and thought how best to frame it. She decided evasiveness might be the best choice. "I'm not sure." Not a complete falsehood; she truly didn't know how Gus Abbott had come to be lying on the warehouse floor. "I think you should wait and ask Mr. Tremaine about it."

"You never answered my question, Lady

Phoebe. Why on earth would you be here now? It can't be to place another order." Now that his initial shock at finding her there had abated, he seemed to relax. His features eased. His tone sounded more congenial. "Unless there is some problem with your orders I'm not aware of."

"No, it isn't that." She smiled, fully realizing if he had seen Fox and Trent, he would have said so, unless his intentions toward them—and her— were less than benevolent. The portfolio once again drew her attention. "What's that? More designs?"

"Again you evade my question, Lady Phoebe. One would almost think you were up to something." He moved closer. "Are you? You really shouldn't be in this office."

"Mr. Tremaine is perfectly aware that I'm here." Caution induced her to combine that bit of truth with a white lie. "I'm . . . looking for something Trent asked for. A . . . photograph that included his mother."

Percy Bateman shook his head. "Ronald Mercer was not a sentimental man. I'd never known him to carry or display photos of his family."

She shrugged as if it were of little consequence to her. "I only know what Trent told me. Perhaps Mr. Mercer didn't wish to appear sentimental. Perhaps he believed it would diminish his authority to admit he possessed a soft heart beneath his stern exterior." She allowed her gaze to sweep him. "I expect it's your position of authority now, Mr. Bateman."

"That remains to be seen," he said with a grim chuckle.

They appeared to be at a standoff, a cordial one, but impassable, all the same. Phoebe wasn't about to tell him what he wished to know, and he seemed equally disinclined to show her what he guarded with such possessiveness within the portfolio.

Mr. Mercer's pattern book? Why else would he be so unwilling to show it to her? But where had it been hidden? Where had he been just now? These were questions she burned to ask, but didn't dare for fear of provoking him. Soon the police would be here and could make whatever inquiries they liked.

The police . . . She had told Percy Bateman they were on the way. If he were guilty of anything, would he still be here, calmly speaking with her? She didn't think so. Unless it was part of his ruse to appear innocent.

She wished Mr. Tremaine would come back inside. Better still, she longed for Owen to arrive, if he'd gotten her message from Julia. She worried about Eva and Douglas—they'd been gone so long now. Had they not yet found a trace of Fox and Trent?

She came to her feet. "If you'll excuse me, Mr. Bateman. I believe you were right, and there is no photograph to be found here. I'll have to speak with Trent again. Perhaps he meant an office his father kept in their house."

"I'm sorry, Lady Phoebe, but I can't let you go." He backed up and closed the door, then came closer to the desk again, leaning slightly over it with a significant lift of his eyebrow. "Not like this. Now sit back down."

CHAPTER 19

Panic hit the back of Phoebe's throat. Did Percy Bateman have a weapon hidden in that portfolio he continued to hug to his chest? She wasn't about to wait and find out. A quick glance down revealed scant few choices for a weapon of her own, but she needed only one. As he continued to lean toward her in a threatening posture, she made her choice.

Snatching the telephone in two hands, she leaned over the desk, swung the device upward, and brought it down on the side of Percy Bateman's head. For an instant he regarded her in startlement. Then his eyes rolled back in his head, the portfolio slid from his grasp, and his legs buckled, rendering him a heap on the floor.

She wasted no time in circling the desk, stepping over him, and hurrying down the corridor. Briefly she considered doubling back for the portfolio, which might provide evidence to prove he had murdered Mr. Mercer and stolen the pattern book, but she had no idea how long she had rendered him unconscious. He might merely be stunned and already could be gathering his sensibilities. Better to get to safety and allow the police to apprehend him and the pattern book.

At the outside door she paused to listen behind

her. No sound came from Ronald Mercer's office. She pushed through the door.

Not a soul inhabited the enclosure, but she hadn't expected to find Jeffrey Tremaine here. He would be in the main quadrangle, or perhaps at the guard gate, waiting for the police. She headed in that direction.

Before she could turn the corner, Mr. Tremaine came around it and she nearly ran into him. She saw him only at the last moment and came to an abrupt halt that upset her footing. Mr. Tremaine caught her, gripping her forearms to steady her and prevent her from going down.

"Are the police here?" The question came out in a breathless rush, barely audible to her above the pounding of her heart.

"Not yet. I thought I'd better come check on you."

"It's Percy Bateman—I believe he's our killer. He's in Ronald Mercer's office. He's got the pattern book. At least I suspect he does. I don't know if he's armed. We must get away from here."

His hands still encircled her wrists, and he tightened his hold. "Please, Lady Phoebe, slow down. What makes you think Percy Bateman killed anyone?"

"We've got to get away before he comes to," she insisted. "And we have to find the others. Eva and Douglas and the boys. Have you seen them?"

"I haven't." Mr. Tremaine steered her into the main quadrangle, hurrying her along with a hand at the small of her back. "Surely, you're wrong about Percy Bateman, though. I can't believe it of him."

"He came into the office hugging a portfolio to his chest, and when I questioned him about it, he was entirely evasive. And then he refused to let me leave. He left me no choice but to hit him with the telephone. But I may have only dazed him. Please, Mr. Tremaine."

"All right, all right. We'll find the others. Everything will be fine, Lady Phoebe, you'll see." He raised his hand to her shoulder, guiding her quickly past the warehouse and the clay-mixing building. "Now if I remember correctly, you told your servants to search this side of the factory. So that's where we'll start."

"Eva!" Phoebe cried out. "Douglas! Can you hear us?"

Mr. Tremaine's hand on her shoulder tensed as if her shouts startled him. He increased the urgency of their pace until they reached the first row of bottle kilns, each one spaced several tens of yards from the next. The doorways, which she remembered as being open when they toured the facility, were now solid walls of brick and sand. Mr. Tremaine had pointed out there were no actual doors to these structures, and that bricks were used to seal each kiln when it was time for the firing. Panic niggled again and sent her gaze skyward. She searched for wisps of smoke.

"You were able to stop the firing," she concluded with a great cascade of relief.

"Of course," he said with authority. "We will not light the kilns until we're sure there is no one in them."

"Thank goodness," she murmured, and called out for Eva and Douglas again. Each time, she noticed, Mr. Tremaine flinched. "What could be taking the police so long to get here?"

"I wish I knew." He guided her around the first one. They briskly circled the perimeter of the kiln, past the firemouths, brick ovens in the walls of the kiln built close to the ground. Here, coal was fed to fuel the fires that would heat the kiln through flues that ran beneath the floor of the structure. Then they moved on to the next. They saw no trace of anyone, other than the footprints of the workmen who had prepared for the firing.

"Mr. Tremaine," Phoebe said, "might we enlist some of your workers to help in the search? Perhaps the warehouse crew?"

"The warehouse crew?"

"Yes, the men preparing the night shipments. Surely, finding Eva, Douglas, and the boys takes precedence over a shipment of tea sets."

"Yes, a good idea, that." But he made no move to retrace their steps to the warehouse. Across the facility other bottle kilns appeared ready for firing, their doorways blocked with bricks. "We should check over that way," he said, pointing.

"Mr. Tremaine, you aren't listening to me."

"Come, Lady Phoebe, we mustn't delay."

It was then the silence, the utter stillness, wrapped a new fear around her. If the kilns were to be fired, where were the men who would feed the furnaces? Had Mr. Tremaine sent them all home when he canceled the firing?

And the men in the warehouse—why wouldn't he ask for their help? What could be so important about the shipments?

Something one of them had said earlier echoed in her memory—something about Mr. Tremaine bringing them shipping labels. Why would the owner of the company perform such a menial task? Weren't there others responsible for preparing and delivering the labels? Of course there were. As they had learned on the tour, there existed a process for every step of Crown Lily's operations.

And yet . . . this evening Mr. Tremaine had delivered those labels himself. And those warehouse workers . . . they had taken such a defensive stance when Phoebe and the others intruded upon their labors—as if they hadn't wanted them to see what was in those containers. Or perhaps not what was in them, but where they were going.

There had been thefts at Crown Lily, with

finished products disappearing in transit to their final destinations . . . And once they went "missing," Jeffrey Tremaine would collect the insurance, not for cost of production, but the price of the final sale plus the shipping fees. Crown Lily could afford to replace the set, while its owner pocketed the profit.

And then there were those leather straps used to secure the crates—the very same used on Mr. Abbott.

"You were in the warehouse earlier," she murmured without quite meaning to say it aloud.

"Did you say something, Lady Phoebe?"

They were nearing the next row of bottle kilns. From the corner of her eye, she saw one with a partly gaping doorway, where the bricks had only been piled halfway. His fingers clamped her shoulder, and he turned her toward it.

"The police aren't coming, are they?" she said.

"Why would you say that?"

"Because you never called them." She tried to dig in her heels. Could she hold out long enough for Owen to arrive? *Would* he arrive? "No. I'm going back. Let me go."

"I've given you every chance to avoid this, Lady Phoebe, and you've refused." He released her long enough to seize her again with two hands, one on each shoulder. With a violent thrust he propelled her forward. "Such a stubborn young lady, it's a wonder your grandparents don't despair of you. Come along now, like a good girl. Why, soon you'll be reunited with your maid. You'd like that, wouldn't you?"

"Eva's in there?" The bottle kiln towered over her, its height blocking out the few stars that had appeared in the purpling sky; its doorway gaped like a toothless grin.

"She is. And so is Douglas. They're waiting for you."

"Where are the boys? What have you done with Trent and Fox?"

"Not a thing . . . yet. But when I find those two troublemakers, they'll regret their meddling, just as you're going to."

They were within yards of the kiln. Phoebe stiffened every muscle in her body to bring them to a halt. "You killed Ronald Mercer, and the others. Why? At least tell me that much before you kill me."

"My dear Lady Phoebe, I'm not going to kill you." He grinned with malevolent enjoyment as he moved his hands from her shoulders to her wrists, locking them viciously within his grip. "The intense heat of the kiln will do that. I suppose there's no harm, therefore, in telling you. Ronald Mercer was about to challenge my ownership of Crown Lily. You see, the war nearly killed this company. We barely hung on, and only did so because Ron Mercer's father lent me a great sum of money. Quietly, with none of our other investors the wiser. When he died in '17, I thought, *Good, the money is now mine, free and clear.* And it was, until Ron found evidence of the loan among his father's financial documents and demanded payment or an equal share in the company. *Equal!* Can you imagine the gall?" With a condescending smirk he shook his head. "I couldn't possibly allow that, could I?"

"So you killed him. But why in the grinding pan?" Recalling something Eva had told her, she gasped. "Gus Abbott said you sent him into the warehouse that morning. Because you knew Ronald Mercer wished to speak to him about altering the clay formula, that he would be in the clay-mixing building . . . that was your chance."

"Indeed, it was. But Gus, he was a man who thought about things too much. He started acting skittish with me, and it wasn't hard to realize why."

"He figured you out, didn't he?" Dread filled her, but she couldn't keep silent. "Trent's dog— Jester. He'd been following you around that morning, hadn't he? He likes you. He didn't go near Mr. Mercer in the conference room that first day, but he went right over to greet you."

"Yes, I seem to have a way with dogs." He chuckled. "He witnessed the whole thing. At the time I thought a good thing dogs can't talk."

A wave of nausea rolled through Phoebe. She whispered, "And Lydia? Why her?" Yet the answer suddenly occurred to her. "She was selling patterns . . . for you. Another way for you to reap greater profits. You sabotaged your own company, didn't you?"

"Crown Lily's days are numbered, Lady Phoebe, and it's time for me to maximize my own profits. As for poor Lydia, she had the misfortune of Miss Wickham putting two and two together and realizing the girl had been selling patterns to the competition. Lucky for me—and for Miss Wickham—her deduction stopped there, or I'd have had to dispatch her as well. As it is, I'm thinking of sacking her. She's too clever by half, that one."

"You killed Lydia for no reason, simply for being found out by Miss Wickham?" The thought of that poor girl's final moments sickened her. Her stomach pitched and roiled.

"Goodness no. I killed her because after she was sacked, she tried blackmailing me." His features twisted into a scowl. "That's enough conversation. Move."

She tried to resist him, tried pulling free, but his grip on her wrists threatened to break her bones. He jerked her forward, half shoving, half dragging her, when she stumbled. The empty half smile of the kiln's doorway mocked her, becoming wider, deeper, the closer she got. She cried out for help, but his hand was over her mouth before she could get out the words, pressing her lips cruelly against her teeth until she tasted blood. The kiln towered over her, filling her vision. Suddenly his hand came away from her mouth, and a blinding pain exploded at the back of her head.

Eva awoke to waves of heat eddying around her, through her, seeping up from the surface beneath her. A vague dread tickled at the back of her brain, but she couldn't name it. She stirred, tried to move, to sit up. Her arms and legs felt weighted and numb, her skirts twisted around her knees. An endless void of inky blackness filled her vision. The cheek that lay on the ground felt as though someone held a hot iron near it.

Where was she?

In the next moment memory flooded back. Douglas had rounded the bottle kiln ahead of her, disappearing from her line of sight. He had thought he'd heard something . . . or someone. Before she reached him, she'd heard a thud and, coming around the kiln, found him on the ground, a figure standing over him. The figure turned to her and recognition had sent a violent shock through her.

And then she'd woken up here in the darkness, unable to move. Her head throbbed, a dull pain that squeezed and released, squeezed and released. She tried to lift it, could just get her cheek off the ground. In the struggle to do so, the restraints on her wrists cut into her flesh. She clenched her teeth against the sting.

"Douglas?" The name left her lips like a swipe of sandpaper. She tried to swallow, couldn't, but tried her voice again. "Douglas? Are you here?"

The words were dry and rusty and stung her throat. She wiggled her body and stretched out her bound hands. The ends of her fingers came in contact with something that yielded slightly as she prodded. Her fingertips identified fabric encasing something more solid. An arm?

"Douglas, wake up. Please wake up."

"Eva? Is that you?" The answering voice, weak and rasping like hers, didn't belong to Douglas.

"Lady Phoebe?" Her heart filled her chest to bursting. A cold and deadly fear swam through her, driving away all sense of the heat.

"Where are you, Eva?"

"I'm here. I can't move. I'm tied."

She heard a shuffling over the stone floor, and then, "Keep talking, I'll find you."

Eva kept up a steady flow of words until, somehow, a pair of hands settled gently on her leg, then worked their way up to her bound hands. Lady Phoebe's fingers went to work on the knots, while Eva clamped her teeth together to keep from groaning each time the thin leather straps bit into her wrists. Her skin became wet there; blood, no doubt, but it didn't matter, not while they were still alive and clinging to some small hope of getting out of there.

Where was here? Oh, yes. The bottle kiln. The bottle kiln that had been lit, and whose fires were even now growing in strength, sending searing heat upward from the network of flues beneath the floor. Jeffrey Tremaine would never get away with it, Eva thought, but then realized he would, of course. He'd order all the kilns fired now, and when they were opened two days hence, there would be no trace that any of them had ever been inside.

"Where is Douglas?" Lady Phoebe whispered as she worked.

"I think he's lying just to my right."

Lady Phoebe's fingers stilled. "Yes, he's here. Douglas?"

"He's still unconscious." Eva hoped, prayed, that was all it was, that Douglas wasn't . . .

"I think I've got it now." Lady Phoebe stopped working the knots again. "Try to pull your hands apart."

Eva put her strength into forcing her bonds to slide free. That further cut into her wrists, but she pushed past the pain until the straps hung limply and fell to the floor. She wasted no time in setting to work on her ankles. "If we could only see something."

"There are tiny chinks of light coming through the doorway. We're behind china saggars stacked in the middle of the kiln. A wall of them, several thick. They're blocking the light from outside."

"I believe I'm free." Eva gave a final tug and was rewarded once again by the last of the leather straps falling away, freeing her legs. She attempted to straighten them. Pain shot through her knees from having been in a bent position for so long, but it passed quickly enough. "Can you help me to stand?"

She groped for Lady Phoebe's hands, found them, and together they struggled to their feet. "Dear God, Eva, he started the firing. We've got to get out."

"We will, my lady. I promise, we will." Could she keep such a promise? She'd use her last breath in the effort. Give her own life in exchange for that of her dear lady.

And yet, it was Lady Phoebe who had already devised a plan. "Let's get back to the doorway and start prying the bricks out of the way. If we can do that, it'll not only let in more light, but will allow some of this heat to escape. And then we'll come back for Douglas."

They felt their way around the stacked saggars until, as Lady Phoebe had said, tiny chinks of light poked holes in the blackness. They headed for them.

"We merely need to push some of these bricks out of the way." Lady Phoebe pressed the heel of her hand against the wall that sealed them in.

Eva did likewise, heaving for all she was worth. Nothing happened.

"They're not moving." Eva kept trying, even as despair filled her.

"We're not giving up." Lady Phoebe took her hands off the bricks and turned away. "Is there something we can use? Anything for leverage?"

Eva, too, turned away from the wall of brick to search their surroundings. Now, in the scant light, she saw the saggars towering over them. Rows of the clay containers lined the walls of the kiln, nearly as high as the chimney some sixty feet above them. The heat surrounded her, seeming to sap her body of all its moisture, leaving her mouth parched and her eyes gritty. She saw nothing useful, only those saggars disappearing into the darkness overhead. "Do you think we could climb up? Could we fit through the chimney?"

Lady Phoebe went to the nearest stack and glanced up. She shook her head. "I don't think they're sturdy enough. They'd come tumbling down if we tried to climb. Besides, even if we got out, it's a good sixty or seventy feet to the ground."

Eva might be willing to chance it, to escape the fate of burning to death, being reduced to ash. She pounded with her fists against the bricks. "Is anyone out there? Can anyone hear me? Help us!"

"The walls are more than a foot thick. So is the doorway. No wonder the bricks won't budge." The hope left Lady Phoebe's voice, frightening Eva more than anything else. "Remember what Mr. Tremaine said that first day. There are at least two or three layers of them, held firm by the sand." Lady Phoebe didn't speak the words, but Eva heard her make the pronouncement, all the same. They were going to die, and their deaths would be horrific.

"These chinks of light prove Jeffrey Tremaine did a poor job of sealing this doorway. It should be a solid barrier, and it isn't." Eva stopped pounding as a thought occurred to her. "Was it still daylight when Mr. Tremaine forced you in here?"

"No. It was nearly dark."

"Well, it's not now. This light peeking through—my guess is the area has been illuminated so the workers can see to resume lighting the rest of the kilns. Lighting only this one would be far too suspicious. Mr. Tremaine must make this look like an ordinary firing."

"Eva, you're right." Lady Phoebe moved back beside her at the doorway and began shouting. "Hello! In here! Someone, help us."

How long they could keep it up, Eva didn't know. The heat drained her energy, left her feeling as though she'd trudged for days through a desert. Once again she turned to search for anything they could use to make noise that would be heard from outside. She saw nothing but all those towering saggars, and the iron bands that ran around the walls of the kiln to strengthen the structure. She doubted very much she could tear one of those free.

Her gaze returned to the saggars . . . perhaps they could make use of those. Eva moved to the closest stack along the wall. They reached well over her head.

Then she would have to push them over.

"Lady Phoebe, help me with this." She heaved against the stack, over and over.

"What about Douglas?"

"He'll be safe. He's toward the back, where I was, behind the saggars stacked in the middle."

Lady Phoebe came beside her and together they threw their combined weight against the stack of containers, each one holding numerous cups, saucers, plates, and bowls. The tower began to rock and teeter, and with a final shove they set it toppling. Eva grabbed Lady Phoebe, whisked her against the wall, and shielded her body with her own. Only a few feet from where they stood, clay and porcelain crashed and shattered, sending a spray of shards in all directions. A cloud of clay dust billowed. A dreadful sound echoed through the kiln, an earsplitting crescendo that lasted only a few seconds before all went still.

CHAPTER 20

Pressed against the wall of the kiln, her back burning from the rising heat, Phoebe coughed against the grit clogging her throat. Eva stayed pressed against her for some moments, utterly still, not even the sound of her breathing reaching Phoebe's ears.

Then Eva eased slowly away. "Dearest Phoebe, are you all right?"

"I am, but never mind me." No, Eva had used herself as a human shield, protecting Phoebe from the flying debris. "Were you struck? Your head? Your back?"

"I don't think so. I'm not in any pain."

"Thank goodness." They moved away from the wall, picking their way over the rubble, a small fortune's worth of broken china. Phoebe could just make out heaps and shards and the swirling dust that was still settling, that had turned the blackness a sickly gray. "Now what?"

"Find any part of a saggar—a lid or a divider from inside—still intact enough that we might use as a wedge between the bricks."

Phoebe went down on her hands and knees, attempting to keep her skirts between her and the slivers of china that littered the floor. Her hands found what felt like a large piece of a round saggar lid. She carefully came to her feet. "I've got something."

She carried it to the doorway and attempted to wedge it between layers of brick. The edge of the lid caught for a moment, but when she attempted to apply leverage, it slid off with a grinding jolt. Eva joined her, having found a piece of curving wall from a saggar. As had Phoebe, she attempted to use it as a makeshift crowbar.

Eva's results were the same as Phoebe's. They kept trying until Phoebe's arms ached, her muscles trembling. All the while as they struggled, the heat continued to swell around them, making breathing difficult, the dry air like a knife against her throat.

"I don't understand it. It's as if he used mortar between these bricks." She let the saggar lid slip from her hands and fall to the stones at her feet.

"They're packed tightly." Eva kept trying as she spoke. "They must have special tools for clearing them away from the openings, once the firing is done."

Each heave punctuated her words. Then she stopped trying to use the side of the saggar as a wedge and simply pounded it against the bricks. Phoebe looked on while hope drained away, as understanding dawned that their efforts would come to nothing.

They would come to nothing in a few short hours, too. Although judging by the growing pain in her lungs, Phoebe calculated they would be dead long before the kiln reduced them to ash.

"Hello?" Eva shouted as she pounded. "Is anyone out there? We're in here! We're—" She broke off, coughing until she doubled over. When she straightened, she pulled back to deliver another blow.

Phoebe reached out and placed a gentle hand on her arm. "Eva, stop. It's no use."

"No, Phoebe, don't give up. Don't you dare." Eva struck the piece of saggar against the bricks.

Phoebe's throat ached and her eyes stung, not only from the heat and dust now, but from the tears pushing for release. "Perhaps it's better to accept it, dear Eva."

Her head bowing, Eva dropped the saggar and turned to Phoebe. "Dearest lady." Her arms went around Phoebe, drawing her close. "A younger sister, a child, a wonderful friend . . . you've been all of those things to me."

Phoebe felt Eva's tears mingling with her own. "I know. I don't know what I would have done these past years without you. I'd have been utterly lost."

"No, you're stronger than that."

"Because of you. Because you've always believed in me, even when few others did."

Like Phoebe's father, Eva had always seen the best in her, had never doubted her abilities. Papa's and Eva's confidence in her had allowed her to flourish, to believe in herself, to do things she might never have had the courage to attempt, otherwise.

But this time she had reached too far. And now . . . "Eva, I'm so very sorry. If not for me . . ."

Eva's arms tightened fiercely. "Don't say that. We're in this together. Everything we've survived, we've survived together. I was never anywhere but where I wished to be."

Phoebe let out a long, searing breath. She had no more words, wasn't sure she could speak them if she did. Her thoughts went to Douglas, still lying unconscious behind the wall of saggars in the middle of the kiln. Should they have woken him? Perhaps it's better he didn't know what was happening. Perhaps he would die without suffering.

She stood in Eva's embrace, returning it with the last of her strength. The bottoms of her feet were burning through the soles of her shoes now. This was her fault, even though Eva would deny that with her last breath.

"My lady, did you hear that?"

Phoebe lifted her head from Eva's shoulder. "Hear what?" Surely, it was merely Eva's hopes conjuring sounds from outside. But then, she heard it, too, or were they both only imagining the clinking sounds from the other side of the bricks?

Eva released her and pressed her ear against

them, wincing when her skin came up against the hot surface. Her mouth opened on a gasp. "There's someone out there."

Phoebe pushed forward, her ear to the bricks as well, ignoring the blistering of her own skin. Ever so faintly she heard voices and a metallic rapping against the outer part of the doorway. "I can't make out what they're saying."

"It doesn't matter." Eva grasped her arm. "Let's move out of the way."

They stood pressed together, clasping hands tightly, hoping against hope. To Phoebe they stood there for an eternity, waiting for the impossible. She began to believe their liberation would never come, at least not in time. But Phoebe realized that if people were out there, they must have doused the coal fires. Could she feel a difference?

She could not. Heat enveloped her. The air continued to sear her lungs, scorch her skin. Surely, surely, they would not burn to death now. She and Eva both tightened their hold on one another. Her fingers throbbed with the pain of it, but she didn't care. It meant they were both still alive.

Finally a voice reached her ears. "Is someone in there?"

"Help us!" she and Eva shouted together.

Bricks began to fall away and light speared through in silver shafts. First Phoebe saw iron crowbars and a sledgehammer chipping away at the barrier. Then thickly-gloved hands appeared, able to find purchase now that an opening had been created. That opening grew, and Phoebe and Eva rushed forward.

"There's someone else inside," Phoebe cried out as those hands seized her arms and pulled her through to the other side. The heated stones burned against her torso and legs, but only for an instant and then she was clear. Bright, electric floodlights momentarily blinded her. Eva emerged immediately after her, and then a man disappeared inside.

"Thank you, thank you." As the words left her lips, she fell to the ground and began sucking in great, cooling drafts of life-giving air.

Eva sank beside her and they held each other again, sobbing and speaking at once. Phoebe didn't quite know what she or Eva was saying. Their ability to speak at all was enough for the moment.

Another pair of arms went around her, and a deep, infinitely comforting voice spoke in her ear. "Phoebe. My God, Phoebe. And you, Eva. Thank God you're both still alive."

"Owen." Without relinquishing her hold on Eva, she buried her cheek against Owen's chest and thanked God and every angel that must have been watching over them for their lives. And then she remembered. "Douglas."

Owen raised his chin from her hair. "They've got him out." He was silent as his arms tightened around her, and then, "He's alive, Phoebe. Thank God for that dreadful crash inside the kiln, or we would have taken much longer to find you."

She thought to tell him that pushing over the saggars had been Eva's idea, but that could wait for now. "Fox and Trent?"

"I found them on my way here," he said, stroking her cheek. "They were on the road, making their way to the police station. They said they had evidence against Jeffrey Tremaine, a motive for him to have murdered Ronald Mercer."

"Are they . . . ?"

"They're fine. And you needn't worry about Tremaine getting away. He had a bit of a mishap with his motorcar just now in his haste to flee Crown Lily."

Phoebe had so many questions that went unspoken. The last of her strength drained away, and she slipped into darkness.

She woke up sometime later—how much later, she could not say. Her head lay on a pillow, her body on a lumpy mattress, which could not have felt more luxurious, not after what she'd been through. A plain white ceiling stretched above her, informing her she could not be anywhere in Lyndale Park, with its coffered ceilings or intricate plaster medallions.

She glanced around her. A curtained screen stood to one side of the bed. A bare window occupied the wall on her left. A plain wooden door with a rectangular window led . . .

To the rest of the hospital, she could only assume. Suddenly the door opened and a nurse came in.

"Awake, I see. How are you feeling?"

Phoebe wasn't quite sure. She tested her voice, only to cough and sputter. She tried again. "I'm all right," she rasped. "Alive."

"Indeed. You're very lucky. We all know what those kilns can do. It's a wonder you survived the heat for as long as you did. You have some minor burns on your legs, but they'll soon heal." The woman shook a thermometer vigorously and slipped it into Phoebe's mouth. "Under the tongue. I'd say you and your friends are frightfully stubborn, in a good way."

"Eva and Douglas?"

"Are both going to be all right. Miss Huntford is already sitting up and asking for you. The young man suffered quite a head injury, I'm afraid. A concussion. But he's also awake and the doctor says he'll be fine as well, given a bit of time."

An urgent thought sent Phoebe upright. Dizziness made her lean back on her elbows. "Mr. Tremaine. He did all of this."

"I know. It's all anyone is talking about. He's in

366

this very hospital, too. But don't worry, he's not going anywhere. He's handcuffed to his bed and there's an armed policeman outside his room."

Phoebe had a vague memory of Owen telling her Mr. Tremaine had had a mishap with his motorcar. "How . . . What happened to him?"

"Well, apparently, he tried to get away in his motorcar, and a young man in a Runabout—a war hero, I'm told—headed him off and made him swerve into a building. It was the one where they mix the clay. But no need to fret over Jeffrey Tremaine. He'll be fine, too, and he'll be heading off to jail soon enough."

Eva opened the front door and beckoned the pair who stood on the steps inside. "Thank you for coming," she said to them, and helped them off with their coats.

"It's quite a place." Moira Wickham walked several steps into Lyndale Park's main hall and turned full about, her gaze traveling over woodwork, furnishings, and the Baccarat crystal chandelier that hung above her. "I suppose your job does have its perks, Miss Huntford. You get to live in places like this."

"Yes." Eva smiled and didn't bother reminding her that most lady's maids rarely saw this part of a great house, as they were typically consigned to bedrooms and the workrooms belowstairs.

Contrary to Miss Wickham's enthusiasm for

the house, Percy Bateman lingered near the door, looking uncertain and ready to flee. "Are we to be taken to task, Miss Huntford?"

The question surprised her. *"Taken to task?* Not at all, Mr. Bateman." She held out her arm. "Won't you both come this way, please."

She led them into the drawing room, where Lady Phoebe, Owen Seabright, and the boys, Trent and Fox, sat ranged around the fireplace. Jester lay curled up in front of the hearth, sound asleep and snoring lightly. Everyone looked up as the new arrivals entered the room.

Lady Phoebe came to her feet. "Thank you for agreeing to see us here today." She extended her hand to both of them, but saved a sheepish expression for Mr. Bateman. "How is your head? I'm so sorry to have struck you with the telephone. But in all honesty, you frightened me. Why did you try to keep me in Ronald Mercer's office?"

"You looked at me so suspiciously, Lady Phoebe, I thought you'd realized the truth of what Miss Wickham and I were doing. I feared if I simply let you walk out, you might tell Mr. Tremaine, and I wanted a chance to explain."

"You might have simply done that, rather than refuse to let me leave in such a threatening manner." Though Lady Phoebe's words were harsh, her manner remained cordial. "It was for that very reason I suspected you. And hit you," she added apologetically.

"Yes, well." He pressed a hand to his head, where, Eva surmised, a bump must still exist. "Hindsight" was all he said. But Eva could sense his vast relief.

Lady Phoebe addressed both of their guests. "Please have a seat. Tea?"

It was Moira Wickham's turn to look wary. "We'd like to know why we're here, if you wouldn't mind."

"Speak for yourself, Moira." Percy Bateman claimed one of the vacant chairs. "I, for one, wouldn't mind being served tea in a drawing room like this. Probably the only chance I'll ever have."

That drew a chuckle from Lady Phoebe, who waited until Moira Wickham had seated herself before returning to her own chair. Eva pushed the buzzer beside the mantel and then took her seat across from Lady Phoebe. "It will be up presently."

"In Crown Lily china?" Percy Bateman asked.

"I'm sorry," Eva replied, "I didn't think to specify to the kitchen staff."

Percy Bateman waved the notion away.

Moira Wickham turned to him with a scowl. "Stop acting the idiot. Do you think they brought us here to ply us with cake? No. We're obviously in some sort of trouble." She regarded Lady Phoebe and Lord Owen, then turned to Eva with a scowl meant specifically for her. "I'm sure you're relishing this."

"You're not in any trouble, Miss Wickham. Nor you, Mr. Bateman." Eva angled her legs and crossed her ankles, leaning slightly forward in her chair. "But we do wish you both to be honest with us. Were the two of you working together to create patterns for Crown Lily, and did you plan to eventually take your combined talent to another company?"

Moira Wickham stared at her for several long moments, her perplexity obvious. "Are you to conduct this interrogation, then? Not your superiors?"

Eva sighed. "It's not meant to be an interrogation. But if you would prefer Lady Phoebe to ask the questions, she will."

"But Eva is perfectly capable, and we are all of the same mind," Lady Phoebe assured her. "Please, Miss Wickham, and you, too, Mr. Bateman, answer the questions. It's important."

"Yes, well . . . all right." Miss Wickham and Mr. Bateman traded glances. He shrugged, as if to say there was no use in hiding the truth anymore. Miss Wickham nodded in resignation. "Yes, we've been working together for some time now. You see, I cannot submit my designs on my own. Percy can. And—"

She got no further, for Percy Bateman bounced forward in his chair, clapped his hands together once, and happily declared, "Moira here is a genius. Together we make a splendid team, and we planned to approach a competitor when the time was right—once our designs had taken on renown at Crown Lily." He sat back again, some of his enthusiasm deflating. "Because you see, Ronald Mercer and Jeffrey Tremaine would never have allowed it. They considered me too young and Moira . . . well . . ."

"Is a woman," Eva finished for him.

"But do you both see," Lady Phoebe said, "that your actions became highly suspicious? We knew you were hiding something—something to do with your work. We believed one of you was stealing patterns from the other, or perhaps stealing from Ronald Mercer. And that, we believed, gave either or both of you a reason to have murdered Mr. Mercer."

At that pronouncement the tea arrived. A brooding silence descended on the room as Carmichael served the refreshments. He had barely crossed the threshold on his way out before Moira Wickham burst out with, "So now you know we weren't doing anything wrong— not criminally wrong, at any rate. Mr. Tremaine murdered Mr. Mercer and the others—God rest them. Crown Lily will be closed forever or will be sold to a new owner. There's nothing that can be done about that. So, will someone please explain why we are here?"

"You are here because we wish to make you an offer," Owen Seabright said.

That drew a frown from Miss Wickham. "And who are you?"

"Miss Wickham, Mr. Bateman, I'd like to introduce you to Owen Seabright." Lady Phoebe smiled over at him. "He is in the textile industry, but is considering diversifying into china production."

"Financially speaking, that is," Lord Owen clarified. "I know nothing about china, which is why we're here. A discovery has been made that should allow Crown Lily to continue as it has been for the past, what is it? Two hundred years or thereabouts?"

Neither Miss Wickham's irritation nor her guardedness lifted even a fraction. "What kind of discovery?"

"One moment." Eva stared down at the dark amber brew in her teacup, then back up at Miss Wickham. "Before we go on, I do have one question. Why did you give Lydia Travers the sack? Did you truly believe her to be selling patterns to a competitor?"

Miss Wickham picked up an enameled box from the table beside her, turned it over to gaze at the bottom, and placed it back on the table. "I did. I know for a fact a few of our patterns showed up on some of Royal Wiltshire's china. She did have a beau there, and it only seemed to make sense."

"I believe we can explain that." Lady Phoebe rose and went to a side table. She lifted a leather-bound book and portfolio, and brought it back to the gathering. "These two items constitute Ronald Mercer's pattern book. They were found in Mr. Tremaine's office. He himself had been selling patterns to his competitors, as well as misdirecting shipments of china, in order to collect the insurance money and reap extra profits. However, he was working through Lydia Travers when it came to the patterns. He used her as a go-between to protect his own identity in these dealings."

This news appeared to render Miss Wickham speechless. But only for a moment. "I was right about her. Why, that—"

"I don't think Mr. Tremaine gave her much choice," Lady Phoebe said. "Once you let her go, she realized her mistake and asked him for enough money to tide her over. Instead he murdered her to ensure her silence."

"Oh, good heavens." Moira Wickham went utterly white. "It's my fault the girl is dead. I surely never meant for that to happen."

Eva went over to the woman, crouched in front of her, and pressed her hand to Miss Wickham's. "No. Mr. Tremaine is at fault. For all of it. You were merely doing your job as a supervisor. You and she were both victims of that man's treachery."

"Still, I wrongly accused her . . ." Miss Wickham blinked back tears. Eva gave her hand a final pat and backed away to resume her seat.

"I want you to know," Lady Phoebe said, "that arrangements are being made for Lydia's sisters. She had been supporting them, which is why, we assume, she went along with Jeffrey Tremaine's scheme."

Miss Wickham nodded, her tears continuing to trickle. After an awkward pause during which the others pretended not to witness the woman's distress, Lord Owen said, "As for the other recent discovery made about Crown Lily . . ." He didn't, however, go on to supply the explanation, but rather gazed across the way to Trent Mercer.

He and Fox had listened in silence these many minutes. Now they grinned at each other, and Trent said, "The Mercers and the Tremaines were once partners in Crown Lily Potteries. It's no great secret, and you might already know that. But then the Tremaines forced the Mercers out a couple of generations ago without proper recompense. But more important, during the war, Crown Lily came under dire straits and the Tremaines appealed to the Mercers for help."

"In the form of money," Fox put in.

"Mr. Tremaine admitted as much to me," Lady Phoebe said to their guests, corroborating Trent's story. "Crown Lily owes money to the Mercers."

Trent nodded. "Heaps of it. You see, after they left the china business, the Mercers continued to prosper for a while in shipping. They were one of the companies transporting Staffordshire china all over England before the war, and my grandfather was a wealthy man. But just as most of the china companies did poorly during the war, so did the shipping companies."

"Is that when the Mercers first attempted to recoup their loan money?" Owen asked.

Trent nodded. "Apparently, yes, except that when my grandfather died, records of the loan went missing. I never knew about any of this. But, somehow, my father managed to recover the documents."

"And wanted the money back?" Percy Bateman suggested.

"No," Trent corrected him, "he wanted a share in the business, to be made a partner, but Mr. Tremaine refused. Said my father would never be able to have those documents validated. But don't you see? This is why my father insisted I leave Eton and learn the china trade. He wasn't going to give up simply because Jeffrey Tremaine proved stubborn. He secretly had a solicitor piecing together the proof he needed."

"And Mr. Tremaine became nervous." Fox shoved a biscuit into his mouth and spoke as he chewed. "So nervous, well . . . we all know what he did."

"I still don't understand," Moira Wickham said, somewhat less testily than before. "What is it you're all getting at?"

"It's this." Eva stood and folded her hands at her waist. "Those shares that should have gone to Ronald Mercer will now go to Trent. This will, in essence, make him Crown Lily's owner. However, he will not, as you can imagine, be running the company—"

"Not yet, at any rate," the boy interrupted. "I'll be going back to Eton." This earned him another grin and a thump on the back from Fox.

"Meanwhile, I'll be buying in as a financial partner," Lord Owen told them. "And while, as I've admitted, I don't know much about the china industry specifically, I can lend a certain expertise when it comes to running a business."

"And the two of you," Eva resumed, "will step in as Crown Lily's head design team, if you're willing."

"*What . . . ?*" Percy Bateman spoke the word like a man awakening from a dream.

Moira Wickham's mouth hung open, until she closed it slowly and swallowed. "You'll have to replace Gus Abbott, you know. You can't resume production without a man like him, and where will you find someone with Gus's knowledge?"

"Let us worry about that," Lady Phoebe said. "What about Eva's question? Are you willing? Crown Lily will need you both."

"You really should say yes." Lady Amelia stood framed in the doorway. For how long, Eva didn't know. She'd been so intent on the conversation she had noticed little else. "You do realize if the factory is forced to close its doors, not only will a lot of hardworking people be out of their jobs, but Queen Mary will be frightfully disappointed. Crown Lily china is her favorite."

Eva went to stand before Moira Wickham's chair. She knew simply by gazing into Percy Bateman's astounded expression that he was ready to take on the position being offered. But Miss Wickham's pride left the success of their endeavor in some doubt. The woman could end matters by walking away, simply to prove a point. Never mind that doing so would destroy her career.

"Miss Wickham," Eva said, "you are needed in this. I don't believe Crown Lily will survive without you." She leaned over and grasped the arms of the chair, bringing her face close to the other woman's. "And you deserve this. Your talent proves you're ready for it. Don't let this opportunity slip away, I beg you."

Eva released the chair and straightened. The anticipation of the other woman's answer set her heart racing. She had meant every word, fervently. Despite Moira Wickham's sometimes-prickly personality, Eva had come to respect her and greatly admire her talents. She wished to see this woman succeed, to take her rightful place among the other professionals in the china industry. It was only fair; it was the only suitable outcome for an otherwise deplorable course of events.

Miss Wickham came to her feet. She extended her hand, reaching for Eva's. "You're right, Miss Huntford. Thank you." Calmly, with so much less emotion than Eva felt coursing through her, they shook hands like two partners in business. "Perhaps someday you'll come back to Crown Lily and work with me."

Eva embraced the other woman briefly. "I'm sorry, but no."

"I'll never be so happy to leave a place." Julia handed her jewelry box to Hetta, who, in turn, placed it in the open trunk at the foot of the bed.

Phoebe, sitting with Amelia near the wide windows overlooking the gardens, raised her eyebrows at her sister, prompting a chuckle.

"All right, yes, I had never been happier than to leave Cowes last spring, but this comes in as a close second."

"But we were right to stay until everything had been resolved. I'm so happy for Trent." Amelia took on a dreamy look as she spoke, and suddenly Phoebe suspected her sister might have developed warm sentiments toward a certain young man. She wondered how long those sentiments would last, and whether Trent had the faintest idea.

She sighed and brushed a loose, honey-golden

curl off Amelia's shoulder. "I'm glad we'll be leaving Crown Lily in good hands. I do hope they'll be able to replace Gus Abbott with someone from within the company. One of his assistants."

"Owen will let us know, I suppose," Julia said. She stared into the open armoire, still holding a few items of clothing yet to be packed. "It's good of him to stay on and help put the company back together."

Yes, Phoebe agreed with that wholeheartedly. Owen would ensure the company's continued success. Although once the news of Mr. Tremaine's villainy became generally known, it would take some doing to rebuild Crown Lily's reputation. She hoped the company's reversion to the descendant of one of the original owners would help in restoring the public's—and Queen Mary's—confidence.

A knock at the door drew their attention to Mildred Blair, standing in the doorway. "May I come in?"

"Of course." Julia beckoned her to take a seat. "Come to see us off, have you?"

"Not exactly." Mildred combed a hand through her bobbed hair and compressed her rouged lips. Phoebe read nervousness in both gestures, and wondered what had brought Mildred here.

Apparently, Julia noticed, too. "Is something wrong, Mildred?" She propped a hand on her hip

379

and smoothed the other absently over her belly. "Has Ernie been making trouble again?"

"No . . ." Mildred's hesitation set off yet another warning bell. Something was not right. "The truth is . . . there's something you should know, Julia."

Julia came over and lowered herself carefully onto the settee on Amelia's other side. "You've got my attention. Tell me what's wrong."

"There's nothing wrong. Well, nothing but what you've been led to believe," Mildred said. "About the house."

Julia frowned in puzzlement. "This house?"

"Of course this house," Mildred snapped. Then, "Sorry. This isn't easy for me. You see, Gil didn't want you to know. Or Veronica or Ernie, for that matter."

Phoebe's patience with this game slipped away. "Mildred, stop talking in riddles, please, and say what you've got to say."

"This house isn't entailed to Gil's estate." Mildred paused to let that much sink in. As it was, the news sent a shock wave through Phoebe. All these months, they had believed the house and the Annondale title to be linked—with all or nothing going to either Julia's male child or Ernie. But now . . .

"So you see," Mildred went on, "even if you have a daughter, it won't necessarily mean she won't inherit the house. Yes, the title will go to

Ernie, but it remains to be seen to whom Gil left the house." She gave a half chuckle. "He even might have left it to me. Although I doubt that very much."

Julia's hand went to her bosom. "How long have you known this?"

Mildred shrugged. "Since Gil amended his will right before marrying you."

"And why didn't you—" Outrage so filled Phoebe, she couldn't finish the question.

"That was very mean of you, Mildred." Amelia spoke sternly and pulled herself up taller against the back of the settee.

"I couldn't tell you. Gil made me promise." Mildred threw up her hands. "Oh, I suppose I could have, but I didn't wish to. And I really did promise him I wouldn't. Anyway, now you know, and it doesn't change anything. We still have to wait until the baby is born before the will is read. Until then, we won't know to whom Gil left Lyndale Park."

Amelia reached for Julia's hand. "Oh, Julia, I hope he left it to you."

"Not me, Amelia," their elder sister said, "but to my son or daughter." Her smile brought a renewed glow to her face. "I suppose we'll see in two months' time."

The cars were loaded, Fenton and Douglas ready to begin the trip home. An extra passenger had been added—or make that two. Trent and

Jester would be accompanying them back to Foxwood Hall, and then Trent would travel on to Eton with Fox, once Grampapa had made the necessary arrangements. Both boys had been groaning over the amount of schoolwork they would have to make up.

Phoebe lingered inside with Owen. "I'd planned to surprise you next month with a visit to Little Barlow," he said with no small measure of regret. "But now, with Crown Lily added to my other responsibilities back home in Yorkshire . . ." His head hung as he shook it.

Phoebe took the opportunity to rise on her toes and steal a kiss. "Then I'll have to surprise you, won't I? Just keep me apprised of where you are, here or there, and I'll see to the rest."

He grinned down at her. "I like an independent woman."

"You'd better, because it isn't likely I'll change."

"I wouldn't like it if you did." He kissed her again, then pulled away. "Before you leave, I have something for you. For all of you, really." He walked briskly to the baize door that led belowstairs and called the name of one of the footmen. Her curiosity piqued, Phoebe craned her neck to see what he was up to. When Owen backed his way out of the doorway, she saw he held something in his arms. Something russet, with patches of snowy white. Something soft and furry. Something squiggly.

With a wide grin he returned to her and transferred the Staffordshire bull terrier pup into her arms. As the chubby body molded against her own, she couldn't help but let out a squeal of delight. "Fox put you up to this, didn't he?"

"No, it was Amelia, actually. This is why we went out together in the Runabout."

A sweet, cherubic face turned up toward hers, and as she felt the graze of a warm tongue against her chin, Phoebe's heart melted.